THE
WHISTLING
ANCESTORS

THE
WHISTLING
ANCESTORS

Richard E. Goddard

RAMBLE HOUSE

ISBN 13: 978-1-60543-329-5

ISBN 10: 1-60543-329-2

Cover Art: Gavin L. O'Keefe
Preparation: John Pelan and Fender Tucker

DANCING TUATARA PRESS #2

The Whistling Ancestors

Introduction by John Pelan

Greetings! This is one of those rare occasions where the editor can speak directly to the reader knowing that the book said reader holds in his/her hand has at least a 90% chance of having been special-ordered.

Chances are that you are either a fan of Ramble House and based on the books you've bought previously, you already know that you're in for a wild ride. Fender Tucker and Gavin O'Keefe have been performing a valuable literary service for a number of years now, bringing back into print some of the most bizarre pulp crime fiction novels including the complete works of Harry Stephen Keeler! To say that Fender and I think along the same lines is probably an understatement; with my own publishing house I've spent the last two decades publishing books that I figured might not exist in accessible editions unless I did them.

My outlook has always been that if I like something well enough to risk a big bag of money producing a new edition, there might be at least 499 other people that will want the book too. So far this has worked out fairly well. Fender and Gavin have done me one better by coming up with an even more affordable route wherein the reader can opt for either a trade paperback or a hardcover. Both states look very nice and while I do lament the demise[1] of the Ramble House homemade paperbacks, the new method can ultimately reach thousands more people.

I was intrigued enough by this to suggest a line of books to Fender. At Midnight House we sort our potential projects into four groups: (1) The no-brainers—collections by the heavyweights like Clark Ashton Smith, Fritz Leiber, and so on fall into this group. (2) The "I like it and so should you" books. These are titles by authors that likely few modern readers are familiar with but are marketable under the premise that if you like most of the books we do, there's a

---

[1] The hand-crafted Ramble House A6-sized paperbacks with jackets are not dead. They've gotten older, like the man who prints and binds them. They can still be cajoled out of him.

pretty good chance that you'll like these too. (3) The Crap file. I don't like it, you probably won't either, and I have no idea who sent this to me or why. (We don't publish these titles and neither should anyone else). And then lastly we have (4) the "Risky Business Books".

The Risky Business Books are best defined as books that I think are cool, but are those titles that I doubt I could sell anywhere near 500 copies. Maybe the book is too overtly non-supernatural (for the most part, our readers expect supernatural horror). Maybe the book has gotten a really bad rap over the years and it just wouldn't be worth the risk. Or, maybe it's something just so weird and off-trail that it just doesn't fit with either of our imprints and therefore doesn't pass the acid test of having a reader say "I didn't like it as well as some of your other titles, but I see why you published it and I guess I'm glad I had a chance to read it . . ."

Now, thanks to Fender, I have a chance to get some of the Risky Business Books out there where people can judge for themselves. The only commonality in this series is that the originals are difficult to come by, I think they're worthwhile titles, and lastly; they're downright bizarre.

When we decided to go ahead with this project, it was a fairly easy decision as to which book to start with, we led off with Sean M'Guire's *Beast or Man?*, a sort of Tarzan in reverse replete with club-wielding gorillas, insane missionaries and the sort of relationships that wouldn't even be discussed in *Penthouse Forum* . . . (Let's face it, if a character is half-man/half ape, in an era well before the advent of artificial insemination it means someone has been up to so some monkey business if you'll forgive the pun).

Anyway, while M'Guire's novel is certainly not without some controversial subject matter, Mr. Goddard doesn't just cross the line of good taste, he rubs it out entirely and plants a garden of poisonous flowers where the line could previously have been seen.

Richard E. Goddard was a British sales guru in the 1930s with the primer *General Cargo: An Introduction to Salesmanship* to his credit. The book is every bit as dry and repetitive as most such titles are, and there's little to indicate the sort of deranged imagination that would produce a novel like *The Whistling Ancestors*.

The Whistling Ancestors is one of those titles that scholars in the genre either like or loathe a great deal. One can picture Everett Bleiler wrinkling his nose in disgust as he typed up the one-paragraph entry that he felt the title merited for his *Supernatural Index*. One can also picture specialist booksellers beaming with pleasure as they type up an entry for the book in their catalogue and wrestle with whether to price it at $400 or $500. You see, another element of the mystique surrounding this book is the genuine rarity of the title. These would pretty much be the elements that cause a book (or an author) to become collectible; strong feelings about the book either positive or negative and scarcity. The two best ways to drive the price of a book up are either glowingly positive or bile-filled negative reviews and then have circumstances where readers can't judge for themselves because they can't find the damn thing. These characteristics are certainly present in regard to this volume (until now).

Let's take a look at the novel itself and see why it ignites such debates over seventy years after its publication . . . The plot pits a poor sidewalk artist against a fiendish mastermind who is not only intent on world domination, but determined to kill all white people and for reasons that are never made entirely clear, wants to create nymphs, satyrs, and other Greek and Roman demigods through the miracle of vivisection! These characteristics alone would qualify Caspar Pettifranc to take his rightful place alongside John Sunlight, Wu Fang, Doctor Death and the other great villains of the American pulps, but Goddard doesn't stop here. The author also makes Pettifranc a master of voodoo who thus can ring in zombies and the pantheon of *loas*. For reasons that the author allows to remain obscure, the loas are given to making odd whistling noises, hence the title of the book.

I can't say much more about the plot without giving far too much away, but suffice it say, there's a lot of action that leads up to the denouement. As with any Ramble House book, you know you're in for a wild ride!

CHAPTER I

I HEAR OF THE WHISTLING ANCESTORS

I SAT cross-legged on the pavement in Sloane Street. In front of me, drawn in coloured chalks upon the stone flags of the pavement, was my silent supplication to the charitable.

I had selected my subjects with considerable care to appeal to the interest of the average passer-by. If I, Patrick Worthing, had to sit behind half a dozen pavement pictures all day, at least they should be such as to arrest attention: a full-rigged ship, an aeroplane soaring over a tropical landscape, and a front view of the Flying Scotsman emerging from a cutting. So far, during the four days I had held my pitch, I had no reason to grumble at my choice of subjects, and I was as reasonably content as an amateur pavement artist could be. During my thirty-three odd years I had emulated the proverbial rolling-stone; I had amassed a character composed of cosmopolitanism, and the capacity for adapting myself to most conditions, but lacked the steady, specialised knowledge which is nowadays demanded if a man is to be a financial success.

I had no particular affliction to capitalise in the matter of blindness or physical injury, and it is difficult for a red head, in good health, even if hungry, to look really miserable. I had a store of matches, and presented a box to such as dropped anything more than a halfpenny into the Indian begging bowl placed beside a caricature of myself saying "Thank you." The only aid to appeal to the sympathetic was a particularly ingenious coat which gave me the appearance of having lost my left arm. The left sleeve was empty and turned over, but there was an inner flap to the coat under which my arm could be stowed away without much discomfort.

I could almost have sung aloud that Thursday morning for sheer joy of living. The early May air was sweet and fresh, and seemed to breeze in straight from the open country, carrying with it the atmosphere of lilac and hawthorn. Up to eleven o'clock I had collected over seven shillings in coppers with a sprinkling of silver, almost treble the amount taken up to the same time on the three previous days.

A very pretty girl had bestowed a shilling and an encouraging smile not ten minutes before, and the policeman on the beat had stood for a second to glance at the ship and had given me a couple of pence and a hearty "Good morning."

If luck held, I might buy a ticket in the Irish or Calcutta sweep and win enough to set me properly on my feet once more. Would I spend the money in fitting out a small schooner and make a semi-pleasure, semi-barter trip to the more inaccessible of the South Sea islands, or buy a business in London and marry the girl who had given me the shilling and the smile?

My train of foolish dreaming was arrested by the pulling up of a number twenty-two bus and the disgorging of four passengers. Among these was a tall, slim blonde with hair like spun silk, straight from the cocoon and done up in an almost old-fashioned roll. She was of the type more often seen on Fifth Avenue or in Paris than in London, as delicately poised as a rapier, yet with lips, eyes and chin that gave hint of a nature as charming as her appearance.

Behind her, and last off the bus, was a huddled-up, brown-skinned crone, wearing a black bonnet trimmed with yellow flowers and a long tweed coat, beneath which I caught a glimpse of a dress made of a kind of Burmese silk, and in colour a shade between orange and pink. Her eyes gave an impression of glowing vitality. They were not particularly large, but the white seemed bigger than usual, producing an uncanny effect and not a very pleasant one. I was trying to place her nationality when, with the slightest backward glance at the blonde girl, who was looking up and down Sloane Street as if waiting for someone, shuffled through the gates near which I sat and went into the church.

I guessed she belonged to one of the coloured West Indian peoples who are extremely religious, when the girl who had given me the shilling turned into the street from the square on the opposite side of the road. A few yards behind her was one of the tallest and strongest-looking dark-skinned men I have ever seen.

The blonde caught sight of my divinity and waved. Their meeting took place within a few feet of my pitch so that I could not help hearing their conversation.

"You haven't been waiting long, have you?"

"Only just this second got here. . . I was afraid I was going to be late," the blonde assured her. "I had to positively wrench myself away from Mrs. Townsend. Why is it, Ines, that being an old friend of one's father makes some people so darned proprietary? Says she doesn't think it right for two girls to be living alone in a flat in

London. I told her she hadn't gotten over her Chicago complex, but she wasn't a bit pleased."

She broke off, suddenly realising my proximity, mechanically snapped open her bag and fumbled in it.

"Lend me a shilling or something, will you, Ines?"

"Thanks very much, Miss, but your friend already gave me something this morning," I said as gracefully as I could.

I stole a quick glance at Ines, hoping she might smile again.

She did, and it was like the sun suddenly coming out from behind a cloud. I decided, definitely, then and there that if the luck turned, it should be the business in London—and Ines.

"Surely that isn't quite usual, is it?" she asked. There was a creamy deepness in her voice which set one's pulses athrob.

"What, Miss?" I returned, knowing quite well what she meant. Out of the corner of my eye, however, I noticed that the big man on the other side of the road threw an inquisitive glance in my direction, then turned and remained gazing into the windows of a shop which displayed lamps and cushions. Subconsciously I felt that he was actually watching the girl—there was a mirror in the shop window; and I wondered why.

"Refusing money when it is offered you?" Ines pursued, evidently puzzled by my attitude—possibly also by my voice.

"I don't like imposing on people," I answered.

She chuckled and produced a shilling.

"Here you are, Bridget. I think honesty deserves to be rewarded."

Bridget dropped the coin into my brass bowl with a fleeting smile. I gathered from her demeanour that she did not quite approve of her companion talking to me so familiarly.

"Oughtn't we to be moving, Ines?" she said to the other, not impatiently, but in a tone that held finality. "I promised Mrs. Townsend I'd bring you back to lunch—she's leaving for Little Barns this afternoon."

"Of course . . . Sorry!" Ines gave me a friendly nod, but turned again.

"I suppose you don't know where the Siena Studios are?" she inquired. "It's that place where they have rejuvenation classes—mind over matter business, run by some queer native doctor . . . Caspar somebody or other," she explained to Bridget aside. "Aunt Mary is dallying with the idea of taking a course."

I thought a second.

"I believe it is off Glebe Place—that is a turning just after Oakley Street near the Town Hall," I answered.

"Thanks. Is it far from here?" She moved a step to placate the other girl who was obviously fretting to be off.

"A penny fare on a number twenty-two bus," I rejoined.

"You're not thinking of going there now, are you?" Bridget interposed.

"No; I just thought I would ask while we were up this way!" and with another nod she went with her companion in the direction of Knightsbridge.

I was not surprised when the big man crossed the road a couple of seconds after and came to a stand before my pictures. I gazed up at him placidly, though for some obscure reason my heart was beating furiously. Of course it might be just a crazy notion of mine—but I had a suspicion that in some way he *had* been following Ines, and that his attentions boded no good for her. Not that there was anything particularly sinister about the man outwardly, except for his bulk. It was something like a radiation that emanated from his inner self which impressed me as disconcerting. I observed, on closer view, that his skin was much lighter than I had thought, and that his eyes were a pale, steely grey. The skin was creepy; in some lights it looked to be the ordinary tint of the mulatto, in others it took on a greenish hue—almost like phosphorescence.

"Not bad work," he remarked, in a gentle slurring accent. "Where did you pick up that particular landscape?" he pointed to the aeroplane over Santo Domingo.

Where my inspiration came from I have no idea, but almost involuntarily I decided that it would be interesting to pretend to be dumb. There was, of course, a risk that he might have seen me talking to the girls, but they were in front of me and it was not very likely.

I took a piece of white chalk and wrote on the pavement with it: "Sorry, can't talk; shell shock. Picture San Domingo."

He nodded and I could have sworn regarded me with a more personal interest as I nonchalantly rubbed the scribble out again. I had an idea that he was going to say something more, when the old woman who had been on the same bus with Bridget came out of the church and he stiffened and moved towards her.

"Maman Constance—you have come then . . . I was afraid you had missed . . . Did you see the girl? Is she fair enough for our purpose?" he demanded, a tremor of something between anxiety and elation in his tone.

She nodded twice gravely. "As good as the best, Papaloi," she answered. Her voice had the same peculiar slurringness as the man's except that the sibilants sounded like leaves rustling in the wind.

I congratulated myself on my sudden hunch. There was manifestly something off afoot.

"You saw the other?" the mulatto asked. "The dark one?"

The woman shook her head.

"A beauty, Maman; a real beauty . . . fit to be the bride of the Great One," he remarked gloatingly. I could have strangled him, but I controlled myself and pretended to be occupied in starting another picture on the stone.

"Tell me, Maman . . . The Whistling Ancestors—did you manage to get a message from them?"

From the corner of my eye I saw the crone go rigid as he spoke. She frowned and cast a sidelong glance in my direction.

"It's all right," he assured her with impatience. "Only a poor fool made dumb by shell shock."

She relaxed a little, but was still uneasy.

"No—in my house there is no private enough place. I tried in one of the parks, but there again, when I sat under the trees, stupid people came and stared at me."

"Well . . . you know how important it is that we should find out if the girl is acceptable or if they want something younger," he pressed.

"I thought perhaps we might try in the church here. It is quiet and a sacred place. If anyone saw—or heard—they would only think it was the birds twittering on the roofs outside," she continued, with a touch of nervousness, and still glancing from time to time at me and one or two pedestrians who passed.

The mulatto nodded. "That's an idea, Maman," he said approvingly. "As you say, it is sacred—though not to quite the same God as we worship." He chuckled very softly and my gorge rose. There was something terrifying in that mountain of flesh shaking like a gross jelly in evil glee.

"You go in and I will join you," he ordered, and then came back to me as she passed through the church doors again.

I pretended to be engrossed with my chalks.

"Here—you . . ." I raised my eyes. Now I was able to examine them more intently, I saw that his were blue—that watery blue so often associated with criminals.

"Do you want a job?" he continued. There was a smile on his lips as though he was contemplating some mischievous practical joke.

"That depends on what it is," I scribbled on the pavement. "Only one arm . . . can't tackle hard work."

"One arm is all I want; that and discretion, and your being dumb should insure that . . . if you're wise," he returned, and though the smile still lingered on his lips, I felt a sudden chill run down my spine.

"What is it?" I wrote.

"I want a doorkeeper for my studio—run messages and see that I'm not worried by the wrong kind of callers," he explained. "The last man I had . . ." he frowned, "gossiped too much. I'll give you three pounds a week if you do the job properly."

"Sorry, I make more than that here."

"The devil you do." He eyed me in surprise. "All right—four pounds."

I added another line. "I'd like to think it over."

"Hm, pretty independent, aren't you?" he sneered. "I don't want anyone who isn't willing. However, if you do decide to do an honest job, come along to this address any evening after seven."

With a gesture of amused contempt he dropped a visiting card and sixpence into my bowl and marched after the old woman into the church.

I picked up the card when he had gone with fingers that trembled.

It was engraved and bore the name "Doctor Caspar Pettifranc."

The address underneath was: "Number Seven, Siena Studios," and at the bottom, in small letters: "Seek and you shall find."

I drew a deep breath. "Siena Studios. Doctor Caspar" . . . unmistakably this was the place Ines had spoken of. What strange connection could there be between the two girls and this peculiar pair of coloured folk.

In spite of the warm sunshine and the sane and commonplace surroundings, something icy and threatening seemed to fill the air. Who were Dr. Caspar Pettifranc and the disturbing old crone? And what were they doing in the church behind me . . . sacred, but *not quite to the same Gods as ours.*

"That could be discovered if I had strength of mind enough to spy on them. I have never considered myself a courageous person; I was none too comfortable at the thought of making an enemy of the unprepossessing Dr. Caspar. Those long, muscular fingers could pluck the tendons out of an arm or the windpipe out of one's throat as easily as mine could wring the neck of a fowl.

A shock passed through me at the involuntary association of ideas. What was the name the old woman had given him? . . . Papaloi! That was it. Recollections of queer things heard during my wanderings in the West Indies suddenly sorted themselves, and I knew why thinking of Dr. Caspar's fingers at my throat, and my own thought of wringing the neck of a fowl, had brought them up from my subconscious mind. The Papaloi was the Voodoo, Chief Priest who officiated when sacrifices were made in the Boumfort or Voodoo temple—pulling the head off the sacrificial cock or dove, or plunging his knife into the goat and sprinkling the blood over the swaying, hypnotised worshippers. Sacrifice! And he had asked Maman Constance whether the blonde girl was fair enough . . .

But this was sheer madness on my part. Such things couldn't happen in London, with taxicabs and brewers' drays with barrels of Guinness's stout on them, and sturdy, phlegmatic police constables to insure law and order and sanity around.

I did not like the idea one little bit, but I felt whatever happened I must investigate what they were up to.

I got up quickly, having made up my mind nothing was to be gained by hanging around. They would probably be in the body of the church and, I hoped, too occupied with their own devices to notice me. I meant to use a small door leading out of the entrance by which they had gone in, which gave access to a room used by the verger as a store. If the doctor saw me, I planned to say I accepted his offer; I had a piece of chalk with me. But, even as I settled on this precaution, I knew I did not fear him one-tenth as much as I feared Maman Constance.

CHAPTER II

I GIVE WAY TO CURIOSITY AND FOLLOW MY NOSE

AFTER THE BRIGHTNESS of the May sunlight the dimness of the church was disconcerting. I halted for a second, there-fore, to accustom my eyes to the gloom, congratulating myself that my footgear consisted of cheap, rubber-soled canvas shoes.

I shot a swift glance into the body of the church. The queer couple were on the far side of the building. They had their backs to me and appeared to be sitting quietly in their pew. The doctor was separated by a gap of about two feet from his companion. They did not seem in the slightest degree uneasy about being interrupted, nor could I make out that anything unusual was happening. If I had come in upon them unexpectedly I should not have given them a second thought and I should have felt I was on a fool's errand had there not been in both of them an air of furtive expectancy. Of the two, Maman Constance looked the less anxious; the man was defi-nitely waiting for some manifestation, and his fingers drummed a devil's tattoo on his knee.

There was nothing in the way of cover under which I could ap-proach them, so I crept down the stone stairs into the verger's retreat, wondering what I should say if he happened to find me.

I found myself in a kind of vestry, for there were cassocks and surplices, kneeling cushions and odds and ends. A small door down another flight of steps led only to the heating system.

I was meditating whether I dared put on the verger's cassock, and risk making my way to the chancel, when I was suddenly aware of an odd sound penetrating into the room. It was not a chirrup, nor yet a whistle, but something which combined the two. It reminded me of the soft noise that occurs if one blows softly against one's upper teeth. I recalled to mind what the old crone had said when she suggested the church: "They would only think it was the birds twittering on the roofs outside."

The sound *was* very like that except that it was softer and the "chirruping" appeared to be detached so that the sounds fell into rhythmical groups—almost as if someone were trying to send

Morse signals by a series of musical hisses. I wondered if that was what Dr. Caspar had meant when he mentioned "The Whistling Ancestors."

I edged back to the stairs, but the sounds were not nearly so distinct, so I moved back and discovered that there was a brass grating along the roof probably intended to provide ventilation. I calculated, too, that at that spot I could not be more than two or three yards from the place where the couple were sitting. If I could get my ear closer to the grating it might be possible to hear their conversation. It was the work of a couple of seconds to secure a couple of hassocks and bring my head within a few inches of the grill.

There was no mistake about the sounds now, they had increased to such an extent that I had the impression of at least a dozen "siffleurs." For about five minutes they continued, then died down to a gentle murmur like the rustling of dried leaves in a soft breeze.

To my joy the doctor spoke.

"What do they say?" he inquired eagerly.

"One said that it would be wiser to keep the two sides of our mission more widely separated; that there is danger if you are not very careful," Maman Constance replied.

Caspar grunted impatiently.

"That isn't much help," he returned. "We have to have some kind of cloak to work under. . . What about the girl?"

"They say she will serve if you cannot find a better, but suggest your waiting until the next full moon, when one who is more acceptable to the Great One will come with an older woman," Maman Constance answered. She spoke as though she were an interpreter translating woodenly into explanatory words the message of the whistling spirits.

I gathered that the mulatto was considering this. "I see no harm in that," he admitted. "We can always use her for—other work." He gave an unpleasantly evil chuckle.

"I could make good use of her if you gave her to me," the woman interposed hopefully. "Properly trained as a priestess . . . or the other dark one you spoke of—"

There was a malicious note in her voice.

"You keep away from the dark one," Caspar snapped, and Maman Constance cackled, evidently amused to have drawn him. "I have my own plans for her. She's far too human to be wasted as one of your lifeless priestesses. Did you ask whether our place in Cornwall is acceptable as a Boumfort?"

"No; the messages were confused a little—almost as if there were some enemy around," she answered.

I held my breath in sudden fear.

"Try again," the doctor suggested. "It's no use laying out good money in buying the place if they don't like it. Though I can't see where we'll find a better. Out of the way spots where you are not likely to be disturbed aren't so easy to locate in this darned country—especially with a sacrificial stone all ready to hand."

"A stone?" Her question showed quick interest.

"Just that," he returned with satisfaction. "Though I don't suppose it has been used for over a thousand years. Faces the rising sun, too; ancient British or Druid, I expect. And there is a good graveyard within two miles that should please Baron Samedi. . ."

"That was clever of you, Papaloi," she purred admiringly. "Could we not go and make our headquarters there?"

"No; there's a lot to be done here before we are ready for that. See if you can get an answer about the Boumfort," he urged.

Another silence followed; the rustlings had died away, but now I heard them returning. This time, however, they seemed to be more concentrated on one note.

"Well?" the mulatto asked impatiently after a while.

"The place is good," Maman Constance pronounced as they died away once more, "but it must be prepared for the greater by the less. Much purification will be needed to dismiss the ancient influences. Grandpere says to use all caution, otherwise the Great One may not come for fear of being defiled."

"That's okay," said Caspar, and I should have been tickled by the prosaicness of his utterance if I had not been so worried.

"I guess we'd better be getting along now. You'd better come along to the studio later to-night and I'll tell you if there's any news about the girl's father."

I heard them scramble to their feet.

"Lucky, too, that the two of them are living together—makes it easier to check up on them. By the way," he added, "I think I've found a doorkeeper in place of Adolf. Pity *he* couldn't keep his mouth shut."

"That one-armed man, hey?" Maman Constance remarked, a touch of disdain in her tone. "Just because he had a picture of your beloved islands . . . when will you be sensible, *mon frere?*"

"Why shouldn't I offer him the job?" he demanded, evidently sulky. "What better kind could we hope to get? Dumb—which means that he can't go babbling; one arm, almost a sign of respectability in itself . . . a war veteran. I tell you he's a cinch for the job," he argued. "Have you anything against him?" he pressed as she was silent.

I could almost see the expressive shrug which greeted his challenge.

"Nothing definite, Caspar—but he stared when I got off the bus and I think he is not so easy as you believe him. That man has been to places—what you told me about his picture of San Domingo proves that. What if he should have heard things which would make him suspect?" she answered, and I could hear she was troubled.

The mulatto laughed. "London doesn't seem to be agreeing with you, Maman; you are developing nerves. I think I'll have to send you down to Cornwall when we've made sure of the girl—and this new one, the ancestors say will arrive. Anyway, don't trouble your head about that 'lapin.' You can rely on me to discipline him. If he gets fresh I'll send him where I sent Adolf," he concluded with an ugly chuckle. "I must hurry, I'm supposed to meet Polynice in Lincoln's Inn."

"You know best, but I still cannot see why you shouldn't use one of the Zombies or our own people," she argued.

"Because, my dear Maman, for a hundred reasons I daren't let the Zombies be seen by the outer circle, and a coloured man might scare the foolish old women who come to be made young again."

I was in a quandary what to do now. If I followed them out I might run straight into their arms. The presumption was that the doctor would not wait if he had to meet somebody in Lincoln's Inn, but I had no guarantee that the old hag would not hang around to look me over again. She evidently disliked me as much as I distrusted her.

Still I could not shelter in the church indefinitely. I would have liked to follow Maman Constance and find out where she lived, but that would be too dangerous.

I lingered for a few minutes and, then, taking a small paper parcel of sandwiches out of my pocket and holding it as if I had just retrieved it from a hiding-place in the vestry, I plucked up courage and walked boldly out to my pitch.

I did not even cast a glance around until I was squatted on the pavement again, trying to carry out the idea by pretending myself to believe it, that I had entered the building to pick up my lunch packet. Fortune had favoured me and I breathed a sigh of relief when, after a space, I allowed myself to look up and down the street, I saw neither Dr. Caspar nor his accomplice were in sight.

As I munched my sandwiches I did a mental summing-up of the information I had so far acquired. It was not very much, but what it lacked in completeness it certainly made up for in interest, though, even yet I was not entirely sure that I was not making rather a fool of myself.

If it had not been for Ines I should have been strongly inclined to think no more about the problem.

During the past half-hour I had procured a series of snap-shots, all of things that appeared fantastically irrelated. A mulatto from Haiti; a studio in Chelsea; a Dolmen somewhere in Cornwall and two white girls, one blonde and the other dark. And, finally, "The Whistling Ancestors."

The thing that bothered me most was the presence of the two girls. Obviously, if the doctor was up to any mischief, they ought to be warned. Yet, even if I knew where they could be found, what warning could I give them at the present stage?

If I were not to abandon the business absolutely and forget the incident, I must follow up the clues with all my energy. Only by doing this and learning something tangible could I hope to be of service to the girls. The first course was undoubtedly the more sensible. I had an unpleasant certainty that neither Caspar nor Maman Constance would stop at anything with anyone who inter-fered with their plans. I was convinced that if Caspar was a Voodoo Papaloi, his companion was the Chief Priestess, or Mamaloi. An old lady who could summon "the Whistling Ancestors" to a respectable London church was not a person to be disregarded lightly.

Nevertheless, if I was to keep any harm from coming to Ines, there was only the one course open, and that was to accept Dr. Caspar's offer of a job. There would no doubt be the devil to pay before I was through, but I had never weighed consequences overmuch once I had decided on a course of action. If I had been in the habit of doing so, I should not have now been drawing pictures in chalks on the pavement of Sloane Street. It would be a pity to give up the pitch. Perhaps Dr. Pettifranc might arrange to employ me for evenings only. I thought before committing myself finally it would not be a bad idea to have a look round the studio.

Funnily enough my spirits had recovered marvellously since I had come to my conclusion. Naturally it would not do to run the chance of the mulatto finding me snooping, but I thought I could overcome this possibility.

In Hollywood I saw a number of extras being made up for a Russian film. I had experimented afterwards for the fun of the thing—even had some of the hair I used—and I believe I could fix up a nice Vandyke which would pass muster in Chelsea studio-land.

With this and both arms I could pass the doctor's scrutiny if I ran into him.

I remembered that Ines had said something about an Aunt Mary wanting to go to the studio and my spirits soared even higher. With any luck I might see the girl there.

In my elation I began to whistle a tune, still making plans for the defeat of the mulatto and his lady friend. How long I had been whistling I have no idea when I was brought back to sudden realisation by the rattle of a coin in my begging bowl.

Looking up I found myself staring into the maliciously un-winking gaze of Maman Constance . . .

CHAPTER III

I TAKE A LOOK AT THE STUDIO IN CHELSEA

IT WAS SHEER instinct that commanded me to continue whistling. Subconsciously I realised it would be fatal to my plans to let the old crone think that I had any interest in her. I wondered if she had been spying on me from a shop entrance, or if she had just happened by again.

She gazed at me in silence for what seemed to be a full minute. It was a disturbing scrutiny; I suspected she was probably a good mind reader and I was scared stiff she might deduce what I had been up to. I therefore endeavoured to make my thoughts blank except for the tune I was whistling. When I considered her presence had gone beyond the bounds of mere curiosity in me and my pictures, I looked up with a forced smile, then picking up my piece of chalk, I wrote on the pavement: "Is there anything I can do for you?"

She shook her head impatiently and I could have sworn I saw a look of disappointment come into her evil eyes. I thanked my stars she had caught me whistling and not humming the tune.

"You were not here five minutes ago—why?"

I wondered what would be the best game to play.

"Fetching lunch," I wrote. "Pub round corner."

"I didn't see you come from there," she replied, evidently baffled.

"I didn't see you," I wrote, smiling cheekily. I had a hunch that she had not been watching after all, but that she had happened to pass by again. "Did you want me?" I looked at her with a perplexed expression after I had written the words.

"No," she hesitated. I took it that she was no more anxious to advertise her interest in me than I was to incur it—now that she was satisfied about my seeming harmlessness.

"Did you see a tall, coloured gentleman pass?" She whipped round and fired the question abruptly, after she had turned to go. I began to have a very wholesome respect for her shrewdness.

I nodded and then wrote. "Yes; gave me sixpence."

"Where is he now?"

I shrugged and replied on the stone. "Last I saw, went into the church."

She nodded at this and I felt I had given the right answer. Then, without deigning another glance, she hurried off across the road. A few minutes later I was relieved to see her back disappearing round the corner of the King's Road. The remainder of the day dragged terribly. I was anxious to have a look at the studio off Glebe Place, but I considered it would be unwise to make any alteration in my ordinary routine. Probably it would have been quite safe, but one couldn't be too careful.

In the usual way I should have gone home to Beaufort Street by the King's Road, but that was too near the Studio, and I did not put it beyond Maman Constance—or the doctor—to follow and see where I lived. So this evening I cut through by various back turnings to the Fulham Road.

It was after seven before I finished my supper and prepared to don my make-up for the evening's adventure.

It took me a good half-hour to get the beard to my liking, but when it was finished I felt I could pass anywhere as one of the young and intensely "arty" painters who frequent Chelsea restaurants. I completed the camouflage by putting on a flowing black scarf, an old black "trilby" and packing a couple of sheets of cardboard under my arm to look as if I was carrying sketches. My pockets contained a length of sashcord, a flashlight and a cigarette case made in the shape of an automatic pistol. The whole thing struck me as rather ridiculous. Since feeding, the events of the morning had in a measure faded . . .

It was only the thought that I might see the girl again that gave me the incentive to carry on.

I turned into Glebe Place with a casual air and turned the corner admiring the old-fashioned little cottages which exist as a relic of the days when that part of Chelsea was almost like Strand-on-the-Green is now.

There was a kind of back lane three-quarter way down the street, running parallel with the Embankment and the King's Road, and a weatherworn signboard proclaimed it as Siena Studios. Underneath, on one side of the wooden post on which swung, half ajar, a rough door, was a small brass plate. It bore the name "Dr. Caspar Pettifranc. Number Seven."

With only the slightest hesitation, I pushed the door open and found myself in a courtyard gazing at what had evidently once been a good sized private mansion. The windows facing me, having a north aspect, were for the most part bare of curtains. On the top floor, however, there were four covered by orange net inside. I decided that this was where Dr. Caspar worked.

It was difficult to do much observation, as I was directly in view of anyone watching from the windows, but I was able to note that on the left there was a high building that crowded on to Siena Studios. But on my right there was only a low garden wall with the branches of trees topping it. It occurred to me that it would be worth trying to get into the garden; later, it might be useful to have a second means of retreat. As I was making for the entrance I heard the sound of a car and, a second later, an elderly woman, very expensively dressed and with white hair, came up the lane. As she went by I caught the scent of a perfume that I knew must be as costly as it was subtle. I judged it must be one of the "doctor's" rejuvenation patients.

It was not until she had disappeared that I noticed that, although there were visiting cards in the niches on the directory board, every one of them with the exception of Dr. Pettifranc's looked as if it had been there for centuries. Either the tenants were of very long standing or else the cards represented people who had lived there once but did so no longer. If my suspicion was correct then the only tenant now was the big mulatto.

I glanced hastily at the board again. Number six belonged—or had belonged—to a Miss Mary Jones; even if—as I had begun to doubt—the lady still had her being there, she could not eat me for calling on her. Humming a tune to reassure myself I climbed the stairs and knocked at the door of number six. There was no reply. A couple of empty milk bottles stood on the landing outside the door. The landing and the stairs up as far as this particular floor were covered with coconut matting, but the next flight, leading to number seven, was resplendent in red stair carpet and brass stair rods. There was also a small oak gate barring the entrance to the higher storey and it, too, bore Caspar's name on a brass plate.

I knocked a second time, more loudly, and as nothing happened I turned the handle quietly.

The last thing I had really anticipated was that the door would be unlocked. But to my astonishment it opened and I found myself staring down a short passage into a fairly large room, furnished in old oak, the whole of the walls, except on the window side, being composed of bookshelves. A couple of easy chairs stood on either side of a fireplace and close by was a tall, standard lamp with an orange shade. The walls were covered with some biscuit-coloured paper which gave the effect of canvas. There were no pictures, but in their place hung three extraordinary looking brass plaques. So far as I could make out there was nobody in the place.

I did not know quite what to do. It seemed rather risky to go into the studio and chance being caught red-handed. On the other hand I very much wanted to investigate; I had a hunch that, although apparently separate, number six and also number five formed a part of Caspar's premises.

I waited irresolute on the threshold for a couple of nerve- racking minutes. I listened cautiously, my hand on the door ready to close it again if anyone came, but I could hear only soft music.

Just then I heard footsteps ascending from below and the chattering of feminine voices. I closed the door and began to light another cigarette though my hand trembled. As the newcomers turned the corner of the stairs I could have cheered. It was Ines and Bridget with an older woman—whom I took to be the Aunt. With an assumption of nonchalant proprietorship I went through the door into number six.

I reckoned that if Caspar was busy with his visitors I had time to inspect the lower apartment.

My first job was to examine the book-lined room, but there was nothing more of special interest. I also examined the plaques. One bore a rather uncanny goat's head in relief; the eyes squinting and formed of two red stones resembling rubies. The other two were a pair and represented a circle enclosing a triangle which in turn enclosed an eye. They gave me the impression of being Egyptian in origin. My gaze was drawn back involuntarily to the centre plaque. The more one came under its influence the more impressive it became. Wherever one stood, once one had realised its presence, the glowing red eyes of the goat seemed to be boring into one and they were absolutely vivid with evil.

I was turning to go into the adjoining room, anxious to get out of range of the eyes, when I caught sight of a cable form dropped beside one of the armchairs. I picked it up and found that it was addressed to Dr. Caspar Pettifranc. I had no hesitation in reading it, but it conveyed very little sense to my mind. It had apparently been sent off ten days previously from Martinique—which I remembered as one of the French islands in the Caribbean. It ran: "All arranged. Yacht with our man due rendezvous tomorrow. Stop. Send cable stating girl in your hands by return. Stop. If all goes well expect to sail for Plymouth next week with new member." It was signed— "Ancestors."

It was double Dutch to me.

The second room contained only a bed, a couple of chairs and a cheap, painted washstand, and seemed to be out of keeping with the well-appointed book-room. The one window gave upon the garden on the right of the studios, but the blind, a green one, was drawn, so the place was in semi-darkness. I switched on my torch to get a better view and something about the bed struck me as queer. For a second I thought I had stumbled upon a sleeping attendant. I held my breath and listened, but there was no sound except the thumping of my own heart.

I crept across as silently as I could. The outline of a figure was plainly defined under the coverlet: I could not see the head because the sheet had been drawn up over it. Trembling violently, I turned back the coverlet, disclosing a pallid face crowned with a shock of grizzled hair. There was no sign of life, nor were there any of the indications of death. If I had not touched the face and felt the con-sistency of the flesh—still firm and resilient—I should have thought I was looking at a marvellous example of wax-modelling. As it was I replaced the coverlet hurriedly, feeling deathly sick.

CHAPTER IV

FURTHER ADVENTURES IN A CHELSEA STUDIO

WHEN I had recovered myself a little, I wondered what was: the meaning of the corpse that was not a corpse.

Leaving the bed and trying not to think of its contents, I made my way out of a door leading from the bedroom and found myself in a small square hall from which a narrow flight of stairs went both up and down. I concluded that this must once have been the servants' staircase and my mind jumped to its useful possibilities. I could see the Thames flowing by in the distance and the neon lights advertising the product of a flour mill across the river. Somehow that heartened me.

I opened the window gently and glanced down at the ground. The wall descended sheer into the garden at least thirty feet below. I bethought myself of the coil of sashcord I had brought with me: doubled, it should be strong enough to bear me. If I could get into the garden I could find my way on to the Embankment. I unwound it, doubled it in two lengths, and secured one end to one of a couple of iron brackets that were let into the wall outside the window. As the bolts fastening them came through the wall on the inside and were secured by a nut and an iron boss, I reckoned they would stand my weight. The doubled cord, when I let it down, was about eight feet short of the ground, but with my own height, I calculated that at most I should only fall a couple of feet.

Then, my retreat secured, I crept softly up the stairs to the back entrance of the studio above.

There was a similar landing and hall-way with a door giving on to a twin of the bedroom I had recently vacated. I put my eye to the keyhole but I could make out nothing more than a patch of dimly lighted wall and a slither of light from a half open door leading into the main studio.

Putting my ear to the keyhole I could hear the mulatto—I was able to recognise his peculiar, soft slurring tones—delivering some kind of lecture. Much of it was indistinct, but I managed to make out enough to know that he was preaching some esoteric gospel.

Suddenly I heard a footstep inside the room approaching the door. Before I could get away it opened and I found myself staring into a pair of vacant eyes set in a white, haggard, and somewhat inhuman face.

I was up, ready to grapple with him if he raised a cry, but his eyes looked sightlessly through me as if he were sleep-walking. Without the slightest sign of being aware of my presence, he closed the door behind him, passed me as though I had been less than a shadow, and slowly descended the stairs. In his hand he carried a vase of daffodils. At the same moment music began in the studio; evidently the séance was at an end.

I suddenly realised that my knees were trembling violently; if I had not caught hold of the balusters I should have collapsed. My sole idea at that moment was to get away from the unholy place as quickly as I could.

The body in the room below was infinitely less terrifying than the man turned into a horrible, soulless, mindless automaton; for there was neither soul nor mind behind that calm face and unseeing eyes. I had seen people hypnotised, but this was not hypnotism; the poor devil gave me a sensation of being completely empty. Something had been done to the man which had turned him into a Robot—a being that would do certain tasks under instruction from its master, but which had no volition of its own . . . a living corpse from which the spirit had fled or been charmed away.

Of a sudden a word used by the old crone came to my mind and, with it, remembrance of legends I had heard spoken with bated breath in the island of San Domingo. They had said that years before, when labour for the sugar plantations in Haiti ran short, certain wealthy Creole owners in conjunction with the Voodoo witch doctors, used to dig up the bodies of those who had recently died and, by their black arts, turn them into Zombies or beings who were animated by the will-power of the Voodoo practitioner and could perform the hard work of turning the crushers in the mills, but had no human faculties. They had no likes or dislikes—being merely mindless flesh—and could be fed on a modicum of offal. It was necessary, however, to prepare their food without either salt or sugar or other strong flavouring, as if they partook of anything highly seasoned they would realise that they were dead and decamp back to their graves. If they reached the latter they would fall into instantaneous putrefaction. It was rumoured that, in certain cases, even white men and women were disinterred to be turned into Zombies. Operations at the graveyard were carried out under an assistant

Voodoo priest, who was garbed in strange ceremonial vestments and was known as Baron Samedi . . .

At the time I had heard the tales I had scoffed at them, but now I had a dreadful feeling that there was more in the gruesome legends than I had been disposed to credit.

If the mulatto and Maman Constance could do a thing like that their powers for evil must be enormous. He had told the old witch, "If he gets fresh, I'll send him where I sent Adolf . . ." I shivered, wondering if by any chance this was Adolf. I registered a vow that on the morrow I would purchase some kind of a weapon, even if it was only a sheath knife.

At the same time I could not make out his objective. There was seemingly an outer circle of clients and an Inner Circle, which was evidently some kind of a secret society. Had it something to do with Obeah or Voodoo or was there a deeper and perhaps more evil motive? Well, if I was spared, I would discover by hook or by crook—even if it meant playing into his hands by accepting the job he had offered me.

I had a suspicion that he probably sought out deadbeats or unimportant members of the community for his servants. Their disappearance would be less likely to excite comment. The figure in the bed was perhaps intended for a Zombie. It looked like another miserable wretch whom nobody cared about and who would not be missed. But there would probably be others . . . like the blonde girl, for example, or—Ines. I went rigid at the thought. They must be protected at all costs. The devil of it was that there was nobody but myself to rely on. If I went to the police they would merely think I was crazy. Suppose they sent to investigate. They would only find a presumably fanatic coloured doctor preaching a doctrine with just enough logic in it to preclude its exponent being locked up as a charlatan. And I had no doubt that the mulatto had some out of the way retreat such as Cornwall, where he could convey his uncanny Zombies. Even as I thought I was considering whether I would follow the ghastly Robot and see what he was up to or beat a retreat and wait for Ines and her friends and warn them of their danger.

I had decided on the latter when I heard the curious shuffling tread of the Zombie returning. I had no fear that he would bother me, but I funked looking into those sightless eyes again. Gazing round I saw an iron ladder hauled up to the roof by means of a pulley and a cord, the latter being fastened to a cleat in the wall. Above the ladder was a trap door, which I took to be a fire escape.

If there was a way on to the roof, there must inevitably be a way down again.

I was hastily loosening the cord to let down the ladder and the bowed back of the Zombie was just appearing when the door of the studio opened and to my dismay Caspar looked out. He had a whip in his hand and I think, for a split second, mistook me for his servant, for he lashed out at me angrily. I suppose the wretched slave had disobeyed orders in sneaking out.

The whip, which had a wicked leather thong, caught me across the shoulder and the tip curled round and raised a weal on my face. It stung like hell, my temper flared, and I turned on him and delivered a hefty right and left with all the force of loathing I felt for the man, intensified by the vicious burning of my cheek.

The mulatto, fortunately, was unprepared. I wished I had knocked him out, but I did not catch him full on the point. My right got him on the forehead, and my left contacted with his jaw, but only struck it sideways. He fell back through the door with a solid thump, clutching at the post. As he subsided he shouted something to the Zombie, who was now on the landing within a foot of where I was standing. If the witless semblance of a man had obeyed his order and grappled with me I should have been done, but he took no notice.

It was too late to release the ladder, so I turned and fled down the stairs, making for the line I had left dangling into the garden from the lower window. As I reached it I heard a crash behind me, which I presumed was the Zombie. I had been only just in time for Caspar's face, distorted with fury, glared from the window as I dropped on to the grass below. I had not attempted to check my descent and my hands smarted agonisingly where the cord had torn through them.

As I picked myself up to dart to the garden gate I cast a glance back at Dr. Caspar and ducked as I saw that a revolver glinted in his hand. Evidently he decided that it would court too much attention to fire at me, for the body in the lower room might have been difficult to explain. Instead, his head disappeared from the window, and as I ran I heard the clatter of his footsteps coming down the back stairway.

By merciful chance the gate *was* open, but I did not relish the idea of remaining in the public roadway, now that dark was setting in, since there might be a back door from the lower floor of the studios. I shot a hurried glance round for shelter, but there was no place to hide, so I doubled round the corner and, breaking into a run, turned into a small road leading to the Embankment.

Luck aided me again in the matter of a taxi coasting idly along. I sprinted alongside and boarded it on the run.

"Victoria Station," I gasped. "Quick; I have a train to catch."

CHAPTER V

I FOLLOW UP THE SCENT

A S MY TAXI approached Grosvenor Road I cursed Caspar for having driven me to flight. He had ruined my plan to intercept Ines on the way from the studio. The odds were right against her passing my pitch in Sloane Street again, and there seemed as much chance of my finding her as a needle in a bundle of hay.

I dismissed the cab at Victoria and went into a tea shop to think things out. I should have liked to get rid of my Vandyke beard, but there was nowhere I could do that without observation at the moment.

With coffee and toast in front of me I settled down to go over the net amount of my discoveries and sum them up, and determine my future plans.

The question of enlisting the police at this stage of the game was obviously out. It was equally clear that in some way I must keep an eye on the two girls. True, there was no actual evidence that the doctor intended them definite harm; but a man who had turned an unfortunate fellow artist into a soulless automaton was not a person one liked to see associating with young and innocent white girls.

I was undecided whether it would be better to take a run down to Cornwall or to concentrate on his lair in Siena Studios. Of course I could get nearer to my quarry by taking the job he had offered, but I had an idea I should be under too strict control to learn much. If I could find out what he was working for, and the activities of the Inner Circle, it might be worthwhile running the risk of accepting a position in the house. But then I should have very little chance of investigating in Cornwall, and I could not help thinking that the suggested "Boumfort" was the place where the more sinister work would be carried out.

Finally, having weighed all the pros and cons, I determined that to-morrow I would go to my pitch as usual and hope a lucky chance might bring one or the other of the girls my way. I would remain there until noon, when I would go to the studio. If I ran across

Caspar, I would explain on my tablet that I had drifted along to talk over his offer. If, as I hoped, he were out, I would find some means of entering and have a look round the top room. I might pick up Ines' address. Then, in the evening, unless I got caught, I would take train to Penzance and see if I could discover anything of the "Boumfort." I reckoned my small earnings were just about enough for the return journey.

The whole of my future actions depended really upon any success I might have at the studio.

I took up my pitch as usual the next morning, but I had no luck as far as the girls were concerned. About twelve o'clock I saw the huge figure of the mulatto loom up at the corner of the Square on the opposite side of the road. He stared in my direction, then made his way purposefully to where I was sitting.

I had no fear of being recognised—my hat had fortunately hidden the redness of my hair—and I chuckled inwardly to see that a patch round his left eye had turned green; evidently my knuckles had caught him just in front of the temple instead of the forehead.

"Still here?" He nodded amiably as he came to a stand before my pictures; the island with the aeroplane seemed to fascinate him.

I nodded and smiled.

"Thought any more of what I said yesterday?" he demanded.

I shook my head, then wrote on the pavement: "I thought you were kidding me."

He frowned. "Not at all. As it happens I have particular need of a decent, honest man at my place and I am willing to give up to five pounds for the right man," he continued.

I pretended to consider the matter, endeavouring to assume an expression of cupidity fighting with cunning. He was waiting for an answer with more eagerness than one would expect. His unknown visitor must have rattled him badly.

"How long will the job last?" I wrote at length.

"Depends on yourself. If you are sensible and don't ask too many questions"—he made an attempt at a wink—"it would be permanent."

I pretended to reflect again. "Would you need me all day?"

"No; not at present, though later, if you suited, I'd like you to live on the premises."

This was what I had feared. Once under his eye there would be no little chance of my getting out on my own devices.

I shook my head and put down: "I wouldn't want to give this up unless I knew it was safe."

His face showed annoyance.

"I wouldn't mind a bit of evening or night work," I added, "so long as I could come here mornings." I felt the bluff was worth trying.

He looked relieved. "All right. I'll try you out in the evening first and we can talk about the other later. I'll want you to wear a commissionaire's uniform—I suppose that isn't going to offend your pride," he added with a malicious grin. I shook my head.

"When can you come—to-morrow night?"

"No; have to see doctor about arm to-morrow," I wrote. "Will Monday do?"

He scowled. "For a beggar you're damned independent," he grumbled. "All right, Monday. Seven o'clock, at the address I gave you."

I had an inspiration. "Sorry, I lost that," I put down.

"Did you?" He glanced at me swiftly. "Never mind. Number seven, Siena Studios, Chelsea." And with a curt nod he strode away down Sloane Street.

I wished I knew where he was bound for. If only I could have been certain he was going to be out of the way for a couple of hours I would have risked another visit there and then.

I fidgeted for a while; one minute keyed up to taking the chance, the next telling myself it would be madness. Finally I tossed a coin; if it came down heads I would go—if it was tails I would wait.

It turned up a head and with a sinking sensation I got up and prepared to catch a bus to Glebe Place.

When I got out of the bus at Chelsea Town Hall my first job was to dive into one of the side streets and buy a hat at a second-hand clothes shop, choosing one that came down well over my red hair.

I had no definite plan of campaign. On the way to the studios I called at an estate agents and inquired if they knew if any of the Siena Studios were to let. They looked through their list and informed me that they understood the property had been disposed of for use as a private house a month or so previously. The confirmation of my deductions hearted me quite a lot.

It was lucky that I approached my objective with more than usual caution. If I had gone straight down the lane I should have been caught and Heaven knows what would have happened. As it was, my timidity drove me to summon up resolution in a small public-house within thirty or forty yards of the lane where, from the bar, I was able to keep an eye on the entrance of the turning to the studios. Halfway through my drink I saw a closed car come round the corner of the street, driven by a coloured man; inside it were the mulatto and Maman Constance. It turned into the lane and I thanked my stars that I had dallied.

Ten minutes passed. Then, strung up to desperation, I decided to have a peep down the lane. Putting on as ingenious expression as I could muster, I crossed the road and, hugging the wall, went along until I was sufficiently near the courtyard to peer at the house.

I held my breath as I saw the doctor and the old woman carrying out of the front door a big, apparently weighty bundle swathed in a sheet. As I stared, risking detection heedlessly, a corner of the sheet slipped and I raw that the bundle contained the body of the man I had seen laid out the previous night. The mulatto cursed and the chauffeur dashed to help, covered up the figure hastily and assisted them to bundle it into the car.

I did not wait after that, but ran back as quickly as I could leg it to the public-house and ordered another drink, A couple of minutes later I was relieved to see the car turn out of the lane and drive off in the direction of the King's Road. Caspar was sitting on the front seat with the driver and Maman Constance kept the corpse company in the interior.

I gave them time to get well out of the way, and then much more confidently set off again for Siena Lane.

CHAPTER VI

I FIND THE ROLL OF THE "ANCESTORS"!

THE rooms of the ground floor studios were open and empty. Bits of straw and sheets of old newspaper lay about in corners. One room on the second floor was locked, but the opposite door opened and I found myself in an apartment furnished in the plainest possible way as a dormitory; three beds with grey army blankets stood along one side of a wall, and there was a washstand in a corner with a bare deal kitchen table on which stood a metal coffee pot and some cheap crockery. In the centre was a vase of daffodils and sitting on one of the beds was the eerie, soulless man I had seen the previous evening. He sprang up as I came into the room, but there was no meaning in his eyes.

"Where is your master?" I asked quietly, keeping an eye on him and also the door. Actually, though the poor devil raised a feeling of nausea in me, I did not think there was any harm in him. For all the effect my words had on him I might have spoken to a block of stone. I realised that I stood no danger from him at any rate.

The door through the further small room to the back stairway was open; this must be the one used by the Zombie; Caspar would scarcely risk his being seen going up and down by the main staircase. The service door of the upper apartment might be unlocked. It was not very likely, but it was a better bid than risking being seen forcing the front door.

I started up the stair, first closing the front entrance and fastening the Yale lock, so that I could get away without losing time if I had to beat a retreat. As I mounted I heard the shuffling of the man's feet following me. Not the least unpleasant part of the Zombie's conti-guity was a deathlike musty effluvium. It was not so much a physical thing as a spiritual one, and I wondered how Caspar could stand having the thing around. But perhaps he had grown accus-tomed to it.

For a second I considered telling him to remain below, then it occurred to me that he probably wouldn't obey, and in any case he was harmless.

It was just as well I had not ordered him back, for when I tried the door to the doctor's apartment it was locked. I was examining the keyhole when I felt a touch on my shoulder and spinning round saw a key which the Zombie was holding out to me.

I stared at him suspiciously, but for the life of me I could not see any flicker of intelligence in his face. No human being could possibly mask every sign of thought or feeling as he was doing.

As I did not take the key the Zombie glided past me, opened the door, then stood dumbly, as expressionless as ever, waiting for me to enter.

I still funked some kind of ambush, but concluded that I would order the fellow back to the lower room. If he obeyed and left the key, I thought I could take it as pretty good assurance that he had no ulterior designs. There was no chance of making a get-away; I had noticed as I came up the stairs that the window had been screwed up on the inside.

"Thanks; you can go back again now," I said curtly. He paid no attention, but when I made a gesture he shuffled slowly back down the stairs.

I waited until I heard him go back into the lower studio, then, taking the key, I stepped over the threshold.

The small room was simply a kitchenette. It was the big front studio that I looked forward to examining. It was shut off from the entrance hall by a *portière* of some Eastern material, and the odour of an Oriental perfume till clung to the air.

I peered round the curtain and stifled an exclamation as my eyes took in the room and its furnishings. By some trick of colour and interior decoration the place had been made to appear almost as large again as it really was. The ceiling was sparrow-egg blue and in it were set small electric, lights with five-pointed, silver reflectors in the form of several of the constellations. I recognised Orion as the central design. The walls were carried out in a light terracotta, and from the floor up to a height of about five feet was a dado bearing a series of figures in groups, which reminded me of some of the Pompeian frescoes.

At the end of the room furthest removed from the window stood a desk of some black wood, and behind it a throne-like black chair. Back of the chair, hanging on the wall, was a plaque of a goat's head with eyes that looked like transparent turquoise. Ranged in seven rows facing the throne were a number of seats. The floor was covered with a heavy, silk pile carpet of glowing orange and a pair of fretted, brass pedestals with ball-shaped censers atop flanked the desk or altar.

I could imagine that at night, lighted only by the constellations in the ceiling, the atmosphere, intensified by the burning incense, would have a decided effect upon an audience. Even by daylight one felt strangely awed.

One had an idea that there were supernatural forces, and these not amicable, present.

There were only three other pieces of furniture in the place. A kind of organ set near the window, a press against the wall near the kitchenette door, and a chest standing by the second door, which I knew led out on to the passage and thence to the main stairs.

Both were of the same black wood as the throne and bore a good deal of carving—some of which was of a frankly obscene nature. They looked to me like native work from Central Africa.

I tackled the press first. There was no sign of a lock, but it was securely fastened. I sought for a concealed keyhole, but concluded that it probably opened by means of a secret spring. I pushed and pulled at every projection in the carving I could find, but nothing happened. I got out my sheath knife and tried to get the edge in some gap at the base of a panel, but without success. So far as any sign of a seam went the thing might have been carved out of a solid block of wood.

Time was slipping by and I dared not remain too long in case Caspar returned. Still racking my brain for a clue I turned to the chest. There was no difficulty with this; the lid was unfastened and, lifting it, I found the coffer contained what I took to be the doctor's ceremonial robes. Underneath a yellow one, carefully folded, lay a long gown of blood-red silk slashed with curious designs in black and a head-dress made of gay-hued feathers and ornamented with a jewel made to represent an open eye.

As I was replacing them I suddenly thought of a Japanese puzzle box which I had one time bought. By pressing up one of the sides one released an inner catch and allowed the lid to slide out in grooves. I went back to the press and tried to move a panel that bore the trace of fingerprints, but could make no impression on it with my one arm. I had kept my waistcoat buttoned, but now I decided that I must have the use of my second arm. When I had freed it I again sought to shift the panel, then I got on my knees to examine the feet, which were in the form of four round balls. Quite at random I noticed that one was movable and alternately pushing and pulling it, I eventually succeeded in bringing it out at an angle. As I did so there was a click and the front of the press swung slowly ajar.

I sprang to my feet excitedly and peered into the press. It was fitted with shelves, divided in some cases vertically into pigeon holes, and at the bottom were a couple of drawers. The first thing that struck my eye was the glint of a thirty-four bore automatic. I took it up gingerly, found it was fully loaded and without hesitation pocketed it. There was an odd-looking bottle beside it which I also stuck in my pocket. Then I turned to examine the pigeon holes.

Several were stuffed with letters, but apart from noting that a number bore foreign stamps, I had no time to spare to go through Caspar's correspondence. I glanced at one or two books, which seemed to be ledgers and cash books, and felt I was on the scent. "Accounts of the Ancestors" was written on the first page of each and one was marked "C. P. Private Account." I put them aside and turned my attention to the drawers. The first contained a collection of bizarre, native jewellery, the "eye "and the "goat's head" motif reproduced in several pieces.

The second drawer was fastened. If what I sought was not there, I was done.

I got out my knife and was about to force it when it occurred to me that one of my own keys might fit. I pulled out my ring and to my satisfaction found that one belonging to an old suit case did the trick.

A second later I was poring over two parchment bound volumes with the first feeling of complete satisfaction I had experienced since I started on the enterprise.

The first was a diary and the entries appeared to concern a number of people, being listed as having "joined the Ancestors," or having joined the "Inner Circle." Large sums of money were entered in brackets under several names. I noted a sum of fifty thousand dollars after a Mr. Sebastian Walton and seven thousand pounds following the name of a Professor I. Singhani. All in all, I estimated the total amount entered must run into a good many thousands of pounds.

I put this aside to examine the second volume. On the cover was a tooled inscription: "The Kingdom to be." There were three sections divided by red cards bound in between the leaves. The first was titled "List of Possible Ministers of the Court," the second "Rank and File, Supemumeries and Zombies, existing and prospective," and the third section bore the heading: "Inner and Outer Circles."

Of greater value still was a large sheet folded into four at the end of the book drawn to represent a kind of genealogical tree. I examined this with great care, and though a lot of it was incomprehensible to me, I was able to make out enough to give me a fairly full idea of the aims and objects of the mulatto and his gang.

The thing was something like a chart; there was a map which I identified roughly as part of Northern Asia bordering on Thibet and part of Turkestan; this was given as the headquarters of the "Inner Circle." A second sketch map covered a swathe of country extending across Central Africa, including the Congo and Liberia. This was the territory ruled by the "Outer Circle." Various names appeared indicating the heads of the two "Circles," including five world-renowned names, of which two were well known Continental politicians and one English. Of the five three were Semitic.

Although I could not make out fully what Caspar's intentions were, I could see that the "Inner Circle" had for its object the establishing of a spiritual and occult world force with headquarters in Asia. The "Outer Circle," on the other hand, was bent on bringing into being a great negro brotherhood—practically an empire—with devil worship as its *piece de resistance*. From notes in the margin it was clear that the mulatto intended to extend his spheres of influence eventually to all countries where there were coloured races.

The ultimate scheme, so far as I could read it, was the fostering of a succession of wars between the white races until finally the white powers were so attenuated that the more virile and untouched negro and Asiatic peoples would be in a position to overcome them—first in Africa and Asia and later in America and Europe. After that the negro and Asiatics would be welded together in a complete imperial hierarchy. Moreover, since good had been tried for several centuries by the world peoples and been found wanting in the matter of bringing prosperity and content, it was necessary that evil should be given a trial. Further, that as the white peoples were the natural expression of the good forces because of their colour, the coloured peoples the natural adherents of the Satanic ones; and that whereas the white were decreasing and the coloured peoples waxing stronger, it was obvious that Satan was the being to be cultivated. . . Money was apparently plentiful for the scheme, and from what I could judge it was being obtained in varying ways, including ransom and blackmail, and by rendering the provider of the money amenable by the use of a drug which was referred to as "S. 17."

Needless to say, Caspar's name appeared at the head of both "Inner and Outer Circles" as "Master," Maman Constance and a

Prince Ali Singh being his principal lieutenants. The latter I had heard of as a one-time ruler of an Eastern state who had given up his throne to seek enlightenment from the masters in the wilds of the Himalayan Mountains.

My mouth was dry by the time I had finished studying the chart. It was so damnably cleverly organised. The tenets of the "Inner Circle" were such as to appeal to all the Eastern races with the exception of militaristic Japan. The work of consolidation would go on quietly and secretly until the moment arrived for the declaration of the "Circles" policy. In the meantime arms were being quietly cached in out-of-the-way places. The mulatto had control of ships owned nominally by small firms in the Levant and Africa. And the "Outer Circle" or its objects must appeal to every semi-educated coloured man who was suffering from the belief that the white races would never allow him to rise socially or economically to complete independence in the ordinary way.

The whole thing was considerably bigger than I had for a moment dreamed. It seemed absurd for me ever to hope to circumvent Caspar's plans alone; yet, if I appealed to Scotland Yard or the Secret Service, by the time I could get them to act, Caspar and the proofs would have vanished. The only thing to do was to learn as much as I could and then trust to luck that I might be able to find help when the right moment arrived. Caspar was the brains and chief priest of the organisation; if need be I should have to make it my business to kill him and Maman Constance.

Then as I was reluctantly refolding the chart I found a slip of paper tucked in between the latter and the back cover of the volume. On it, in pencil, were written three names:

Mrs. Montague Whitfield. Cadogan Terrace, S.W.
Miss Bridget Westerham. 123, Queen Street, W. 1.
Miss Ines Bellenden. 123, Queen Street, W. 1.

Following Miss Westerham's name was a note—"For the Stone if better unavailable," and against that of Ines, "Self will deal with."

CHAPTER VII

I PUT AN ENEMY OUT OF ACTION

I EXTRACTED two pages from the diary relating to the money obtained from Walton and the others. This done, I restored the book to the drawer, relocked it, closed the door of the press and was congratulating myself when I heard somebody coming up the back stairway. It was not the Zombie, nor did I think it was Caspar.

A bold bluff seemed the best solution. If I knocked at the front door and said I had come to see the doctor, I should get a glance at the newcomer. He would tell the mulatto that I would report for duty in the middle of the coming week. This would leave me a few days free to carry out my investigation in Cornwall. And, by declaring my presence, he would be less likely to question the Zombie, if he had heard me in the room.

I shut myself on to the landing and knocked.

Almost immediately the door opened and I found myself facing a young buck negro of the type sometimes seen swaggering down the sidewalks of Harlem or the main streets of Sierra Leone. He exuded impudent vulgarity from the tips of his shining, patent-leather shoes to the crest of his brown derby, set at a cocky angle on one side of his fuzzy head.

I think he was almost as startled as I.

"What d'ye want?" he said.

"I want Dr. Caspar," I returned sharply. "He told me to call."

He surveyed me in a puzzled way and then answered: "Well, he ain't here, so you'd better call again. Doc' gone out of town; he won't be back till to-morrow," he went on in a surly tone. His eyes roamed over me again. "Say—what kind of a guy are you at all?" he pursued. His hand reached out and plucked aside the unfastened under lapel of my coat, disclosing my left arm folded across my chest. I cursed inwardly and drew back, but it was too late.

"Sure! You're the guy the old dame spoke about. . . said you were dumb an' couldn't talk, but she reckoned there was su'thin' crooked about you." He had grabbed me by my coat in his excitement, and in doing so the bottle I had taken from the doctor's cupboard could be seen sticking up out of my inner pocket. His jaw dropped; either in fear or indignation, and his voice took on a brutal note,

"Where d'you get that?" he demanded, loosing his hold to point at the bottle. "That's what ah come for. Did he send you fo' it, too?"

His stupidity played into my hands. I nodded.

"You're a liar," he cried suddenly, and with a gunman's celerity whipped a revolver out of his hip pocket and levelled it at me.

"Stick up your hands," he ordered, viciously.

"What for?" I tried to look mildly surprised and lifted my right arm, but with every nerve alert to put him out. "Say, this is a fine way to treat a chap after the boss telling me to come along for a job," I continued in an aggrieved whine.

He glowered at me, but hesitated, and I could see he was uncertain.

"How come yo' pretendin' to have only one arm when yo' got two?" he rejoined, curiosity getting the better of him.

"You mean this?" I nodded my chin in the direction of my doubled-up left arm and grinned cunningly. "It's there okay, but it ain't no use—paralysed. Only if people saw it they might not believe it so I keep it out of sight. When you're begging you've got to appeal to folks as best you can."

"Sez you," he jeered; then: "Does the doctor know?"

"Of course," I answered.

"Yeah, but what about that bottle?" he returned with an access of his previous venom. "Yo' say he sent you to fetch it?"

"I don't know what you're talking about," I replied curtly. "I said the doctor told me to come to the studios about a job. As for the bottle—it's whisky. Look for yourself if you don't believe me."

He hesitated then, shifted the gun to his left hand and came forward. It was what I had prayed for, but I had thought he would have ordered me to show it myself; perhaps he feared I might draw a gun if he allowed me to drop my arm.

As he approached I practised a trick I had seen used in a fight between two dagoes in Brazil—launching a kick with all my force at his stomach. It caught him fair in the solar plexus and he went over like a ninepin, the revolver clattering along the floor as he fell. I dropped, too, overbalance by the kick, but whereas I was unhurt, he was doubled up with pain. I scrambled to my knees, pushed shut the studio door behind me, and before he could get up was at his throat.

He was a shade smaller than I, but every inch of him was wire and sheer black murder. I had knocked his gun out of reach and we were at it, equally matched, tooth and nail—for he used both without compunction.

Writhing together on the floor, I had no chance of giving him a knock-out punch. We both had one another by the throat, and though I was uppermost and contrived every now and then to give his head a whacking thud on the floor, the carpet and the thickness of his skull saved him and the bangs only rendered him more vicious.

I felt my eyes bulging and my tongue swelling as he wrapped his legs around mine to give his claw-like fingers a better purchase, and retaliated by raising myself up as far as I could and dropping down again on his stomach to drive the wind out of him. It was a double-edged manoeuvre because it gave me a pretty good jolt, too, but I was prepared and could render the muscles of my diaphragm rigid.

As I came down on him with a thump for about the fourth time, the bottle worked itself out of my pocket, the glass stopper flew out and rolled along the floor, and a good half of its contents, a viscous, green fluid with an aromatic odour, went into his open mouth and over his nose. He must have seen it coming, for he gave a wrench to avoid it, and a gurgle of absolute animal terror. Some of the stuff was spluttered on to my face; it stung sharply and I shut my eyes thinking it might be vitriol. I felt his throat gulp convulsively between my fingers and his hand gradually relax. A second later, when I dared open my eyes, he was lying without a sign of movement.

For a space I had an idea that he was shamming, so I still kept my hand on his windpipe. Though his body was inert, his eyes appeared to be alive and they glared into mine wildly in the most appalling horror. As I stood him up I saw the negro's eyes begin to close very gradually. I watched breathlessly, more interested now than scared, and as I stared his face grew calm and the lines round his eyes and mouth began to fade. In less than two minutes more he appeared exactly as the man I had seen the night previously . . . the swathed figure that Caspar and the old crone had taken away in the car.

I felt better as I realised that I had not deliberately killed him. Something would have to be done about him, but that could wait for a little while. It would be a pretty problem for Caspar when he did find the nigger; he might believe that the fellow had had an accident with the bottle, but I considered him too astute for that.

I got up shakily and straightened my clothes, and then went into the kitchenette and bathed my aching throat and washed away the blood from the scratches. Curiously enough the battle had driven away most of my fears. Winning this trick had heartened me for future trouble.

I found a pot with coffee in it and I warmed it up on the' gas stove and purloined some biscuits from a tin. After I had consumed these and smoked a cigarette, I felt something like my old self. Then I went back into the studio to think what was the next thing to be done.

I could scarcely go lugging a thing that looked like a corpse on my shoulder or in a taxi to my room; and I had no idea how long the effects of the drug would last. I might hide it in the chest—there was ample room—but Caspar when he found it would be more inclined to suspicion than if I left the body on the floor. The only alternative was to carry it down to the vacant, first floor flat. I had noticed an empty, wooden coal bin in the back room, and I believed the body would just about fit into it.

I knelt down to examine him again more carefully There was no sign of rigor, but his flesh was as cold as the death it simulated. When I raised his eyelids I observed that the pupils had turned upwards almost out of sight and the eyes closed again slowly when I released the lids.

I thought I might as well go through his pockets whilst I was about it.

There was a wallet with about seven pounds in English and American notes and a driving licence made out in the name of Antonio Barley. There were one or two letters, a rabbit's foot, two bunches of keys (one of which bore a silver tag with Caspar's name on and the studio address), cigarettes, a pocket knife, some loose change and, in one of the waistcoat pockets, a curious disc, made of silver, with the goat head motif and the number 23 stamped on it in copper.

I replaced all the items but Caspar's keys and the badge. That latter I pocketed, thinking it might be useful, and the keys I dropped in front of the ebony press. I picked up the revolver and replaced that in the man's hip pocket, taking the precaution of removing the cartridges first.

Then, after restopping the bottle carefully, since about half the contents remained, and tying the neck and stopper with my handkerchief, I went to the front door to reconnoitre. I hoped to be able to carry the body alone, but it would have to be by the front stairs. As the staircase seemed quiet I thought I could take the risk. It was a pretty stiff job hoisting him on my shoulder, but I managed it after two or three shots, by propping him up in a chair like a sack of coals.

Within five minutes of leaving the studio, Mr. Antonio Barley was reposing in the coal bin of number one studio with a gap sufficient to prevent his smothering. I scattered some of the loose straw and newspapers around the bin to cover up traces of my hard work, shut both room doors, and hopped up as quickly as I could to Caspar's place again.

The thing that now most worried me was the spilling of some of the mulatto's "medicine" on the carpet. However, it had dried out practically clear, though the smell still hung around. When I had rubbed the place with a duster from the kitchen, for a few minutes, and revived the pile of the carpet, it looked quite normal.

Then I had a final glance round to see that I had left no traces and, five minutes later, I was on the top of a bus on my way back to Sloane Street.

CHAPTER VIII

I CALL ON THE LADY OF MY DREAMS

MY SAFEST PLACE for the next couple of hours was the Sloane Street pavement. I had also come to the conclusion that I must refuse the mulatto's offered job.

My immediate plan was to remain on my pitch till the morrow, when Caspar was due to return, and then send him a line to say that I had taken a job in the country and myself disappear. I cursed Barley: if he had not turned up there was practically every chance of my visit to the studio never being suspected.

I was thoroughly nervous, and kept a wary eye open for anybody who passed more than once. There was one woman who turned up twice between two and four P.M., and she got on my nerves to such an extent I wanted to bolt forthwith. When, a few minutes before I had made up my mind to go and call on Miss Bellenden, she sauntered along for the third time, I got the wind up completely.

Probably she was only waiting for a friend, but I had had more than enough of her. At the same moment a Piccadilly-bound omnibus turned the corner and without waiting to see if she had reappeared, I dashed across the street and took it at a run. I felt a little happier when I alighted at Knightsbridge and saw no trace of her.

In case I happened to be followed I doubled round Shepherd Market and approached Queen Street from the north, cutting through some mews. I found the house was one of the old, converted aristocratic residences. A neat maid answered the door, informed me that Miss Bellenden had recently come in, and asked me to take a seat.

She disappeared through a doorway facing the first floor landing—one of a couple—and I dropped into a settee by the wall and stared at a coloured print of Frith's Derby Day, trying to compose some suitable way of opening the interview. I had fortunately a card with me—relic of my better days—and had sent that in by the maid.

She returned within a few minutes, said Miss Bellenden would see me and ushered me into a large, well-lighted room with two windows overlooking Queen Street.

There was nobody present so I took it that Miss Bellenden was in the bedroom beyond the folding doors. From the general atmosphere I judged that the suite was let furnished. The personal touches consisted only of a large photograph in a leather travelling frame of a fine-looking elderly lady and a profusion of flowers and books. I was endeavouring to make out the titles of a pile on a small table nearby when the door clicked and Miss Bellenhem came in.

I was too interested in her face to take much notice of her dress, but I believe she was in a filmy semi-evening gown of coral trimmed with grey. She showed no surprise as I stood before her and I inferred that the maid had given her own description of me.

"Mr. Worthing?" she inquired in the voice I had memorised so well.

"Yes—you must think it very extraordinary of me . . . calling on you like this, but the matter is terribly important," I began in rather an incoherent rush.

If she thought that I had come to solicit money or help, she showed no sign of it on her face.

"I've seen you before, Mr. Worthing—haven't I?" Her brow wrinkled, then she smiled. "Sloane Street corner, wasn't it? Of course, I remember perfectly . . . Won't you sit down?" She indicated a chair near a big divan and turning to a side-table took a box of cigarettes and brought them across to me.

"You'll smoke, won't you?"

"Thanks." I accepted and, as she took one herself, lighted it for her; then she dropped on the divan.

"I haven't come here to ask for anything—please don't think that," I blurted.

Her glance gave me grave consideration. "No; I didn't think you had . . . but suppose you tell me why you have come. . . By the way, how did you discover my name and address?"

"I didn't follow you—if that is what you infer." My tone was curter than I intended, but I hated her to believe I was a footpad or a crook. "I got it from Dr. Caspar Pettifranc's private diary at his place in Siena Studios," I explained. "Actually, I broke in and pinched it."

That startled her.

"But why?"

"Well—it is rather a long story," I answered. "Can you spare, say, a quarter of an hour? I assure you I shan't be wasting your time."

She glanced quickly at a small clock and nodded. "Yes, I have to go to a cocktail party near here at seven, but I haven't anything to do until then. Before you start I think you'd better have a drink. Which would you prefer, a cocktail or a whisky and soda?"

"Neither, thanks, unless you are going to have one yourself."

"As a matter of fact, I was . . . orange juice," she returned, "but if it will make you more comfortable, I'll make it two cocktails."

"No, please—have the orange juice and I'll have a chotah peg—whisky and soda."

"India, too? I knew there was something mysterious about you yesterday in Sloane Street," she smiled in a friendly way. She was getting up, but I saw the orange juice all ready in a glass on the side-table, together with a decanter and glasses, so I forestalled her.

"By the way, before I begin, do you mind telling me whether you knew Dr. Pettifranc before you went to his studio the other evening?" I asked.

She shook her head. "No; that was the first time I ever saw him as far as I am aware."

"You didn't know he was following you in Sloane Street when you met your friend, Miss Westerham?" I pursued.

She frowned. "No—was he? Why?"

"Did Miss Westerham know that she was also being followed, on the bus, by a native woman?"

"No, I don't think so. I'm sure she didn't or she would have told me."

"Would you mind telling me how your Aunt heard of him?"

"I—I'm not quite certain," she pondered. "I believe some friend of hers said he was clever and that there was a lot in what he taught. You mean you think"—she looked pretty incredulous—"that he made her go and take me and Bridget—but how could he?"

I noticed with joy that she was no longer on her guard, delicately disguised as it had been, but was treating me now as an equal.

"I think just that," I answered, steadily. "I'll tell you why."

I then related as concisely as I could the events following on our meeting in Sloane Street and the conversation between the doctor and Maman Constance in the church.

" 'The Whistling Ancestors,' " she interrupted me. "What a peculiar name. What does it mean?"

I explained all I knew and went on to tell her of my subsequent operations. Until that moment I had not realised the damnable indictment it formed on the mulatto and his accomplices. Her eyes sparkled as I narrated my tussle with Caspar and I could see my own first horror reflected in her face as I described the Zombie and the figure on the bed. She shivered as I recounted the effects of the drug on the negro, Barley, but did not say anything herself until I had brought my story up to the moment when I had decided to call on her that evening. In relating the thing I had kept to myself the information contained in the chart. It was too vital to run any chance of being talked about at present.

I had expected her to evince some apprehension but, so far as I could judge, her manner conveyed more of curiosity than fear.

"But—what would he want to do to us . . . or with us?" she began. "I mean . . . you don't honestly think he really intends to—to sacrifice Bridget?"

I shrugged. "If you'd seen him as I have you wouldn't put anything past him," I said. I had not told her of the mulatto's intentions regarding herself—it was too beastly to talk about.

"Do you think we ought to go to the police?" she asked.

"I'd considered that, but you see the devil is so clever. There's no evidence that he is anything but a medical lecturer; you bet he has plenty of alibis. And even if they got hold of the Zombie, Caspar would probably persuade them that he is merely some wretched mental case he's treating. And then—" I stopped.

"Well?" she prompted.

"There's a good deal behind his activities that I haven't fathomed yet," I temporised. "I'd rather not bring in the police so far as the studio business is concerned. I'm rather keen on following up the big thing myself, and if the police went nosing round the studio, Caspar might bolt. Also, if they discovered the chap I laid out, they're much more likely to stick me in jail than Caspar."

She nodded. "Yes, there is that. I wish I could take a hand."

"I'd much rather you went off to some place where I knew you'd be safe," I returned soberly. "I'm certain London isn't healthy for you while he's around."

"I'm not a child," she said, indignantly. "And, anyway, if the doctor is so clever and we can't tell the police all we know they wouldn't stand a chance against him and the woman. You'd be far more of a protection than they would."

"I doubt it," I said.

"I'd rather trust you than them," she rejoined and I glowed inwardly. "Suppose—" her gaze dropped and she flushed a little. "Suppose I engaged you as a body guard," she suggested.

"I'd do all I could to deserve your trust," I answered, "but, frankly, I shouldn't feel happy."

"Is it a question of money? . . . I mean, if you're broke—and I suppose you are or you wouldn't be working as pavement artist," she continued, looking very embarrassed.

"Partly—but I expect I'd manage somehow," I returned trying to put her at her ease. "If necessary I can always burgle Caspar's place again," I grinned. "But I'd feel more comfortable if there was a good hefty private detective looking after you."

She considered this for a space and then began again, "Very well—I'll ask Aunt Mary to see about one—but only on condition that you'll let me engage you unofficially as well. You say Dr. Caspar offered you five pounds a week . . . Bridget and I can easily afford that and not miss it. Her father is one of the richest men in America." A startled look flashed across her face. "I can see why he might be interested in Bridget."

"How do you mean?"

"He might be going to blackmail Mr. Westerham by kidnapping Bridget."

The telephone bell shrilled and she went to the little lobby to answer it. I could not help overhearing the conversation and her very first words sent a wave of apprehension through me.

"Yes, Mrs. Townsend . . . No, she left here at twelve o'clock . . . she hasn't arrived?" Her voice took on a note of concern. "Oh, no, I'm sure nothing could have . . . She may have decided to call in somewhere, or her car may have broken down . . . No, she was driving herself in the Bentley she bought last week." There was a pause.

"Yes, please, I wish you would—that seems the only thing *one* can do at the moment. As you say, there's plenty of traffic on that road. I know; if she doesn't turn up in another half-hour I'll drive out myself and see if I can find her. You'll ring me up, then? Thanks, and I'll do the same." There was another pause.

"Oh, but that's absurd; of course it isn't your fault. I expect she will turn up safely, though she is rather a long time overdue . . . Very well—in half an hour. Good-bye."

She replaced the receiver and when she came in I could see she was having a hard task to maintain her composure. "It's Bridget," she said tonelessly. "She left at twelve o'clock to motor to Mrs. Townsend's near Hartley Row in Berkshire. She hasn't arrived and Mrs. Townsend is worried. You'd have thought she'd have telephoned if she had been all right." Her voice tailed away in a pathetic break.

"Oh, no—it couldn't be," she gasped, as something in my face chilled her. I was remembering Caspar's drive to Cornwall. He must have passed her on the way, and what more favourable opportunity could he have of abducting her?

"When did Miss Westerham decide to go?" I asked.

"Yesterday at lunch Mrs. Townsend asked us both, but I had another appointment, so Bridget went alone."

"Did you happen to mention it at the doctor's last night?"

She nodded. "We were telling Aunt Mary, but I don't see how he could have heard." Her face was strained. "You said he was taking that body to Cornwall—he'd be on the same road. But—he couldn't . . . not in broad daylight," she added piteously.

I took it upon myself to pour out some whisky for her.

"I expect it's just coincidence, but I agree with you it's damnably worrying. I know . . . ring up the Automobile Association and ask if they've had any report of a breakdown or accident in the neighbourhood of Hartley Row," I suggested.

"Please, will you?"

When I got the man in charge he said there had been no information of that kind; could I give him a description of the car and the driver? I did this and he was exceedingly kind and sympathetic and said he would call several A.A. scouts on duty in the neighbourhood and let me know.

"Thank you, Mr. Worthing," said Ines. Her face had lost its scared look and now held something that appeared to turn her into an entirely different person. There was a strange, almost exalted determination mirrored in it now I was able to see and appreciate the sterling quality and depth of her inner self.

"Can you drive a car?" she asked quietly.

I nodded.

"Will you go with me to look for Bridget?"

"Of course; but it may mean making for Cornwall."

"Do you mind?"

"I? Lord, no. I was thinking about you. Why not let me take the car? I'll phone you all along the road," I added recklessly, forgetting the meagre limits of my immediate resources.

"I shouldn't dream of it. I suppose you're afraid I might let you down. Believe me, I'm not quite so helpless as I look. Father taught me to ride and shoot and I've stood up to leopard and buffalo, and they require nerve . . ." She stopped, suddenly scarlet.

"I wasn't thinking that at all," I replied, hastily.

"Then—it's settled. Thanks. I'll phone and call the party off and then we'd better scratch up something to eat, whilst we wait for Mrs. Townsend to ring up. After that, if Bridget hasn't turned up, we'll start. All right?" She looked at me questioningly.

"All right with me," I said, more optimistically than I felt.

She started for the phone, but stopped and came back.

"I've been puzzling over how we heard of Dr. Caspar. I've suddenly remembered it was a chambermaid at the Carlton . . . we were all staying there before we took this flat."

"A chambermaid," I echoed; it sounded innocent enough.

"Yes. She had a card of his that she said had been left behind by one of the guests who had been to his séances, and she was telling us how he had made her look at least twenty years younger—" She broke off as she saw my face.

"Was it a young woman?" I inquired.

"No, about forty, I should say. The intensely respectable type. Why, do you know her?"

"Was she . . ." I described as adequately as I could the "intensely respectable" female whom I had suspected of shadowing me during the afternoon.

"It sounds like the same, but I couldn't be sure."

"You may not be, but I am—practically," I said warmly. "And if it is"—I had a queer, totally irrational hunch—"I'd almost bet my last penny she's hanging round somewhere not far from the house right now!"

By common impulse we started to the window; I checked myself in the nick of time and let Ines go alone.

"Pretend you're just glancing out casually," I cautioned, but she had forestalled my warning and merely took in the street as an incurious accompaniment to moving a vase of flowers.

"On the other side of the road," she said, "as if she were waiting for someone to join her."

We stared at one another in silence for a space, then her mouth twitched and we laughed—more from nervousness than amusement.

She pulled herself up abruptly. "This is terrible," she exclaimed.

For a moment I was afraid she was going to the opposite emotional pale and burst into tears, but she didn't.

"Anyhow, that settles it, we've got to go," she said on a note of finality.

"Yes, that settles it," I echoed.

But I did not like the situation one little bit. The mulatto's intelligence department was too far flung for my fancy.

CHAPTER IX

I GO ON AN EXPEDITION WITH A LADY

MRS. TOWNSEND'S promised call came just after Ines' preparations were completed. The chauffeur had driven back as far as Bagshot, but had not seen nor heard anything of the missing girl or her car.

It would, of course, have given the show away completely if Ines and I left the house together. I had a suspicion that the "intensely respectable" woman had not followed me to Queen Street, but had come to keep an eye on Miss Bellenden.

We arranged that she should ring up the garage for a man to bring round her car. Starting off alone, she would wait for me at Notting Hill Gate tube. She was to tell the maid fairly loudly that she would be back about ten, and I did not think our shadower would trouble to follow.

As soon as the car arrived she went off, leaving me to wait for the phone message from the A.A. I was also to take her suitcase with me.

The message came through some ten minutes later. An A.A. scout had seen Miss Westerham's car pass through Staines. A second piece of news which disconcerted and puzzled me was that the same car had been left at Egham. The garage proprietor had stated that the young lady seemed very worried as she had to go to Plymouth by train to meet somebody who was ill.

I made sure before leaving that the watcher was not lurking around. At Notting Hill Gate I kept well in the background by the bookstall until I was sure Ines had not been followed.

She told me that the woman was close to the door when she set out and must have heard her say she would not be back till ten. As her car had turned the corner she had seen the "respectable person" walking sedately down the street.

Ines was even more perplexed than I over my information. Miss Westerham's mother was dead and her father was in New York and had no intention of visiting England There was certainly nobody else regarding whose health Bridget would have been likely to go scuttling off to Plymouth. However, we could do nothing until we saw the garage proprietor at Egham.

The long, almost summer twilight was deepening by the time we reached our first goal. The proprietor had gone to supper, but a lad fetched him and we explained our mission. He was a good fellow, but he knew no more than had already been conveyed to me by the A.A. official. He took us in to see the car and there was no doubt whatever that it belonged to Bridget.

"Did you notice if the lady was with anyone or if there was another car near?" I questioned.

He shook his head. "No, sir. I was busy getting the Bentley into place, so I didn't see her leave myself. Joe might have done," he continued. "He was outside putting some oil into a crank case for a customer. Hi, Joe," he called.

The lad came in and I questioned him. He had seen the lady go and said she walked along the main road for a hundred yards. There was nobody with her nor had he noticed any other car waiting.

"Which would be the nearest station to pick up a train for Plymouth?" I next demanded.

The proprietor himself answered. "Either Slough or Maidenhead, sir, would be most handy."

While I was questioning him, Ines was poking about in the car. Just as I was about to ask for a time-table, she gave a little cry and held up a crumpled piece of paper: it was an inland telegraph form. Our eyes devoured it together.

It read as follows: "Pick up Miss Bridget Westerham without delay and bring to Plymouth meet Ile de France. Father on board seriously ill and asking for her." It was addressed to "Scotson, 27 Lincoln's Inn Fields, London," and signed Westrigg. Apparently it had been sent off from Plymouth at ten A.M. that morning.

"But it can't be true," Ines argued breathlessly. "He wouldn't have left New York without telling her."

"Do you know Scotson or Westrigg?" I asked her.

"Westrigg is the code signature for Mr. Westerham's American firm—Westerham, Briggs & Company."

"I see; so, naturally, bearing that signature, she would take it as proof of authenticity," I reasoned.

"You don't think it may be genuine?"

"It may," I replied, "but, we can soon tell if Mr. Malden can lend us a morning paper."

He hurried off into the office and came back with a *Daily Express*. I looked to see if the Ile de France was listed amongst the coming arrivals, but there was nothing in the paper.

"What shall we do now?" Ines asked irresolutely.

"Go on to Mrs. Townsend's as we decided. We can put a call through there to the Royal Hotel at Plymouth, they'd know if the boat came in to-day. It's too late to get anyone at the London office."

We thanked Malden—he wouldn't accept a tip—and got back into the car again. It was getting dark, but I thought it would be worthwhile having a look in the lane. I got out when we turned the corner, went up one side for fifty yards or so and started back on the other, examining every foot with a big electric torch from the car. About halfway down on the return journey my light flashed on a small bottle. The cork had gone and there was no label, but an odour which clung to it reminded me of an anaesthetic. There was no evidence that it had belonged to Caspar, but I was pretty certain, particularly when I saw, a yard or so further on, an oily tyre mark which finished abruptly at almost right angles to the road on the path, and a second imprint which separated from the first in a kind of V—the sort of track one leaves when one backs on to a pavement to turn a car in a constricted area. A little further along I found a film of oil in the road where the car had been parked and a drip had set up from the gear-box or some other point.

Ines did not need me to explain the inference.

Mrs. Townsend was nearly in hysterics when we arrived. She tried to persuade us to remain the night, but admitted, when we showed her the telegram, that it was perhaps better we should go on. Ines put a call through to Plymouth, and I saw by her face directly she came back that our suspicions were correct—the Ile de France had not docked, neither was she due. Having fortified ourselves with a quick drink we made our escape as quickly as possible.

As we turned out of the drive gates I felt that our real adventure began.

We headed the car for Basingstoke—I was driving—and covered a couple of miles in silence.

"How long will it take us to get to Carbis Bay?" Ines interposed suddenly.

I made a rough calculation.

"It's about two hundred and forty miles from here via Wilton and Exeter. It's getting on for eleven now . . . with luck we ought to be there before eight to-morrow morning."

"And then?"

"I don't know."

Alone I would have run any wild risk, but I could not take chances with Ines.

"Cheer up," she comforted. "I'm only trying to get things straight in my own mind."

I nodded. "Same here. I have an idea we ought to have some kind of backing, but I would rather wait and ask the police on the spot to help us if necessary. If Caspar goes back to London to-morrow, it should leave the coast fairly clear."

"I know a man at St. Ives who might be useful. He's an artist—quite mad, but a heart of gold and brains to match. You'd like him. He has made a study of early British remains round the moors and what you were telling me of the sacrificial stone reminded me of him. His name is Penberthy. I'm sure he'd be tickled to death to help if you cared to bring him in?" Ines glanced at me tentatively.

"The very man," I assented with enthusiasm. "He'll probably be able to put his finger on the spot straightway. And being an artist, they wouldn't be nearly so likely to suspect him if they saw him snooping around."

"Good," she said, and snuggled back with a sigh of relief. "We'll leave everything until we get to St. Ives."

"Tell me," she broke in again, as the car swung into a steady fifty, "what do you think Dr. Caspar's object is . . . I mean the 'Ancestors' and this talk of sacrifices and all that? Is he insane, or is there some purpose behind it all?"

Her tone was easy, but I could feel her underlying nervousness.

"I haven't been able to make up my mind," I temporised. "I'm pretty sure, though, it isn't insanity. The man is a very intelligent mulatto. That means that he has an inborn hatred both for white people and coloured. Being neither one thing nor the other himself, he has an inferiority complex where the white race is concerned and yet can't bring himself to be happy with the coloured."

As I talked I tried not to be aware that her shoulder was cushioned against mine. Apart from the gravity of our mission I was infinitely content to be driving through the mellow sweetly-scented night with her by my side.

"And the—Zombies?" she asked.

"I don't think they're genuine Zombies," I fibbed. "The real Zombie was a resurrected dead person; the one I saw might have been that, but I rather fancy he was man who had either been drugged or hypnotised—perhaps both."

We slowed down a little through Basingstoke, but soon got into swing again when we left the main thoroughfare behind.

I think Ines shared with me the exhilaration of the swift rush through the moon-brightened country.

"Ever driven all night before?" I asked at length. For a few miles her eyes had been closed and I wondered if she had fallen asleep. In a way I hoped she had, for though I loved the creamy cadences of her voice, there was something intimate and fascinating in having won her confidence sufficiently to nestle beside me and go to sleep.

She opened her eyes and smiled. "As a matter of fact, I was thinking it was the first time I ever had—in England I did once in India when I was there with Daddy. I was thinking how different it was and yet how very much the same."

I nodded. "I know—I hadn't considered it myself, but I can see now you mention it."

I sniffed; there was a faint tang of burning leaves in the air. "On the Grand Trunk Road in India, it's chupatties and the odour of baked earth—here, it's freshly cut grass and burning garden stuff."

"Tell me something about yourself," she prompted.

"There's nothing to tell," I replied. "Just a rolling stone."

"That in itself is interesting, isn't it?"

"Oh, I don't know." I made my reply as casual as I could. "I am beginning to think that perhaps in chasing moonbeams I've missed the more worthwhile things."

"Such as?" she said interrogatively.

"A home and a definite purpose in life."

"It isn't too late to go in for them yet, is it? You don't look so terribly old to me." Her eyes studied my face amusedly. Yet I believed that there was something more than mere amusement in her scrutiny.

"Opportunity knocked three times at my door and I didn't offer it hospitality. I'm afraid it isn't likely to repeat the experiment," I returned. I should have hated her to think I harboured self-pity.

She sat silent, staring in front of her for a long time. I wondered if she had the slightest inkling of how much she meant to me. In spite of our unusual meeting I could not be regarded by her as anything more than a ship passing in the night.

After a while she looked at me again.

"I shouldn't worry," she said. "Everything will work out all right; I am sure of it. No, really," she emphasized as I grinned dubiously. "I'm as certain of it as I am that you'll rescue Bridget and bring that

rotten doctor to justice. If you do that, Mr. Westerham must . . ."
She bit her lip and broke off suddenly.

I knew instinctively what she was on the point of saying, but I
was grateful that she had thought enough of me to leave the sentence
uncompleted.

"At least I'll have something to give me a start," I returned
jocularly, avoiding her eye. "You did say you would pay me five
pounds a week whilst I was looking after you, didn't you?"

I felt her shoulder stiffen and she looked at me sharply. It was not
until the idiotic words were out that I realized how ungracious they
sounded.

"Of course; that was understood," she answered, "but I meant
something more substantial than that.'

"Thanks, but I'm not doing this for a reward," I continued, per-
versity and the knowledge that I had flung her desire to help me
back in her face, driving me to burn the last boat.

"I know—I'm sorry . . . I didn't mean that at all," she interposed.
"It was only that—" she hesitated, seeking for the best way to express herself without further wounding my pride. "It was only that I
would like to do something to help you to—get what you want . . .
the 'more worth-while things.' "

It was as much as I could do to keep my gaze riveted on the road.

"I know and—thanks," I said gruffly. "Only you see—I wanted
this to be purely—my party."

She nodded. "Very well. I won't say any more about it. But
promise me that if we succeed, and something should turn up, you
won't let foolish pride prevent your considering it."

"Yes. I can safely promise that," I said.

She settled back in her seat again, relaxing with a sigh of content.
For a while she sat dreamily watching the road, but as we passed
through the practically deserted streets of Andover I saw by her
steady breathing that she was now really asleep. Her head had
dropped on to my shoulder and her hair—she had taken off her
hat—brushed my cheek.

I could have kissed her without her ever knowing, but I dared not
trust myself to touch her.

And so we passed Salisbury and Wilton and took the rising
ground towards Shaftesbury. In a very short while we should have
covered half the journey. I wished it could go on forever, but as we
drew nearer our destination I deliberately tried to shut her out of my
thoughts and busied myself with plans for the circumventing of Dr.
Caspar.

CHAPTER X

WHAT HAPPENED TO MISS WESTERHAM

TO SAY THAT Bridget Westerham was surprised when she was stopped by a man dressed in uniform and greeted by name was to put it mildly.

There was a second man who came forward and introduced himself as Mr. Scotson of a legal firm in London who did work for her father's house of Westerham & Briggs. Mr. Scotson apologised for holding her up, but explained that he had received a telegram stating that Mr. Westerham was arriving on the Ile de France, that he had been taken ill, and was anxious for his daughter to meet him on arrival. He then went on to explain that he had telephoned Miss Bellenden in London and in the circumstances the best thing had seemed to follow to Hartley Row as quickly as possible. There were at least three loopholes in his story that occurred to Bridget at a later date, but at the time the narrative seemed perfectly plausible.

True she was surprised to learn that her father was on his way to England; but he was a man of quick decision and the telegram was irrefutable.

Mr. Scotson would drive her to Reading, where they could pick up a fast train for Plymouth, and he suggested she should leave her own car at a garage at Egham whilst he telephoned to Mrs. Townshend.

After she had completed the handing over of her car he met her a little way down the road and told her that his office had radioed the ship and learned that Mr. Westerham had developed appendicitis. They reached the car and even when her eyes fell upon the face of Dr. Caspar, set in a half amused, half triumphant grin, Bridget was surprised but not actually alarmed. It was only when she saw Maman Constance staring at her balefully that she drew back. But it was then too late; she uttered a cry as Scotson seized her and threw her into Caspar's lap. As she did so the woman wrapped round her head something that gave off a pungent odour. After that all was blank.

"Quite a nice piece of work, Polynice," Caspar congratulated the man called Scotson, when after a few convulsive jerks the girl's form lay inanimate over his knees. "Did anybody see you stop the car?"

"No, we were lucky. She turned up when the road was quite clear."

"Fine. You'd better give me back the telegram."

"I gave it to the girl!"

They made a hasty search of Miss Westerham's vanity bag.

"She must have left it in the car," Polynice remarked. "Shall I go back and look for it?"

"No," Caspar replied. "It doesn't really matter. There's not a chance in a million that it will be found in time to do any damage. If you go prying round now it would only give the garage hands a chance of identifying you when inquiries are made. I'll find some way of removing it on my way back. That's all right. I should have warned you . . . You'd better get off back to London now. Don't go by Staines; pick up a train at Chertsey. I'll ring you up when I get in tomorrow. If all goes well we should be able to make our first big coup within a couple of weeks. Go to the studio as soon as you reach town and see if you can find what has delayed that nitwit Barley. He ought to have met me at Staines. Since I found that artist snooping round the other night I've been wondering if somebody has got something against us."

Maman Constance gave a shrill cackle of derision. Caspar glowered at her, but said nothing.

"But who could?" Polynice asked in surprise. "Nobody on this side knows what we're after."

"Not unless one of our milk cows has kicked over the pail," Caspar replied. "I dare say it's nothing—some idiot looking for a studio . . . though it's queer he should have provided himself with a rope. Anyway, have a look round and telephone me about eleven o'clock if every thing is okay. I intended returning by the early train when I'd got the girl and Walton settled he nodded in the direction of a peculiar looking figure with a large wideawake hat pulled down so that its face was almost invisible, bunched up as though asleep, beside the driver. "But if you think there is anything wrong I'll come back by car right away."

"Very good, chief," Polynice answered, and closed the door of the car.

"What's been amusing *you* all this time?" Caspar demanded with some irritation of Maman Constance.

"Nothing, Caspar. Only that for a clever man you do some amazingly foolish things," she retorted with a caustic grin.

He grunted. Then: "Such as?" he inquired.

She shrugged her shoulders. "That one-armed man. I told you he was no good for you. And Maman Constance always knows . . . though you pretend not to believe her except when it suits your purpose," she responded. There was no animus in her tone—merely an "I told you so" intonation that gave him a sensation of nervousness.

"All right; if you think that I'll have no more to do with him," he said placatingly. "What makes you so sure?" he continued.

"I felt it—coming from him like a hot wind," she said. "To-night, when we get to the house, I will ask the 'Ancestors' and you will see. I tell you my friend, though you may scoff, that once a thought of suspicion is aroused in the mind of a man—or woman—who has a strong will, it is like the ripples in a lake caused by a stone thrown into the water. The thought aura pursues its path in the ether to be caught by that one who has the ears to hear."

"That's easily stopped," he commented with a frown. "When he comes along on Monday I'll do the same with him as we did with Adolf. Will that please you?"

"The girl too—not this one but the other—she whom you intend to make your principal—wife," Maman began sourly. Caspar stiffened.

"You're not going to say that she is in league with him and dangerous, too," he scoffed. There was an expression on his face that implied her accusation was due to jealousy, but she controlled her emotion.

"The Great One—who claims help from the Greatest of All to make him an earthly king, with powers undreamed of by those who do not worship the sign of the goat—should be above all mortal women, except to satisfy his bodily desires," she remarked tonelessly.

"Who said I intended her for any other purpose?" he demanded with a sudden access of sharpness.

She smiled with thin lips, but would say no more, and the remainder of the journey passed in silence. Caspar was busy with his thoughts and the old crone with hers—though from time to time she looked down, with a kind of gloating satisfaction, on to the relaxed body of the girl which lay on the floor at her feet.

Shortly after nine o'clock they turned off the high road into a narrow, apparently little used lane which ran between high banks, part rock and part earth. Here the driver stopped, and getting out walked on ahead where the lane gave on to a patch of rolling moorland. In the distance looking to the right, could be seen the shimmer of the sea. Small solitary lights shone here and there along the coast and a couple of tiny ones could be seen inland. But for the most part the country to the left of the lane appeared deserted, only a dusky, uneven waste of furze, stone outcrops and occasional patches of turf. After pausing for a few moments to make certain that there were no stray intruders, he took an electric torch and flashed it on and off five times with a gap of a couple of seconds between the third and last two signals. Then he waited developments.

In the car Caspar and Maman Constance made a careful examination of Bridget, raising her up between them on the seat. The anaesthetic they had used appeared to possess some powerful and peculiar qualities. Her breathing was normal and her body perfectly flexible, yet capable of maintaining any position.

Caspar now produced a leather case from his pocket containing a couple of small bottles, a hypodermic syringe and a roll of cotton wool. He charged the syringe carefully from one of the bottles, then removing the stopper from the second, poured some of its contents on to a pad of wool. The old crone, with a contemptuous expression on her face, raised the girl's skirt, and taking a portion of her thigh between her talons stretched the skin tight. The mulatto swabbed this surface carefully with the wool then inserted the needle of the hypodermic.

For five minutes nothing happened, then Miss Westerham opened her eyes, looked from the doctor to Maman Constance and smiled.

"Wonderful," the old woman said admiringly.

Caspar grinned triumph. "Thank you," he remarked with a touch of irony.

He turned to the girl between them. "All right?" he asked.

"Perfectly, thank you." She smiled again confidingly. Her utterance was the self-composed diction of a nicely brought-up child. "I shall be glad when nurse brings my supper, though," she added with a touch of naivety.

Grinning complacently at Maman, Caspar handed her a small package of biscuits. Thanking him Bridget opened it and began to munch them. It was as if she had suddenly been turned into a little girl of seven or eight.

"Do you know who this is?" the mulatto asked her after a pause, pointing to Maman Constance.

"No; ought I to?" Bridget put her head on one side, mouth full of biscuit.

"Yes; it's your new nurse—Maman Constance."

"Maman Constance," she repeated, then put her hand out politely. "How do you do, Maman Constance," she said, taking the latter's claw-like fingers in her own without any sign of distrust.

"I'm your new uncle—Caspar," he continued quietly, but with a ring of authority in his tone. "You are coming to stay with us for a time whilst your other friends are away, so I hope you will be a very good girl and do exactly what you are told so that I shan't have to punish you."

"Very well, Uncle Caspar," Bridget murmured, gazing at him for a moment, and then returning to her packet of biscuits.

A few seconds later an extraordinary procession came off the moor, led by a short stout negro with a pair of simian-like arms and a twisted nose. He was dressed in some kind of uniform and carried a brutal looking leather whip with three knotted thongs.

He halted and grinned amiably. The procession following him drew up in a serried cluster as he cracked the whip sharply once. They looked like a herd of animals half-tamed, hanging on their master's commands. All had unshod feet and held a handle attached to a kind of litter.

"Oh, it's you, Carol," the chauffeur greeted the little negro. "I didn't know you were back . . . Did you have any luck?"

Carol chuckled wheezingly. "Yes: Baron Samedi was generous. Two. They're up at the house waiting for the master . . . fine stout bodies; one was a sailor killed by the boom cracking him on the skull. The other was a farm labourer from Zennor way. Not like this lot of skin and bones"—he made a gesture in the direction of the silent group behind him. "We can get some real work out of my pair when the master has waked them up. Did you bring the girl?"

"Sure—but you'd better keep your eyes away from that direction if you don't want the master after you. Bring your crew along and pick up Walton. I don't think we were seen coming, but we don't want to run any risks. How long will it be before your darned Zombies finish digging out that passage to the old ruins?" He went on leading the way back to the silent company shambling along at a crack from the negro's whip.

Carol grinned. "Now, don't you start complaining," he returned. "I'll finish it soon enough when the master gives me that pair of new guys with some muscle behind them."

Arrived at the car the figure from the front seat was removed on to the litter. Caspar and Maman Constance, each holding one of Bridget's arms, alighted and set out along a track evidently known to the mulatto, but invisible to Maman Constance. Carol, with his detachment of strange, silent litter bearers, came on in the rear.

As soon as they had gone the driver backed the car out of the lane, and drove for another four miles along the main road to where a moderate-sized, one-time farmhouse was rented in the name of Professor Polynice who had taken up his residence there some three months back in order to write a book on the early British remains in Cornwall.

The chauffeur garaged the car, locked up and whistling cheerfully set off to join the mulatto in the big house.

CHAPTER XI

THE MANOR ON THE MOOR

APART FROM a few shepherds, farm hands and a stray hikers or so, it is doubtful whether more than half a dozen people between St. Ives and Penzance knew of the existence of the big, grey-stone, castlelike house set in a little valley, between two stony hills and for years deserted.

Caspar, seeing it advertised, had been struck with its possible suitability, had secretly inspected the place, and later, through Polynice, had rented it at an absurdly low figure.

There was only one possible source of gossip within a radius of three miles of the house—an aged, nondescript one-time farm hand, who lived by himself in a lodge at the gates.

The lodge-keeper, so Caspar found out, had no claim to his dwelling. His disappearance would not have caused any stir with the exception that some enquiry might have been made by the St. Ives Post Office, whither he went weekly to draw his old age pension.

For a week or two the mulatto left him in peace, but the old fellow started prowling round the manor. Being an old man whose principal distinguishing characteristic were his ragged garb and a face that could hardly be seen for hair, Caspar had no great difficulty in preparing a "double" from one of his own followers. The doctor then gave the rightful pensioner a bottle of poisoned port wine and the patriarch passed away in the finest fuddle he had ever known.

Certain alterations in the interior of the house rendered it apparently empty except for the west wing. There, at night, the blinds were left undrawn and in a comfortable room a quantity of respectable-looking old gentlemen were in the habit of playing cards. Actually they were four of the mulatto's Zombies dressed up for the occasion. It was extremely unlikely that inquisitive people would wander round the manor after dark, but Caspar had provided a charmingly normal scene.

The gate-keeper, on hearing Caspar call him, held a lantern up to identify the visitors.

"Any news, Alfonso?" Caspar asked.

"No, chief, except that the professor's been telephoning from the house every few minutes during the past hour asking why you hadn't arrived," the man replied.

Dimly illuminated by the side rays from the lantern he carried he loomed, a gargantuan figure. He had been a promising South African candidate for the world's heavyweight championship until Caspar had enlisted his services under promise of much greater fun. The doors of the Manor were well guarded.

Caspar nodded. "You needn't close the gate; Carol is just behind," he remarked. "Go on in front; Maman Constance doesn't know the way yet, and I don't want her or our new friend here to risk their necks on the wires."

Alfonso nodded and went on, stopping every now and again and holding up the light to indicate a zigzag of stepping-stones let into the driveway. At these points he would wait until the party had passed over the stones, holding the girl between them so that her feet should not touch the ground on either side. On arrival at what was apparently the back of the house, Alfonso made a slight detour to one side of a flight of stone steps, thrust his hand into a niche in the balustrade and pushed over a small lever then swung his lantern in signal to go ahead.

Maman gave a little nod of satisfaction.

"You're cleverer than I thought, Papaloi," she remarked pleasantly. "It would be a very shrewd man who caught you napping. What eventually happens if you omit whatever Alfonso did?"

The doctor smiled. "Two of the steps would turn over and you would drop at least fifteen feet on to a very hard stone floor studded with sharp spikes," he replied, "in which case your lamentations would certainly announce the arrival of an unexpected visitor . . . that is, if you were not killed outright."

The old crone's eyes gleamed cruelly. "I should like to see it in operation one day," she murmured involuntarily.

"Perhaps you shall," Caspar said, amused.

They were in the outer hall now, between the inner and outer stout, oaken doors. Maman Constance's native love of warmth and colour was repelled by the grim, granite walls and the few sparse furnishings of antique oak, whilst her shrewdness approved the strength of its defences. But as soon as they passed through into the inner hall, she nodded unqualifying appreciation.

The walls were panelled to match the parquet flooring. Luxurious Turkey rugs were laid, and in a wide, old-fashioned fireplace an enormous log fire crackled cheerfully. There were brass sconces on the panels of the walls fitted with amber coloured electric lights. A couple of settees and a number of armchairs upholstered in red leather gave a club-like atmosphere. If the outside were sinister, this part of the house did its best to create an entirely opposite effect.

Facing the fireplace, on the right as one entered, was a wide stairway which curved into a kind of bridge, affording access to a gallery on either side. There were two doors on the lower floor above and below the fireplace, and two more opposite. Leading off the gallery were three doors on either side and more rooms were indicated by two corridors, disappearing under carved wooden arches to right and left.

The only unusual note was struck by a massive, altarlike erection of carved ebony at the far end of the hall, set upon a dais covered with a heavy, black silken carpet. Above it, in a niche was a statue of bronze some eight feet high, representing a figure with two goat-like legs, the middle and shoulders of a man, and a head, human except for the horns sprouting from a mass of shaggy, bronze curls above the pointed ears.

Maman Constance without further preamble made her way to the most comfortable chair near the fire. She was of the type that, seemingly, never ages, but the journey had tired her. She took no notice of a coffee-coloured elderly maid who had appeared as the inner door closed upon them, and now stood waiting for Caspar's orders, but in very feminine fashion drew up her skirts and proceeded to toast her knees.

The mulatto frowned; although a mamaloi and, in certain respects almost as important and powerful as himself, he resented Maman Constance's self-assurance and independence.

A white mamaloi—and here his eye turned reflectively upon the glowing fairness and beauty of Bridget Westerham—if she could be trained to interpret the messages of the "Ancestors" would not only be more effective in the negro principality he meant to institute, but far more pleasant. And, whereas Maman Constance was honestly afraid of the powers and therefore incapable of twisting their messages to suit political conditions, the girl, under his influence, might be rendered more amenable.

As he turned to the maid to bid her put the white girl to bed, he did not notice the quick, malicious glance that the old woman shot at him. As she had said, "a thought aroused in the mind of a man or woman of strong will, pursues its path in the ether, reaching the minds of those capable of receiving its message." She grinned serenely into the blaze of the comforting fire. She had disapproved all along of his mixing up self-glorification and politics with the spiritual aims to establish Satan and his court as a power on earth again that animated herself and at least three-quarters of Caspar's followers. Up to a point she had deferred to him, but when it came to a question of setting himself up as the Great One ... that was a different matter, especially if he was fool enough to think he could throw her on one side.

Still—possibly he was merely rendered a little foolish by the dark girl. Let him have her if it pleased him, so long as he did not make the fatal mistake of trying to possess her soul as well as her body.

Bridget, having been led away perfectly docile by the maid, Caspar moved with a friendly smile to the side of his associate. It was better to conciliate rather than antagonise her until his plans were riper; besides there were certain things that only she could do.

"Well, Maman, here we are. Now you have seen it tell me what you think of the place? At least we can make you comfortable so far as warmth and food are concerned." He took his stand with his back to the log fire.

"It seems well enough," she replied noncommittantly, "as a residence or meeting place, but hardly suitable for use as a place of worship ... unless," she continued, as a gleam came into his eye, "there is another building."

He nodded. "Exactly, Maman; a building over nine hundred years old, within a quarter of a mile from here, set in a hollow in the moor and surrounded by a patch of boggy ground that insures its privacy better than anything man devised." His voice thrilled exultantly. "A sacred temple that, when we have finished the excavation and the underground passage from the cellars here, will make Stonehenge pale in insignificance. To-morrow I will show you, and then we will together call upon the "Ancestors" to say if the Great One will not be pleased with our work."

"A passage—underground?" she repeated. "But this house is not ancient."

He chuckled. "So far as I can judge it must have formed the store chambers—or maybe a hiding place—for those who dwelt near the temple. When this house was built part of the foundations crossed the passage. The masons dug out a few feet on one side, clapped an iron grating on top and used it to ventilate the cellars. They had bricked up the end of the niche, but in exploring the underparts of the house I could not account for the different texture of the side stones of the ventilating well. Curiosity led me to set the Zombies to

pull out the bricked portion, and it was then I discovered—by following the direction outside through the kitchen garden on to the
moor—that it led to the ruins . . ."

He broke off suddenly as one of the upper doors was flung
noisily open and a quick patter of feet was heard moving towards
the balustrade.

"Caspar . . . is that you, Caspar? Why the deuce didn't you send
word you had arrived? Didn't Alfonso tell you I've been nearly out
of my mind with anxiety?" A pair of nervous, clenched fists
thumped the oaken rail angrily. "Keeping me waiting just when I
need your assistance to carry out the final experiment."

The voice, a thin, almost falsetto one, stopped.

"I'm sorry, Professor—very sorry, but we were delayed a little
on the road," Caspar grinned up at the balcony from which the irate
speaker was glaring down at him. Only his head could be seen with
a bald, dome-like cranium long narrow lantern jaws, and a pair of
large horn-rimmed glasses which flashed vindictively in the fire-
light.

"All right," the head disappeared abruptly, and the feet were
heard stamping in the direction of the stairs.

"Professor Kucynski," Caspar murmured in answer to a glance of
interrogation from Maman Constance. "Probably the greatest ex-
perimentist in vivisection the world has ever known."

"The Russian you enlisted at Stamboul?"

"As you say—enlisted." The mulatto smiled at the word.
"Though actually he is a Pole—or was until they found what they
believed to be his dead body in the Bosphorus. Through him, if he
succeeds, as I think he will, the master"—he made a curious salute
in the direction of the bronze statue—"will have once more a train
of his beloved fauns and satyrs when he holds his royal court."

CHAPTER XII

THE EXPERIMENTS OF PROFESSOR KUCYNSKI

PROFESSOR KUCYNSKI fumed peevishly all through supper. Maman Constance did not eat, but consumed a large jug of fresh milk, looking as she sipped it like an intensely malevolent black cat masquerading as a woman, her glowing eyes fixed speculatively upon the professor.

Not more than five feet three in height and spare in frame, he was as electric as she in the energy he radiated. His body, as an expression of humanity, had no significance. The thing that mattered was the almost blinding mental power which indicated where he happened to be. And his individuality and that of the mamaloi, a couple of seconds after they met, coalesced with a flash that was almost visible. They were, so far as an infinite capacity for devilry was concerned, one person.

Caspar, watching the pair furtively, was surprised, then amused, and finally a shade uneasy.

When they set out to visit the laboratory it was Maman Constance who led the way unerringly as if every twist and turn of the place were familiar. Her hand had stretched out and taken Kucynski's; in the dim light of the stone stairway that led to the underground workshop their clasped fingers looked like skeleton hands. Their shadows silhouetted, as their positions shifted in relation to the lights, had an eager, grotesque air—as if a male and female vampire were setting out on a love tryst.

They resolved themselves into their true forms again—a resolute, self-contained, elderly woman and a dapper-bodied, agile man—as they emerged through a massive stone door padded with green baize on both sides into laboratory.

It was a huge room occupying almost the whole space between the foundations of the house, painted a dull white and gleaming starkly beneath a battery of daylight lamps. All down one side was a row of steel cages similar to the ones used in the newer prisons.

There were eight of them each just large enough to take a narrow stretcher, a chair and a small drinking fountain.

Along the opposite wall were a series of glass cubicles resembling incubators, only large enough to contain a kind of operating couch-bed. The glazed front of each cubicle could be raised or lowered by means of a lever and chain.

Several of the steel cages were occupied—the inmates, with one exception, having the lifeless expression of the Zombies. This exception was a young man of perhaps thirty. His expression was one of horrified incredulity, of which, nevertheless, a trace of grudging admiration could be seen.

In the glass cells, all of which but one were filled, the occupants were stretched out, bound in different positions by ligatures of gut or rubber.

The mulatto went across to speak to the young man.

"Well—have you decided yet to be sensible?" Caspar inquired.

"If, by being sensible, you mean allowing myself to be a party to these devilish practices—no."

"Oh, come, Doctor," the mulatto returned smoothly. "Aren't you, as a surgeon of acknowledged brilliance, being rather foolish? After all, you have seen for yourself that our . . . operations are quite painless. That your nerve is perfect is demonstrated by the fact that you have not lost your mind whilst you have been here. I don't mind telling you that you are the only one of five, so far, who has managed to preserve his balance. Think, man—with your nerve and the professor's knowledge, there is nothing—absolutely nothing—that you could not do. If only you would be sensible, I can give you more power than ever you have dreamed of."

"I don't want that kind of power," he snapped with some spirit. "Good God, man—are you a devil that you can let that madman do such ghastly things?"

He averted his eyes as Kucynski, who had wheeled a patient from a cubicle, gloatingly began to remove some bloodstained bandages.

"The devil is a good friend of mine, I admit," Caspar chuckled. "As for being a 'madman' that is a debatable point. If super-genius is mad, then your accusation may be in order. After all, you know, Dunkerley, you'd far better join forces with us. These little experiments"—he made a gesture in the direction of the table—"may seem a trifle unusual, but they do serve to teach us something of the possibilities of transmuting flesh. It isn't as if we were working on the living: every one of these cases has been resuscitated, after the patient was accepted as a cadaver by the doctors who attended until life was pronounced extinct."

A strange sound, half bleat—half whinny, came from the operating table and a spasm of horror passed over the face of Dunkerley.

"No," he gasped. "No; I can't. God knows there are enough monstrosities in the world. A decent man should try to eliminate rather than increase them . . ."

Caspar shrugged. "I'm sorry," he said and his tone held genuine regret. "In you I thought I had at last found a perfect team-mate for the Professor. It is unfortunate—for both of us—if I am mistaken."

"Can't you leave me alone?" Dunkerley breathed.

"Very well. I'll give you another twenty-four hours that is all I can spare. It would be a pity if I had to bring pressure to bear through that charming fiancée of yours in Edinburgh . . . but if you still persist in being stubborn, we shall have to see whether her presence here will change your views."

He turned abruptly to join the Professor and Maman Constance.

"The best yet," Kucynski chuckled as Caspar stood beside him. "The others—good, yes, for purely decorative symbols, but nothing to what we are on the verge of producing. If only you can procure me a capable assistant . . . Gospodi! if only I had four pairs of hands!"

"Well, if anyone can produce that phenomenon, you can," the mulatto returned, admiration in his tone.

Bound to the table by rubber thongs lay a creature whose height would be about five feet. Its face was shaggily bearded and two small, black horns sprouted just above the pointed ears. The upper half of the torso was that of a man but from the waist down the figure followed the hindquarters of a tawny-skinned goat. A pair of yellowish, bovine yet humanly malicious eyes stared squintingly out of the mass of coarse hair that hung down over the low forehead.

Every now and again the lips parted, a red tongue flickering between them, and the semi-bleating, semi-whinnying sound arose. It was gruesome and eerie, but there was no distress; rather it gave the impression of the creature trying out its vocal capabilities.

"Beginning to sit up and take notice, eh?" Caspar remarked in approval. "Do you think you'll be able to teach it to speak?"

"Who knows? Time alone will show," the Professor lied. "At least it has the desire to express itself, whereas all the others are like oysters. In a couple of days we will take it down to the stables and see what reaction it produces amongst the previous ones. Note, my friend," he went on, pointing a stubby finger at a place just above where the goat thighs merged into the man's waist and several rudimentary patches of tawny hair were sprouting. "How nature, so much stronger in the beast than the man, is striving to take control. My problem is going to be, not to produce your Satyrs and Fauns for you, but to prevent the purely animal instincts from submerging the human intelligence. You know," he glanced at his employer thoughtfully, "the linking together of a man and a goat has been so easy that I am almost tempted to believe that nature herself has done nine-tenths of the work. Something is working to bring back these particular creations into the world again . . . ."

Caspar smiled grimly. "It is quite possible," he said, and exchanged a glance with the old woman. "And the Nymph . . . how is she progressing?"

Kucynski's face fell. "Alas, my friend—she is no more. There was one very delicate piece of work required to complete the operation. I enlisted the assistance of your young friend there"—he jerked his hand in the direction of Dunkerley's cage—"with his aid I could have rendered the incisions and graftings absolutely painless. He agreed, but in the middle of the operation he plunged a scalpel into the patient's heart. A pity; she was a nearly perfect reproduction of one of Praxiteles' nymph statues."

Maman Constance raised her red-glowing eyes and grinned.

"Your fair girl would look well as a nymph," she said in a would-be casual tone. Ageless in mind, her actual years were nearly seventy. One of her secret hopes had been that when the Great One was summoned to His Court with proper ritual, He might be prevailed upon to restore the rounded limbs, firm young breasts and girlishly-glowing face she had possessed fifty years ago. She had been able to maintain her body in a state of almost violent vitality, but the existence of that vitality was in itself a curse when she was no longer attractive in the eyes of men.

If through Kucynski she could exchange the life stream of a young and lovely creature like the blonde girl for her own—that, together with the darker arts should procure the result she desired. Then . . . she could charm Caspar with her youth and beauty and bodily lures and experience against any white woman, and together they could rule the coming kingdom as Emperor and Empress!

These thoughts were cut short by the entrance of the man, Carol.

"The two bodies I got ready for you and the mamaloi are in the small chapel at the back," he announced to Caspar. "Maria says that if you don't deal with them soon it will be too late. And Mr.

Polynice is on the telephone in the library speaking from the studio; he says it is very urgent."

"I'll come at once," Caspar replied. "Will you deal with the bodies, Maman? You'll find everything ready and Maria can help you."

She nodded assent and he hurried out and, after another speculative glance at Kucynski, who was brooding over his newly-completed Faun with all the pride of a doting parent, followed Carol out to the chapel.

~ ~ ~ ~ ~

"Well?" Caspar demanded.

"Is that you, chief? . . . I'm speaking from the studio," Polynice's voice said.

"What's the trouble?" There was tense anxiety in Caspar's tone: a sensation of impending disaster came over him.

"I don't know exactly, but one or two queer things seem to have happened. There's no sign of Barley, but your keys were lying at the foot of the ebony cupboard. No sign of the bottle you sent him for, and the key of the backstair door was on the inside and the door unlocked. Just as I was leaving Mrs. Jansen turned up to report that the dark girl had left Queen Street telling the maid she would be back by ten. Mrs. Jansen went to Clarges Street, where the girl directed the chauffeur to drive, but says she never arrived there. She found out from one of the maids that the lady had been expected, but telephoned to say she was called out of town. Mrs. Jansen wants to know what your instructions are. As ordered by Maman Constance, she kept an eye on the man at the corner of Sloane Street. He was away between half-past twelve and half-past two, but came then and remained until getting on for six. She says his chin was scratched as if he had been in a fight, but otherwise there was nothing suspicious about him."

"I never thought there was," Caspar commented. "It's just because Maman has taken a dislike to him . . . Damnation take it—if only one could be in two places at once. Something always goes wrong if I don't see to it myself. The girl couldn't have heard anything about her friend to make her anxious . . . You *did* telephone to that woman in Hartley Row, I suppose, before you met the blonde, to say she wouldn't be able to keep her appointment for luncheon?" he went on with quick anxiety.

"Telephone . . . you never told me to telephone anybody, chief," Polynice's voice replied. There was such perfect sincerity in his tone that Caspar had no choice but to believe the statement.

"My God! I must be losing my wits. Hell and damnation—that blasted cat-burglar at the studios the other night must have rattled me more than I knew." He paused for a moment, then: "I'll be right back," he announced curtly. "Lock the caretaker in the dormitory . . . you know who I mean. Tell Mrs. Jansen to report to me there at eleven o'clock to-morrow morning, meanwhile to find out, if she can, if the girl returns to-night. You'd better meet me there, too."

"Very good, chief," Polynice replied.

The mulatto stood for a couple of minutes trying to imagine the meaning of what the other had told him. Miss Bellenhem's summons out of town *might* have nothing to do with the non-appearance of her friend at the place in Hartley Row. And Barley might have placed the key to the back door on the inner side of the lock and forgotten to fasten it when he left. But . . . what had become of Barley?

The non-delivery of the precious bottle of S.17 was disquieting. Now, until he could prepare another lot—the drug being both poison and antidote, according to the manner of its application—the man Walton couldn't be handled. And Walton, head of an American armament concern, could not be used without an injection of the drug in its antidotal capacity.

Then there was Mr. Westerham, due within a week; there should be a cable any minute from his two men in St. Lucia whose job it was to advise the millionaire that his daughter was held to ransom.

And, finally, there was the first official meeting by the Sacrificial Stone at the coming full moon. That must be carried out if they were to make use of the presence of all those African notabilities who had come over to attend that fortunately timed Political Conference called by great Britain and France to settle the question of the independence of certain East African territories.

He went to tell Maman Constance the gist of the telephone message. She would have to look after things here while he returned to London.

He found her carrying out her awesome rites on the first of the bodies which lay on a low, deal platform, arranged like an altar at one end of the chill, stone mortuary. At the head of the body were three stone vessels containing an oil made from human fat in which cotton wicks were burning. A circle had been drawn in chalk round the platform and seven more lines, traced in goat's blood, forming a seven-pointed star, intersected the circle. A wooden bowl of goat blood stood handy. In the charge of the maid, Maria, who stood just outside the circle and whose neat white cap and apron and black dress looked grotesquely incongruous, were two doves and a little black kid.

Maman Constance had not donned the feathered headdress and scarlet robe of the mamaloi, but a monstrous obscene garb—stark naked except for a black morning coat and a top hat. Above her ankles and knees she wore ruffles made of white cock feathers and two white circles were painted round her eyes. She represented the Voodoo, "Keeper of the Gates of Death," and in this guise "wrestled" for possession of the corpse.

Small platters containing fruit, corn-cakes, sugar and an open jar of wine were arranged in the corners of a pentagram drawn on the table at the feet of the body.

If the "Keeper of the Gates" was in a good mood, he would allow Maman Constance, as his self-constituted deputy, to resuscitate the corpse and use it for her own purposes and satisfy himself with the refreshment provided in the cakes and wine. If the "Keeper" happened to be in a bad mood, then nothing would happen and the body would have to be reinterred.

Maman and the mulatto were, however, very rarely disappointed in their hideous rites: only when the body was that of a young man or woman did they fail.

Caspar stood silent, whilst she flittered round the body murmuring incantations and looking, in the flapping black tail coat, like some nightmarish crow. Then she clapped her hands three times sharply and poured some of the goat blood into the open mouth of the body, closing it afterwards by lifting the chin and then massaging the throat so that the liquid was forced down into the stomach.

Finally she lighted two little piles of powder which lay on either side of the figure's head and with a dried palm leaf fanned the smoke so that it was driven up the body's nose. After this had continued for a few minutes she suddenly seized one of the doves, lifted it above her head with both hands and started spinning round on her toes faster and faster. Then, with a convulsive motion which shot through her twirling body like an electric flash, she tore off the head of the dove, sprinkling its blood on the recumbent form and uttering a command in a spasmodic shriek.

As she did this the previously lifeless figure on the altar seemed to tremble violently, opened its eyes and a second or two later rose to a sitting position. It was then taken by the hand by the maid and led out of the chapel to be herded with its fellows.

Caspar waited until the old woman had recovered from her exertions, complimented her on her success, and then told her his news.

Her eyes, notwithstanding her weariness, snapped viciously. "What did I tell you," she said. "I knew that idiotic one-armed man of yours would bring evil on us."

"But that is absurd, Maman," he argued. "How could he have anything to do with Barley and the girl leaving her rooms? Mrs. Jansen said he was in his usual place all the afternoon."

"Have it your own way, my friend," she retorted with a touch of peevishness. "But some way or other he is at the bottom of this business."

He shrugged irritably. "Anyhow, it is damnably disturbing. We have only about a week before the meeting and I had hoped to get everything set—money and transport arranged for our people to the coast—before it took place, so that we can get things started on the Congo. . ." He thought moodily for a space. "However, we'll hope there's nothing in it really. I'm driving back to town at once. Can you look after things while I'm away?"

"I can do my best, Papaloi," she returned with a mildness that was more indicative of scorn than humility.

"Thanks, then I'll start right away." He suppressed a yawn. "Blast Barley or whoever it is that has muddled things; after all the work we've had to-day, I did hope for a decent night's rest." Nodding a final "good night," he strode gloomily out of the chapel.

Maman Constance continued chuckling to herself for some seconds then, as if summoned by a voice audible to herself alone, grew rigid and raised her head in a position of tense listening.

A deep silence ensued; even her breathing was scarcely apparent, until, suddenly, the odd, soft chirruping sound of the "Whistling Ancestors" could be heard filling the chamber.

For at least five minutes she stood riveted, interpreting the message that was being given to her, her face gradually growing more and more awed. It was the first time that the "Ancestors" had ever broken in upon her of their own volition. Finally the sounds ceased, but the mamaloi still remained, her eyes staring perplexedly at the wall of the chapel.

Then with an abrupt jerk she pulled herself together and set off quickly to the room in which Miss Westerham had been put to bed.

Arriving there, she switched on the light and crossed furtively to the side of the girl who was apparently fast asleep.

Maman Constance was tempted to seize her by the shoulder, but she refrained and, putting out the light, stole away again.

Her mind was in a turmoil. For, unless the "Ancestors" were fooling her for some purpose of their own, the message she had just received had emanated from the sleeping girl.

"Father . . . Father . . . please come to me . . . a man here has done something to me and I know I am in danger, but my body won't do what I tell it. Won't you please come and help me . . ." That was the message through the chirrupings that carried with them the thought vibrations.

Had the drug administered by Caspar driven out the girl's soul so that it had temporarily joined the "Ancestors", or had the drug intensified her will power and enabled her to send out the message consciously or subconsciously?

CHAPTER XIII

FURTHER ADVENTURES ON AN EXPEDITION
WITH A LADY

I T WAS CLOSE on midnight when Caspar left the Manor.
Electing on this occasion to drive himself, with two quick
changes of gear he shot into a full thirty that rapidly accelerated
to a forty mile an hour average. He was still uneasy, but rushing
through the night air under the almost tropic moon was an anodyne,
and stimulated his faculties even whilst it soothed his nerves.

Polynice was always inclined to panic. Barley's disappearance
was odd, but it was possible he had been inveigled in for a drink
somewhere, and ended up blind to the world. It had happened once
before.

An ironic fate willed it that Ines and I passed the doctor about a
quarter past three between Chard and Honiton, both having to make
a sudden swerve to avoid crashing. We were both holding to the
crest of the road. This curved between two high banks and it was
only as Caspar's car turned the corner that its headlights were mirrored in the beam from the car I was driving.

Had Caspar realised who was in the second car I am certain he
would have had not the least compunction in steering to wreck it.

By the time he had recovered from the jolt to his nerves be was a
couple of hundred yards away. Immediately the vehicle had passed
my mind raced to the possibility of the solo driver being Caspar. I
came to a screeching standstill, but the turn in the road precluded my
identifying the rear number-plate of the north-bound car.

My first impulse was to turn about, but it would not do to risk
anything with Ines in my charge. Bridget was not in the other car
and if she had been kidnapped she was more likely to be incarcer-
ated in Cornwall than anywhere else with Maman Constance in
charge.

As I switched into forward gear again Ines opened her eyes.

"What is it?" she asked sleepily.

"A car passed us—we should have crashed if we hadn't both
swerved. I had an idea it was Caspar."

"Why didn't you stop him? Was Bridget . . .?"

"No, he was alone—I'm almost sure it was he. I thought we'd get in touch with your friend, Mr. Penberthy, and then I'll do a bit of scouting. With Caspar out of the way it means only Maman Constance in charge."

"But, supposing . . ." she hesitated, ". . . they take you prisoner?"

"If I don't turn up within a few hours you'll know I'm snaffled; then you and Penberthy can call in the police.

"I don't like your taking so much risk," she said uneasily.

"Oh, I don't think there's such an awful lot," I replied—though I was by no means as confident as I pretended. "If they believe that we are wise to their little game, I fancy their first thought will be to insure their own safety."

I pulled out the small disc and showed it to her.

"Unless by bad luck I run into the old hag, this may give me the entry to the house. I found it on the negro Barley."

She handed it back to me with a shudder.

"I don't like it," she said, "somehow it seems to emphasize the beastly side of their operations. Kidnapping is damnable but, at least, it is cleanly criminal. What the people are after is sheer vileness." A scared look came in her eyes. I could see she was thinking of Miss Westerham, but there was very little I could say to banish her fears. I slipped the disc hastily into my pocket again.

"Anyway, Miss Westerham is bound to be all right until the 'doctor' goes back," I soothed her. "And before he does it won't be my fault if we haven't got her safely out of their clutches."

~ ~ ~ ~ ~

We drove up to Penberthy's cottage, about a quarter of a mile out of St. Ives, a little before seven in the morning.

We found him already up busy doing something to his rose bushes and whistling cheerfully. From the cottage a most appetising aroma of fried ham, toast and coffee came and mingled with the morning fragrance of the garden. I suddenly realised that I was starving.

At first sight Mr. Penberthy did not impress me very much as a prospective ally against the mulatto and his gang. He was shortish, fair-haired and freckled. On his upper lip was a weedy ginger moustache, and he looked to me none too robust. But I reversed my opinion when he recognised Ines and leapt forward to greet her.

"Of all the unexpected sights at this hour of the day. How are you? I'm delighted. You will have breakfast, of course."

His glance took in the car, me, and probably half a dozen indications which informed him that we had been motoring all night.

"Mrs. Thompson—Mrs. Thompson," he called in a robust voice out of keeping with his appearance. Then, as a stout, red-cheeked female of the cook-housekeeper type appeared hurriedly in the doorway: "There will be two extra for breakfast."

"Well, well, well, I can't get over it," Penberthy began again as the woman disappeared. "You'd like to brush up, though, I'm sure, after your journey. . . Mrs. Thompson," he hailed again loudly, and as the woman put her head out of the door: "Put some clean towels in the bathroom and see that the spare room is all right for Miss Bellenden. Tidy mine while you're about it for the gentleman . . ."

"Worthing. Patrick Worthing," I interpolated.

"For Mr. Worthing. You don't mind using mine, do you?" he added. "But our accommodation is limited."

"No, but really," I began.

"Couldn't dream of it, my dear fellow—custom of Cornwall," he grinned. "Besides—how can one talk business"—he surveyed us with uncanny intuition—"after travelling all night unless one is comfortable . . . Let me show you in."

My eyes caught Ines' as we turned. I nodded vehemently in answer to the unspoken query in hers, backed by a glint of amusement.

He chattered gaily all the way up the quaint old narrow and steep staircase; purely, I was certain, to make us feel at ease. He was as good as a tonic and I felt far more hopeful for our enterprise now that there was a likelihood of enlisting his help.

"Breakfast in a quarter of an hour—if it's urgent; or if you want a bath first, three-quarters," he concluded at the door of the spare room.

Ines consulted me with a glance.

"It is rather urgent," she answered.

"Right," Penberthy said. "In a quarter of an hour, then."

He fussed around for a few seconds in his own room, putting a spare brush and comb at my disposal and pouring out hot water. "Something badly wrong, eh?" he remarked at last in a tone that combined both question and comment. I gave him a rough outline of the situation as brief as I could while I shaved. His eyes hardened as I told him the plans I had heard the mulatto make in regard to Miss Bellenden.

"Pleasant sort of cove, the doctor," he commented when I had finished. "No wonder Miss Bellenden is a bit under the weather. Marvel is how she's managed to bear up as she has."

"Yes," I agreed. "She is as fine as they make 'em."

"I'm glad you came here," he burst out after a short pause. "Of course I'm with you to the last fence, only—if you don't mind me suggesting it—you'd better dig in with me rather than go to the hotel. For one thing your names would be printed as 'visitors' in the local rag, in the second place you'll be safer."

"That's darned good of you," I replied.

Springing up, he crossed to the window and peered out across the hills.

"I wonder," he said suddenly, almost to himself.

"It's just occurred to me that the Old Manor House might be the place," he went on, with something like excitement in his tone.

"The Old Manor House?"

"Yes. It's been empty for ages, but I heard someone had taken it about three months ago as a home for mental deficients. It's a gloomy old barracks tucked away out of sight among the moors about four miles from here. Just the sort of spot your man Caspar would pick on—and the only possible one this side of Penzance. There are some old British barrows and dolmens quite close. I dropped on them by chance some months ago and did a bit of exploring, but the Manor was empty then."

"Sounds as if, thanks to you, we've holed out in one," I said.

"Anyhow it's worth investigating," he returned, becoming diffident again now his momentary excitement was over. He nodded as Ines was heard going downstairs, shot me an encouraging grin, and went out.

She was tackling ham and eggs when I entered the sitting-room.

"Mr. Penberthy tells me you have given him particulars," Ines commented presently. "He thinks it would be better if we stayed here for the time being."

"I'll be tremendously relieved if you will," I answered, "but, though I'd like nothing better myself and feel it better for me to be foot-loose. Caspar knows me and I don't think Maman Constance loves me. Secondly, I may have to dash back to town if what we're after isn't here. And thirdly, it strikes me it will be better to have someone in reserve to take 'requisite' action if necessary."

Penberthy nodded. "There's a good deal in what you say," he admitted. "But why not let me do a bit of scouting round the Manor

and you and Miss Bellenden stay here. I know the lay of the land and
I shouldn't arouse suspicion even if I were seen."

"I agree," I said, "but on the other hand, because Caspar has not
met you yet, Miss Bellenden will be safer with you."

"What do you suggest?" Penberthy asked.

"I'll go straight off to the barrows," I replied. "From what
Caspar said to the mamaloi, I have an idea there may be some
connection between the ruins and the house; if there is, I may be
able to find it. In fact, if Caspar is in London, I shall try and bluff my
way into the Manor by pretending I have a message from him to
Maman and see if Miss Westerham is there. If she is, I'll do my best
to get her away. Give me until four this afternoon; if I don't turn up
by then or get a message to you, you'll know there is something
wrong and can take whatever steps you think best to follow me."

Penberthy considered this plan in silence for a few minutes. Ines
did not speak; she was obviously a little annoyed at being given no
active role to play.

"Speaking from a purely common sense point of view in relation
to Miss Westerham," he began at length, "there is one bad flaw. If
you don't come back we shan't know whether or no she is at the
Manor. There might be half a dozen alternatives to the kidnapping
theory. But if she is not at the Manor and you don't return we are
still in the dark. Caspar and the old woman may have a private feud
with you and might claim they were justified in detaining you and
communicating with the police. And in that case we might only be
doing you harm if we got the police to raid the place. . ."

"You're quite right," I put in, admiring his sanity. *"If* I am
wrong—though I'd bet a hundred pounds that I'm not—your interference would do none of us any good. The chances are that Miss
Westerham would turn up safely, possibly suffering from loss of
memory. I'd be clapped in jail for breaking into Caspar's studio, and
the thing I'm keen on smashing . . . the big thing—would go un-
disturbed."

"What big thing?" Penberthy questioned.

"I'll tell you that later."

I paused, trying to plan some way of letting Penberthy know if
Bridget was at the Manor.

"Does the Manor look on to the moor or is it shut in?"

"Shut in, in the middle of about five acres of garden. There is a
wall and you can't see the building for a plantation," he replied,
dashing my hopes of signalling from a window.

"That makes it more difficult," I said glumly. "Jove, though, I have it! If they get me they're sure to go through my pockets. I'll write two letters, stamp the envelopes and seal them as if for posting. I'll address it to my landlady in Chelsea telling her that I've been summoned out of town for a few days and that if a gentleman calls for me, she is to ask him if it is regarding the Siena Studio case? If so, she is to say I investigated the place but could find nothing to suggest that his wife is in any danger from the methods of rejuvenation Dr. Pettifranc was teaching. The second one will be to a fictitious firm of solicitors in Chancery Lane, saying that in reference to the case I am of the opinion that the young man had gone off for a motoring tour of Cornwall with a girl from a London theatre chorus and that I will telegraph his father, the Count, as soon as I have located them. That will give Caspar the idea that I'm a private inquiry agent. If they decide to hold me, it is ten to one they will post off the first letter, to my landlady, because it exonerates Caspar. They may, or may not, post the second letter; it doesn't matter.

"If Miss Westerham *isn't* at the Manor, I'll find some way of destroying it; if she is, I'll see that they get hold of it. To-morrow morning you can ring up Mrs. Dobbs and find out if the letter has arrived. In that case you will know Miss Westerham is at the Manor. If there is no letter you can be pretty sure I've drawn blank, though you'd better ring up in the evening. That's the best I can suggest. What do you say?"

"It seems to meet the bill," Penberthy allowed. "It may hold us up for twenty-four hours, but I can't think of a better alternative. If Miss Bellenden won't be staying here quietly by herself, I can take a stroll over the moor before dusk—if you haven't turned up. I can get the lie of the land in case we have to form a storming party and there is always the chance I might pick up a clue—" he broke off with a sudden grin.

"I know," he went on. "I'll call at the lodge and see if the old patriarch is still alive. I used him as a model once or twice. I'm not to know the place isn't still empty. People are accustomed to see me trudging over the moors; they wouldn't dream of suspecting an ulterior motive."

I suggested if he would supply me with paper and envelopes, I would get off the two letters.

Within a few minutes I had completed my task, given him my landlady's phone number and was ready to be off. He had ordered Mrs. Thompson to make up a packet of jam sandwiches and would have set me on my way. I thought it better to go alone, however; I had a wholesome respect for Caspar's intelligence staff. So he drew a rough map which I memorised.

Ines shook hands and seemed more depressed than circumstances warranted.

"Don't worry," I said to her as we stood at the garden gate. "I'm sure everything will be all right."

"I'll try, but I shan't be really happy until you're safely back," she answered and then turned quickly away as Penberthy reappeared carrying a stout-looking ash walking-stick.

"It's loaded," he explained, swinging it to demonstrate. "You can knock a heifer down with it. I thought you might find it handy. And—don't worry over Miss Bellenden. I'll see no harm comes to her. By the way, do you know what the cry of a seagull is like?" He gave an apparent imitation of one.

"That should do," I grinned. "I've seen enough of them," and answered his call.

"Fine; if you hear it, it may be the real thing or it may be one of us . . . well—good hunting!"

"Thanks. I'll hope to see you about four or earlier."

CHAPTER XIV

I EXPLORE SOME RUINS
AND SEE SOME STRANGE THINGS

I T TOOK ME nearly an hour to reach the patch of moor where the ruins were situated.

They lay in a huge crater, invisible until one reached the lip.

Gazing down upon the ruins from the ridge of gorse-covered ground I could distinguish a series of low, stone walls forming a circle from which radiated passages, that apparently terminated some distance under the banks of the crater. Penberthy had explained that these were the "runways" to the living quarters—chambers not more than eight to ten feet square at most. The actual burial mounds were further away, and I could not place them. I noted, with a quickening of my pulses, that although most of the side passages were almost overgrown, the centre of the village had the appearance of being recently cleaned up. Plumb in the middle were two upright monoliths, and some ten feet in front of and between them was another big block of stone set lengthwise—the sacrificial stone.

I had done the last stage partly crouching and partly on all fours as the ground rose to the rim of the crater. I was anxious to get an idea of the position of the Manor House before making my way down into the cup. I waited a few minutes, but the place seemed quite deserted. Except for the song of a lark, a distant murmur which I knew must be the sea breaking, and the whisper of the wind amongst the bushes, I could hear nothing.

As soon as I rose I saw the plantation on my right a hundred yards or so off situated in another hollow. The house itself was invisible, but I made out a portion of the wall. The smooth grey stone offered very little chance of climbing without a rope or ladder unless I could find a tree whose branches overhung it. I marked down in my mind the most likely point of attack and then scrambled down to the ruins.

Closer inspection assured me definitely that work of tidying up and excavation had been carried out within the past few days.

Moving warily I made my way to the stone slab and observed that it had been carefully scoured, and that there were some rough carvings at one end flanking a series of chiselled lines radiating fanwise from a bowl-like centre cavity about eight inches in diameter and a couple of inches deep. It resembled a conventional figure of the sun and its rays. I felt suddenly chill as I observed a couple of chains on either side of the stone, one end of each terminating in a ring and the other anchored by a steel spike to the ground. They were old and rusted, but I was convinced that they had been quite recently fitted; the heads of the spikes showed the freshness of the hammer marks.

I think that, more than anything that had gone before, set the seal on my determination to carry out my own brand of justice on Dr. Caspar.

I faced round in the direction of the Manor and saw that one of the passages which had recently been cleared ran towards it. For about ten yards the path was open to the sky, then it dipped and became a dark tunnel about four feet wide. If there was a communication between Caspar's house and the barrows, this was the most likely opening.

I was on the verge of entering it when something caught my ear. It was more of a vibration than an actual sound and only rose at intervals. I took a few steps into tunnel, but it disappeared entirely. Then I put my ear to the earth and at once it became clear—an intermittent underground thud. There was another tunnel running at a slight angle to the one I was in and here the sound was much more distinct. I hesitated, but curiosity drove me on and I traversed the opening for some way, when it came to a stop. When I examined the face with my torch, I found the original runway terminated there. However, I had undoubtedly located the hammering; when I put my ear against the face I could hear the blows of the pick being used.

There was nothing to be done in that direction, so I returned to the first opening and warily, torch in hand and loaded stick at the ready, I set out to find what was at end of it.

I had barely got under cover when I heard people scrambling down the crater and, peering out, I saw half a dozen weird figures carrying spades and picks with another man—a short, very black negro—armed with a vicious-looking whip, who was obviously in charge. One of the poor creatures stumbled on a loose stone and the negro overseer lashed out at him. The fallen man gave a moan, but did not attempt to get up: the others stood riveted, watching with impassive faces.

"Get up, blast you," growled the negro, raising the lash again threateningly. Whether or no the Zombie was frightened, stunned, or had broken an ankle in its fall I could not tell, but it was too much for my feelings when the overseer, still cursing, started to rain vicious blows on the prostrate creature's shoulders. In an ordinary way I could not have attacked even a brute like that from the rear, but in dealing with Caspar and his crowd there was no room for scruples. At least, however, he had his chance, because he turned as I came near, thinking, probably, that it was one of his charges.

His whip was raised, but it fell abruptly as he saw my face. Even then, if he had stood up to me, I might have tried other tactics, but instead he swerved round, caught one of the Zombies and swung him towards me to trip me up. I stumbled over the Zombie, but as I did so my arm with the loaded stick flew up and providence brought it down on the top of his head just as he had drawn his gun. He fell without a groan. The Zombies stood silently by like a flock of uninterested sheep. The negro's skull was pretty thick and looking at him I reckoned he would come round in half an hour or so. I could not remove him anywhere and equally I could not murder him in cold blood. Then I bethought me of the chains by the sacrificial stone . . .

I signalled to two of the Zombies, made them understand what I wanted and they carried him to the slab. As I had no rope I removed his trousers and tore them in strips, which, twisted and attached to the chains, enabled me to bind him safely. Then I gagged him with a portion of his own shirt and left, hoping he would not be discovered for a few hours.

My next trouble was the Zombies: they appeared to regard me as their natural protector and whenever I made a move they started to follow me.

Suddenly I thought of my ham sandwiches and the legend I had heard regarding the effect of salt or spice upon the Zombie. I distributed a sandwich to each of the six, then I took the remaining two myself and started to munch. In a couple of seconds their jaws were all moving.

With quickened pulses I sat waiting. The vigil was getting on my nerves and I lighted a cigarette and got up with the intention of having another look at the spreadeagled negro.

Almost as if my movement were a signal one rose—an old bearded fellow dressed in a tattered frock-coat—and into his face came a look of the most unutterable horror I have ever seen on any human countenance. His jaw dropped and saliva ran down the

corners of his lips; then a groan issued from his throat, and with a
kind, rigid determination he turned about and strode up the crater
and across the moor. As I scrambled up to see where he went, the
remaining five passed me, walking stiltedly and following the first.
Whither they were bound I had no idea; I only saw that they moved
like automatons, in single file going straight as homing pigeons until
they were lost to my view beyond a rising knoll.

In spite of the gruesomeness of the notion, I chuckled to think of
the stir that would be caused locally if they were truly animated
corpses and were seen returning to graves. I wondered, too, if this
particular batch of creatures represented all of the mulatto's slaves
or if there were others.

I redeemed my torch which, fortunately, had not suffered
through my fall, and then went to have another glance at my captive,
who was evidently on the point of regaining consciousness. I tried
the improvised lashings and tightened them a little. I also tore off
another piece of his shirt and bound that round his jaws to keep the
gag in place. Then I decided to search his jacket pockets and came
across a small chain to which several Yale keys attached. These I
annexed.

Before leaving to explore the tunnel curiosity drove me to the top
of the crater again to see if there was any sign of the Zombies. I was
relieved to observe a line of small, dark figures, mounting a rise in
the moor and still pursuing their self-set path. With luck, if they
were not turned back by any of Caspar's people, they would be well
away within another half-hour.

~ ~ ~ ~ ~

The tunnel ran fairly straight, slightly downhill for about fifty yards
and then rose a little. At one or two spots I could hear the rever-
berations of the digging in the second passage. I had to go carefully
because every contact of my feet with the stone floor created an
echo. I could have shouted with relief when, after traversing as I
believed a good quarter of a mile, the tunnel veered abruptly to the
right and I found myself in another corridor that gave me the impression of a moat which had been bricked over, and was lighted
dimly by iron grids in the roof.

From the look of the stones forming the walls, which were much
smaller and cemented together, whereas those in the first tunnel
were large and simply set one on top of the other, I concluded I had
reached the Manor House. A newly installed electric light by the

entrance clinched my belief that it was being used by Caspar as a private exit. My main fear was that I might be interrupted before I found an entry. The sounds of digging had returned much more plainly.

I waited long enough to get my back straightened, then slipping my shoes in my coat pockets, I set out even more cautiously than before along the new corridor. There was no sign of a doorway in the house wall until I had passed the entrance to the second tunnel. I could see the glimmer of lights reflected on the walls some distance down, but beyond the steady, slow tapping of the pick there was no sign of life.

Just beyond the opening on the right I saw the entrance I had been hoping for; but there were two—set about seven feet apart. One was of rusted iron with a few holes bored through the upper part for ventilation; the second had, apparently, only recently been put in. The brick-work surrounding the frame was new and the oak door was still without varnish.

Every nerve alert, I crept up to it. There was handle, but the light from the grating showed me the round, brass boss of a Yale lock. As I was examining it I became aware of a curious smell. It made me think of a stable, and yet there was a ranker tang to it—not unlike the odour one finds in a menagerie. It seemed to me quite within the bounds of possibility that Caspar might protect the place with a wild animal. It would not be too good if I opened the door only to march into the claws of a ferocious beast.

Sniffing to try to locate the scent I discovered it came from a ventilator situated close to the iron door; when I went closer the smell was overpowering. By its strength it seemed to me that no single animal could be responsible.

The second key I fitted did the trick; I pushed the door gently open. I saw nothing more alarming than an empty corridor with a slip of coconut matting running along the floor and two electric lamps burning in the roof.

I was now inside the enemy's camp.

The passage ran straight for a short distance and then turned abruptly to the right. On the left-hand side two doors, both of metal, painted grey. It all looked very innocuous, but for some reason my spine started to creep. I held my breath, striving to make out what the odd sounds were that disturbed me; they seemed at one time like the bleat of a kid and at another like a horse whinnying. All at once my uneasiness cleared. It must be one of sacrificial animals used by the mulatto and Maman in their religious rites.

I was so pleased with the solution that nothing would suit me but to confirm it. By the direction, one of the metal doors on the left of the passage should give on to the stables. I examined it and found that it was fastened by a flat iron bar on a hinge, which dropped into a slot in the brick setting. Apparently it could only be operated from the corridor. A somewhat louder bleat coming to my ears reassured me; it was undoubtedly a stable.

Without further hesitation I lifted the bar, pulled open the heavy panel and peered through. For a second I could not make out much in the dim light that came from a single blue electric bulb hanging from the arched roof. Then, as my eyes became accustomed to the, gloom, my heart contracted in deadly disgust at the beastly spectacle before me.

It was a stable right enough, complete with stalls and troughs in the place of mangers, and halters by which the inmates were tethered. But instead of the goats and other domestic animals I had expected to see, I found myself quivering under the glare of a dozen pairs of malevolent green and yellow eyes that belonged to a number of creatures that looked as if they had been transported direct from the mythical groves of Mount Olympus. There were some I recognised as fauns, several satyrs, and a couple that I could not identify. But all were utterly horrible and unearthly and bestial to the verge of madness.

I think I should have flopped in a dead faint if it had not been for the uproar that my appearance created. Each and every one started to give vent to its own particular voice—from the deep bass of one of the larger ones, whose human upper part and goaten extremities were dead black, to an evil kind of reedy chuckle that came from one of the nameless brutes—a pinkish-white monstrosity with female breasts and legs like a sheep, covered with grey wool.

My mortal fear of the alarm being given was stronger, fortunately, than my bodily weakness. I slammed the door shut, dropped the iron bar into place and then subsided, my legs dropping from under me, with my head reeling and my body breaking into a cold sweat. A burning indignation mastered me and did more to overcome my physical weakness than anything else. But I had to force my mind to keep from remembering the awful eyes the brutes had turned upon me as I opened the door. They were human eyes, but out of them glared all the evil passions and foul animal desire that civilised man has endeavoured to forget.

There and then I resolved that if needs be the first bullet from my revolver should be for Miss Westerham if there was no other way of getting her out of his clutches.

I set out, so blazing with fury that I forgot to go warily to explore the rest of the cursed place. All thought of circumventing the doctor's big scheme had vanished. I was in berserk rage—only desirous of, first, insuring Bridget's escape and then killing as many of Caspar's crew as I could before I was killed myself.

I took the remainder of the corridor and the stairs—fortunately carpeted—that I found on turning to the right, at full speed. At the top of the first flight I passed a door covered with shabby green baize from behind which came the low mumble of voices. There was little doubt that this communicated with the servants' quarters.

Followed another short flight of six stairs which bore to the left and brought me to a small square landing. There was a window in one wall overlooking a patch of garden. Facing the stairs up which I had come was a pair of double swing doors and, continuing into the upper regions, another flight. I pushed one of the doors slightly ajar and found, as I had anticipated, that it led into the main hall. I was in two minds whether to slip across and make a dash for the main stairway that led to a balcony which I could gee above, or take the servants' stairs. I decided that there would be more chance of bluffing there than if I was found in the owner's part of the house. I halted a couple of steps up and put on my shoes again.

At the top of the stairs was another small landing with a window looking on to the same bit of garden, and pass doors similar to those giving on to the hall. Everything appeared quiet, so I pushed them open and found that on the inner side, where they gave on to the balcony, they were made to resemble the panelling of the walls and were almost indistinguishable.

My quandary now was where to go next. Miss Westerham might be in any of half a dozen rooms—and so might the mamaloi.

At that second I was brought up with a horrible jar by a panel at the other end of the gallery opening and the emergence of a little man with a high bald pate and popping eyes. He wore rubber gloves and a kind of white smock, and over his nose and mouth was a surgical mask and in one hand he carried a stethoscope.

He looked harmless enough and I was confident I could tackle him easily if he gave any trouble.

He pattered along the gallery in my direction, so preoccupied that he did not see me until he was nearly upon me. My impulse was to close with him, then I thought a bluff ought serve better.

"Excuse me, sir, but do you know where Maman Constance is?"
I asked as he came to a sudden stop on realising my presence.

"Eh—what . . . what's that?" he snapped irritably, his protruding
eyes goggling at me shortsightedly. "Who the devil are you—damn
it all, I've left my glasses behind," he continued.

I pulled out the disc I had taken from Barley.

"I'm number 23, sir," I returned politely. "Dr. Caspar sent me
with a message for Maman Constance. He,"—I hesitated then went
on—"he's anxious about the girl he brought last night and wants me
to remove her to a place where he thinks she'll be safer."

"Don't know what you're talking about," he retorted impatiently.
"You'd better speak to Maman Constance."

"The fair-haired girl the doctor and Maman Constance brought
here last night," I pursued. "I thought perhaps you might have been
examining her," I added.

His queer, pale eyes blinked at me, puzzled.

"Oh—you mean the patient who's suffering from amnesia.
That's right—just gone over her—nothing wrong except that she's
apparently had a shock or something."

I nodded. "The doctor said he thought that was what had happened," I lied. "Where is she?"

"Second on the left," he snapped, stepping to one side to get past.

"And Maman Constance?"

"Last room on the left," he jerked his head towards the balcony
and pattered down the stairs.

CHAPTER XV

I FIND MISS WESTERHAM AND FALL INTO A TRAP

I BREATHED a sigh of relief as the little man disappeared. I now knew that Bridget was in the house and where to locate her. I was about to tiptoe across the gallery when it occurred to me that it might be well to leave some trace of my presence in the house where Penberthy could spot it—supposing my retreat was cut off.

I dodged back on to the landing and looked out. At one time a rose garden, the ground was now merely an untidy mass of briars. The path disappeared into an overgrown shrubbery and behind that I could see the stone wall surrounding the grounds. I judged the distance from the window to the wall to be at least a hundred feet. If I could get into the garden and back I might throw my kangaroo tobacco pouch over the wall on the chance of Penberthy finding it. But there was no way down short of jumping.

Then I noticed a flower bowl containing narcissi supported by a glass ball.

It did not take half a minute to empty the tobacco into my pocket and replace it with the ball. I then made a sling of my handkerchief, took a couple of trial casts, and putting all I knew into the swing, let go. The pouch cleared the wall by a good yard.

The gallery was still quiet when I returned. I waited a second, and then legged it at full speed as softly as I could through the swing panels in the opposite wall. Here was a wing apparently at right angles to the main building and I thought at the front of the house. In comparison with the main hall and gallery it was shabby and miserable-looking. The floor was covered with a length of cheap threadbare stair carpet. There were several windows, but all the blinds were drawn.

I made a bee-line for the second door on the left. Before turning the handle I put my revolver in my left-hand pocket so that I could fire it through my coat if necessary, and placed my stick under my left arm. Then I walked into the room as calmly as I could, closing the door behind me. I found myself looking almost into the eyes of the girl I was seeking. She was sitting up in bed playing with a large, black doll.

At the same instant a youngish, coloured woman in a nurse's uniform sitting on the far side of the room rose quickly. She did not appear startled, but I meant to give her no opportunity. There was another door opposite and it seemed to me that it probably communicated with Maman Constance's room.

With a warning glance at Bridget—I assumed as professional an air as I could muster and beckoned to the nurse, at the same time placing my hat and stick down on a chair by the bed and reaching in my breast pocket for the bottle of stuff I had purloined from Caspar's safe and had suddenly remembered. The woman came across the room quietly.

"The doctor has sent me with some special medicine." I whispered.

She nodded respectfully. "Do you want the hypodermic?" she asked, lowering her voice to match mine.

"No it—it has to be administered through the nose," I replied. "I don't want to frighten her in her present state, so you had better go in front of me as if to give her a drink," I said hastily, noticing a tumbler of orange juice on a bedside table. "Then I'll drop this handkerchief over her face." I picked one up and surreptitiously poured a generous dose of the drug on to it. "As soon as I tell you, hold her arms in case she struggles," I continued, and placed the bottle on the table as I spoke.

She nodded again and turned without showing any sign of suspicion.

As she bent over the girl, I drew every nerve taut and, clutching the handkerchief in my right hand, I threw my left arm round her throat from behind and pulled her backwards, at the same time levering my right knee into the crook above her left calf.

The pressure of my arm on her throat prevented more than a stifled gurgle and the next moment I had rammed the handkerchief between her teeth and clapped my hand over her chin and nose so that she would be forced to swallow the fumes and some of the drug.

She struggled viciously, but I held on like death. My principal fear was that Bridget would call out. Alarm came into her eyes as she watched the nurse, but I murmured reassuringly—"Don't be frightened, Bridget. We are only playing," and set my whole strength to keep the coloured woman from struggling. The nurse, instead of relaxing, seemed to grow more violent and my muscles were taxed to the uttermost. All at once, however, I felt a shivering tremor run through her and in a couple of seconds more she lay limp in my arms.

Miss Westerham's gaze was still riveted upon me and its lack of intelligent interest chilled even whilst it relieved my mind. She had no idea of what had happened to her, which was a blessing; at the same time it destroyed my hope that she might be able to co-operate with me. For one thing I was immensely grateful—her eyes did not hold the appalling emptiness of the Zombies. They were bright and sane, but held merely the interest of a very young child in what was going on.

I smiled again and made a gesture with my head in the direction of the woman. "She's gone to sleep," I said softly, "so I am going to put her to bed."

Bridget nodded and moved slightly to one side as if to make room. "In here?" she asked, copying my whisper.

"No, in her own room," I answered, glancing quickly around for a convenient hiding-place. The only cupboard was fitted with shelves and it looked as if I should have to stow the nurse under the bed. As quietly as I could I lowered the woman to the floor.

"Can your doll talk?" I inquired, struggling without making too much fuss to unfasten the nurse's dress? her cap had already fallen off. If I could get Miss Westerham into the uniform there might be a wild chance of leading her out of the place.

"Only to me," Bridget smiled.

"What is she saying now," I continued, going down to my knees and working feverishly. The woman was lying on her back and I had to turn her.

Miss Westerham listened gravely; her face growing rapt.

"She—she seems to be asking where Ines went," she replied. "Do you know?" she questioned, eagerly.

"Yes," I said, as I managed to roll the nurse over. "I am going to take you there in a minute, but we shall have to borrow nurse's dress."

"Why?" she demanded.

"Because . . . you see, she is expecting nurse, and if you didn't have her dress on she might be disappointed."

She nodded gravely, "All right. Do you want me to get up now?"

"No—not for a minute." I was shaking with anxiety in case we were interrupted. "Wait? " I handed her the woman's cap. "Roll up your hair so that it won't be seen and put this on," I instructed.

Considering it a good game, Bridget busied herself doing up her hair whilst I stripped the nurse of her blue dress and apron. I was sweating violently by the time I had finished and pushed the body underneath the bed.

"Now—hurry," I adjured, passing her the uniform and casting an anxious glance in the direction of Maman's door. There was no time to stand on ceremony, so I helped her to put it on.

I was worried about her shoes in case she made too much noise in the corridor, but if we met anybody her bare feet would have excited more suspicion. I had adjusted the bedclothes so that a casual glance might deceive anyone into thinking she was still there and asleep.

The only way out that I knew offered comparatively free egress was the route by which I had come. I hated the idea of taking Bridget anywhere near those foul creations of the mulatto's evil arts, but it seemed the only thing to do.

As we stood, her hand in mine, preparing to make a dash, a telephone in the hall below started to ring. I drew back cursing under my breath as I saw the door I was watching open and the old woman appear. However, the interruption might be all to the good, if she were kept busy for a few minutes.

I glanced along the corridor of the wing again and a brighter thought came to me. If it was Caspar on the line and he had by any chance discovered the body of the negro, it was more than possible that he would have the wind up and warn her to be doubly on her guard. If the wing of the house, where we were, was as deserted as it appeared, might it not be better to hide Miss Westerham in one of the rooms and myself go and get reinforcements? We could then force the mamaloi or Caspar to restore the girl to her proper senses. Supposing I got her away from the mulatto and Maman decided things were getting hot for them, it would be an appalling situation if we could not find an antidote for the drug and Bridget was doomed to spend the rest of her life as little better than an infant.

I grew more worried. I could hear the old woman talking at the 'phone and, by the sharpness of her tone knew she was flustered, but I was unable to catch what she was saying. Suddenly she called loudly—"Antoine . . . Antoine," and as there was no immediate answer, began to ring a bell that clanged like an alarm through the house. There was the sound of a door being thrown violently open and footsteps hurried along the hall.

"What is it, mistress?" a gruff voice inquired.

"It is Joseph—the doctor's chauffeur . . . He says that he was out on the cliffs and he has just seen the Zombie workers going across the moor. He says they were all walking in single file and looked very odd and didn't appear to have anyone in charge of them. He wants to know if anything has happened to Carol. Have you seen him all?"

In spite of her self-control I could hear she was shaken.
I could have chuckled at her consternation if I, too, had not been upset, for it prevented our escape by the barrows. In a few minutes they would find Carol bound to the stone and then the hunt would be on in earnest.

"No, mistress, not since he went out to the meeting-place half an hour or so ago," Antoine replied. I could not see him, but I judged by his voice that he was of the heavy, ruminative type.

"Then go and see if you can find him, and come back at once and let me know if anything appears wrong. Satan!" she continued as Antoine shuffled hurriedly away, "if anything has gone amiss Caspar will never forgive me. Are you there," she went on more loudly, speaking into the 'phone again. "I have sent Antoine to the meeting-place to find out . . . where were the Zombies going? Not the town, I hope."

"What?" Her voice jumped a couple of tones?

The graveyard! Oh, but this is appalling. If they get there and anyone should see them: Go at once and see if you can head them back. In the name of the Great One, don't stand arguing," she added shrilly, "go and make sure." She banged the receiver into place, and I heard her cross the hall and pass through a door which slammed after her.

"Come—I'm going to give you a ride," I said to Bridget, and put her across my shoulder. She gave a little squeal, but it was childish pleasure and I silenced her by saying that we should not find Ines unless she was quiet.

I tried each door, risking the chance of running into someone. The first three rooms were empty, but I wanted to find a place with a window that could be seen from the garden walls. If I could leave a curtain or blind awry it would enable me to spot it from the outside. It might be possible for Penberthy to bring along a ladder and get the girl down. I did not think Caspar would go so far as to murder her if he found the house besieged, but there might be hiding-places and there was only my word that she was there against his and the mamaloi's.

The next door I tried was locked; then came a small passage leading to a narrow, uncarpeted stairway, and finally another pair of swing panels which gave on to the main gallery again. Unless the second flight of stairs offered sanctuary I was done.

I deposited Bridget at the foot and raced up, finding myself on a landing about six feet square. There was a window facing the stair and in the ceiling over my head a trap-door. There were two doors opening off the landing; the first showed a small, dark chamber filled with bits of old, broken furniture and other rubbish. The second was more promising. It was carpeted and there was a child's cot in one corner. While piled up, haphazard, were a number of toys. There was an old, chintz-covered couch and chairs to match, and though the place had evidently not been used for years, it looked cheery and comfortable.

I called to Miss Westerham softly to come up, drew the blind, opened the window and found I was gazing down on to a kitchen-garden and orchard. I noted that we were in a kind of square tower which rose above the rest of the wing. It should not be diffi-cult to spot the turret. Bending over the sill, I saw that there was a gravel path, running down to a gate below. I closed the window again and drew the blind, but left a sufficient opening to light the room, and turning, found Bridget quite happily sitting on the couch playing with one of the new dolls.

"Are you going to be a very good Bridget and stay here quite quietly until I come back to take you to Ines?" I said seriously.

She nodded. "Yes, I like being here. Only—I don't like being alone too long," she added.

She was obviously content for the time being and almost too docile. I smiled reassuringly, patted her shoulder and as she raised her face expectantly, kissed her. I saw there was a key in the lock on the outer side of the door, so I turned this, but did not remove it. The chances were that unless anything alarmed her, she would play with the doll until she got tired and then go to sleep.

I next gave my attention to the blind on the landing; cutting a diagonal piece from it from top to bottom and hiding the slip in the lumber room. I judged it would enable us to identify the window in case the other wings were also crowned with turrets.

The corridor was still in silence when I went down, but I could hear some kind of activity in the main hall and concluded Maman Constance was getting busy. I had hoped there might be another service staircase near at hand leading to the ground floor of the wing, but I could not discover it. It looked as if, after all, I should have to risk crossing the gallery again.

I thought perhaps there might be a way out by the roof through the trap. Going up the steps again I examined the trap in the ceiling. Here I was once more checked. I could not reach it as I stood, and if I brought a box from the rubbish room there would be no way of removing it after me.

I heard a sound in the passage, dodged back into the room, and clutching my stick held my breath anxiously. Then followed what seemed an interminable pause, broken by the sound of a heavy article being moved into the corridor. A second later the newcomer set off down the passage, pulling something with creaking wheels. I tiptoed down the stair and gazed furtively after the retreating figure.

It was the little man I had taken for a doctor. Behind him was an odd-looking contraption like an old-fashioned bed-chair fitted with a number of metal joints and arms. The creaking came from the wheels of a small trolley upon which it was set. I watched him turn the corner and then enlightenment flashed upon me as I caught a side view and saw that there were strong straps dangling from the arms of the machine and a kind of iron collar fastened to the hood-shaped top.

I waited long enough to let the doctor get out of the way and then slipped through the door he had left open. The place was window-less and I could see no way out. Then I observed, as my eyes grew accustomed to the gloom, that behind the door was a lift. It was a pretty solid affair and from its appearance must have been recently installed. There was room in the cage for two people and I saw there were three buttons in the right-hand panel. I took it that if I pressed the bottom one I should be deposited somewhere near the ground level. As was no other alternative I got in after shutting the room door behind me, pulled to the expanding iron gate and pushed and pushed the button.

The thing started off, passing two landings on its descent, but the lift did not stop. When it reached a lower level I found I was looking on to a white tiled alcove in which an electric lamp was burning. This was no good, so I pressed the second button and the thing began to ascend, but apparently there was no means of stopping it at the ground floor. Feeling rather like Alice in Wonderland, I pressed the lowest button once more, hoping I might be able to pull up by opening the expanding gate and make a jump for the landing. The speed was too fast, however, unless I wished to risk a broken leg, so for the second time it arrived at the alcove.

Emerging from the lift I found myself before a sliding door faced with chromium, the upper part of which was glazed and looked upon a brilliantly lighted, white-painted chamber, along both sides of which were cages and glass cubicles with beds in them. For a moment I thought I had come upon another stable, but a second cautious peep showed me a couple of operating tables and glass-fronted cases containing a battery of surgical instruments. I knew then that I had stumbled on the mulatto's laboratory.

The place seemed to be deserted but for the patients strapped to their beds; I did not think there would be any danger from them. In any event I had either to find a way out through the laboratory, or return by the lift to my starting point.

Before venturing into the room I went back to the lift and wedged the gate so that the switch buttons were rendered inoperative.

I knew that I might expect to find some of Caspar's monstrosities in the making; at worst they could hardly be more noxious than the finished products. Actually, except that several seemed to be straining and moving uneasily under their bonds, there was nothing very horrible about those in the cubicles.

The cages on the opposite side were filled with either mental deficients or Zombies sitting or lying apathetically on their pallets. Some system of purification of the air had, I concluded, been installed because the usual unpleasant odour was absent.

I was passing them, almost unconsciously, my mind being fixed upon another glazed door at the further end of the laboratory, when one of the figures, suddenly turned and I found myself gazing into a pair of glowing, entirely human eyes. I halted as if I had been shot, a shocked "Good God," escaping from my lips.

He glared at me.

"All right," he said, and there was a despairing recklessness in his tone, "you can tell the doctor I give in—so long as he swears on his word of honour not to touch Sheilah."

I suppose something in my expression told him that I was not connected with the mulatto; his own changed and a quick glimmer of hope tinged his tone. "Don't you belong here?" he breathed.

I shook my head. "No. I'm after a girl that swine Caspar has kidnapped. Are you a prisoner, too?"

He nodded. "Yes. Dunkerley's my name—I'm a surgeon. They're trying to force me to assist that lunatic professor . . . said they'd get hold of my fiancée if I refused." His mouth twitched. "I held out until I found that he tracked her down . . . For God's sake, if you can, get me out of here, too."

"I'll try," I said quickly, "but you'll have to wait until I've got in touch with my friends from outside."

"I can't stand much more of this," he groaned.

"It is quite probable you'll be better able to help me than I you," I continued. "I ran into one of the keepers this morning and swiped him and released the Zombies. They've all gone over the moor and the alarm is out; it's a hundred to one chance I'll be able to pass the guards. That's why I left the girl for the time being. If I don't show up my friends will carry on. Do you think you can pretend to agree to what they want? You'd be one ally in the house when the others turn up."

He stared at me, half-suspiciously, half-hopeful. "You're sure you *are* what you say and not a friend of that devil?" he growled.

I had an inspiration. "Are you a Mason?" I asked, and as he nodded, "on my word as a brother," I said offered him my hand.

"I'll do what I can, but for the love of God get a move on," he replied. A twisted grin crossed his lips, "I've been holding on to my reason by sheer will power for the past two weeks and I'm scared of cracking if I have watch to the professor at his beastly work much longer."

"Is that the little man with the bald head and like a rabbit?"

"That's the scum. Though there's no real harm in him except that he's crazy on vivisection. Amazingly brilliant, but," he shrugged, "mad as a hatter."

"Do you know the way out of here?" I asked.

"No, not an idea. But you got in all right . . ."

"That road is too dangerous now. Still—I'll find one with luck. I can rely on you then, if anything happens and I'm pinched?"

"If you aren't too long," he said grimly. "I'll tell the professor I'll do what he wants, but I don't promise I'll be able to stop myself killing the rat if you don't get me out soon."

"Cheer up," I said. "Everything is going to be all right."

I spoke confidently, but there was plenty to be done still before we were out of the wood. So far my luck had been so good that I was beginning to get scared. An inner sense of disaster set my heart thumping furiously as I made my way through the far doors.

I went along blindly, now almost running in my anxiety to get into the open. The brightly lighted, silent passage with its thick, felt carpeting that muffled my own tread was horribly nerve-racking. I brought up sharp at a flight of stairs as a door clanged above, followed by the sound of shuffling feet and heavy breathing.

I glanced round wildly, but there was not a sign of cover. Then I heard a voice and recognised as that of Maman Constance.

"Be careful of that corner," she adjured somebody, who grunted as if carrying a heavy burden. "Let Joseph get her legs round first. . ."

It was the evil in her tone—a gloating note—and the word "her" that sent my discretion to the winds and made me go forward and on up half a dozen steps. I stopped then, partly in sheer dismay, partly because the way was blocked by two men bearing a girl's limp figure between them, whilst behind was the mamaloi, grinning maliciously to herself.

I knew that it was Ines even before I recognised her dress. Something inside me cracked and in a hoarse voice I called "Stop," and drew my revolver.

"Well, well—if it isn't the red head," Maman Constance remarked almost conversationally as the two men stopped dead on the stairs. "I shouldn't shoot, young man," she continued silkily. "You will only risk injuring your sweetheart if you do." She ducked as she spoke so that she was shielded by Ines' shoulders and head.

"Go back and put Miss Bellenden down—if not I swear I'll put a bullet in your men and through you." I moved up another step.

She cackled and at the same second the lights went out. I made to collar the first man, but my foot slipped and the next instant a weight descended on my head as the fellow nearest dropped Ines' legs.

~ ~ ~ ~ ~

When, aching in every joint, I opened my eyes, I found I was tethered by chains in one of the compartments of the stable, the unnatural inmates of which were jibbering and bleating excitedly. The reek of the place nearly sent me off again, but I clung to my senses desperately. As I straightened myself painfully to examine my bonds I caught sight of another human figure fastened to the other side of the stall, and a sickening sensation of absolute despondency settled over me. Ines, and now Penberthy; my last hope.

He smiled grimly as our eyes met.

"Pretty ghastly, isn't it," he remarked quietly. "I was wondering when you'd come round . . . I found your tobacco pouch and was just off to get help when I ran into a regular army corps. They wouldn't give me the chance to explain and hustled me off to your friend, Maman Constance. I thought everything was going to be all right and she would accept my story when some swine came rushing in with Miss Bellenden. Said he'd spotted her walking along the road.

"It didn't take your old hag two seconds to conclude we were acquainted. I guess that threw sweet Maman a bit off balance and she didn't quite know what to do; anyway she told the men to take me away and hold me until she consulted someone, and they brought me to this cheery den. You were shot in about half an hour after. You know I—I was only half convinced by what you told me this morning," he went on, "but when I saw these ghastly freaks" —he jerked his head in the direction of a satyr in the stall facing that was whinnying and glaring at us with its malignant green eyes—"I realised just how bad things were. I'd have cut my heart out rather than they'd got Ines—damn them."

"It wasn't your fault," I returned. "As a matter of fact everything would have been perfectly okay if I hadn't run into a nest of Zombies, swatted the keeper and let them escape."

"The other girl—I take it from the pouch—that she's here, too?"

"Yes, but she's all right," and I explained the situation.

"A hell of a fine mess," he groaned. "It looks like being the end of everything. And I was so confident we'd pull it off. Damn, oh damn the whole brood. I wouldn't care a hang about myself, but I've let you down—and Ines. . ." There was utter misery in his tone.

"The chance may come yet," I said, and told him about our new ally, Dunkerley.

"Did they take the letter you wrote?" he asked suddenly.

I nuzzled my inner pocket with my chin; it was the only way I could ascertain if they had searched me.

"Yes, I'm afraid so," I said, feeling it was empty.

"That stops any chance of your landlady making inquiries."

I nodded. "Though she wouldn't have done in any case. She'll only think I've gone off without paying the rent."

"Oh, well," he continued, "I suppose the best thing to do is to set our grey matter to work," and I was more than ever satisfied that in him I had as staunch a companion as one could desire.

"Can we get at one another's chains, do you think?" he asked. We tried, but even with our arms pulled almost out of their sockets there was still a good ten inches separating us. We gave up, panting, at last, and leaned back to rack our brains for ideas.

I was not able to think very coherently because fears for Ines kept popping in and out all the time. I do not know if Penberthy was in a similar case, but what with the excitement of the morning's chase and the black disappointment I presently found myself overcome with a desire for sleep that nothing I could do would conquer.

I tried to speak to Penberthy, but my lips would not frame a sound. I wondered vaguely if I had been drugged or if the reek of the stable was acting as an anaesthetic; whatever the cause I found myself nodding at short intervals and fell into a heavy doze standing.

Eventually, after a nightmarish space, I returned to consciousness. When I looked across to where Penberthy had been tethered he had gone.

CHAPTER XVI

DOCTOR PETTIFRANC SPEEDS UP ACTION

AT SIENA STUDIOS Caspar paced to and fro like a caged panther. Polynice sat in one of the pew-like chairs. The mulatto had gone over every inch of the apartment, but had not been able to find a clue to the whereabouts of the missing Antonio Barley. Polynice had already been to make inquiries at the vanished man's lodging. Caspar stopped and faced his companion.

"It doesn't make sense," he said irritably. "A man like Barley doesn't vanish unless there is a reason. Even if he'd gone on the drink—he would have contrived to get back to his rooms by this morning. Something has happened to scare him, or else he has been made away with. . . If anything happened here, he should have seen. . . The key of the back door was in the lock, so that he must have come in that way; but—why was the key on the inside? . . . I tell you, it doesn't fit whatever way you look at it."

Polynice could offer no solution. Caspar resumed his march for a few minutes, then halted once more.

"If that man who was prying round the studio the other evening had met Barley," he began, "then one or the other probably got hurt, eh?"

Polynice nodded, watching the mulatto curiously. Sweat broke out on the big man's forehead as he closed his eyes and strove by exercising the powers of his witchdoctor ancestors to visualise what had occurred. Then he opened them again.

"No use," he grumbled. "I'm too bothered to be able to concentrate on anything, except that I have the feeling somebody did meet Tony here and that there was a fight."

He went over to the press and examined the base and then the panel. Suddenly he started and gave a grunt.

"Somebody *has* been here," he said; "do you see the scratches where they've tried to force the door open?"

"It does look rather like it," Polynice admitted.

"We'll have another look round to see if we can find Tony. He may be hidden in the house or he may have been taken away. Whether Tony got the better of an intruder or not, the winner had to do something with the loser's body. There may be a clue on the stairs now we know what to look for."

He hesitated whether to go by the front or back stairway. "If the body had to be carried, the back stairs would be safer, but he'd have to pass Adolf, and the steps are narrow and difficult for anyone with a weight on his back."

They examined every inch of the landing and went carefully down the stairs and through each apartment on the two floors below the mulatto's studio. At the entrance to number one, Polynice called his chief's attention to a scratch on the doorpost.

"Isn't that new," he asked.

Caspar looked at it closely.

"Certainly looks that way."

The place seemed exactly as the previous tenants had left it. It was Polynice, on his way to the kitchenette who stooped suddenly and picked up something from amongst a litter of straw on the threshold.

"Found something?" Caspar demanded.

"Only an old rabbit's foot." Polynice returned

"That's Tony's," the mulatto said hoarsely. "I've seen him with it a hundred times."

With a common impulse they pushed through the door together, and the next second had lifted the lid of the coal bin and were gazing down on the negro's crumpled body.

Caspar bent over the edge and raised Barley's chin gently; then, with one hand supporting the head, he drew up one of the man's eyelids.

He bent over still further and sniffed. "He has been given a dose of the drug I sent him to fetch ... This is more serious than I thought," he continued, releasing the unconscious man's head.

"You mean . . . somebody knows what we are planning?"

"I can't think of anyone on this side of the world who has even a glimmering notion of our existence. It may have been that burglar fellow . . . but I can't see what object he has."

"Why don't you revive Barley and get him to tell us?"

"Because I can't, you fool," Caspar snarled, losing his poise for a flash, then recovering it again as quickly. "Until I can get hold of the bottle Barley had, or have time to prepare some more, I'm done. I don't mind so much about him"; he jerked his head in the direction of the coal bin. "He's no use except for carrying messages, anyway; it's Walton who worries me. Until I can bring him round, we're held up on that matter of the new gas he got hold of in Switzerland."

"Couldn't you find the man who invented the gas?"

"Maybe Maman Constance might—through the Whistling Ancestors," Caspar answered curtly.

"Did Walton . . .?"

"No; he died quite naturally. Tuberculosis. He was an old friend of Walton's and gave him the formula because Walton had staked him in his experiments. Oh, well? " he cast another callous glance at the coal bin, "we must decide what is to be done. I'll have to ring up Maman and tell her to be doubly on guard. We may have to alter some of our plans." He motioned to the studio door.

"Aren't you going to bring Tony along?"

"Why? We can't do anything for him until we find the drug, and he's less likely to be found here than anywhere else," Caspar returned coolly. "It's his fault for being taken off his guard. By God, though,"—the muscles in his throat knotted tensely—"I'd like to get my hands on the meddling swine who did this."

He nodded warningly to Polynice to remain silent as the sound of footsteps were heard. He relaxed again, with something like a sigh, as Mrs. Jansen came round the corner of the stair.

"Is anything wrong?" she asked, startled, as she saw him.

"Plenty," he replied shortly, "but we'll talk of that upstairs. Have you any news? Is the dark girl back?"

"Not yet, but I think it must be all right. The maid at her apartment said she often went out to stay with friends at a minute's notice." Caspar grunted. "But I've found the fair girl."

"What fair girl? Not Miss Westerham?"

Mrs. Jansen stared at him in surprise. "Of course not. You got her yesterday . . . didn't you?"

Caspar grinned almost apologetically. "Yes, of course. Sorry—but one or two annoying things have happened and I'm a bit off balance . . . What girl?"

"I thought you said you wanted a really pretty blonde of not more than sixteen or seventeen for one of your houses in Brazil," Mrs. Jansen explained, obviously puzzled the other's distraction.

"Oh . . . yes; that's right. Have you found one?"

"I have; and quite by chance. She's a wonder, Dr. Pettifranc—much more attractive than the Westerham girl. An orphan, too, and no friends. I ran across her on the Embankment about midnight. She was going to jump into the river. I thought there was something funny about her—and I stopped her just in time," she rattled on ingratiatingly, as Caspar led the way into the studio.

"Poor devil; broke, I suppose," he commented.

Polynice's lips tightened, but he kept his face averted so that his real feelings were masked.

"Yes," Mrs. Jansen replied. "She was in a revue chorus for a time after her mother died: apparently mother and daughter came from South Africa. They had a little money, but the mother invested it in some dud company. The girl was too pretty—that was her trouble; no business firm or shop would engage her. Then the manager of the revue wanted her to live with him and she ran away. . . I told her a friend of mine was looking out for good-mannered, pretty girls for mannequin work in Rio de Janeiro. She's at my place now—quite happy," she concluded with a leer that turned her veneer of respectable virtuousness into something horribly depraved. And yet, such was the peculiar character of the woman, she would have been appalled had she known that the mulatto's object in finding the girl was a quick and painless death as a sacrifice to a God—rather than a living death as ministrant to the baseness of man.

"Good. I'll discuss her later. You might go into the pantry and make me a cup of coffee whilst I do some telephoning," Caspar remarked. "I've been driving all night and had no breakfast yet."

"That dame gives me the creeps for all she's been useful to us," he commented to Polynice as Mrs. Jansen went through into the kitchenette. "Maman Constance doesn't like her either," he added, going to the telephone and putting in a trunk call for the Manor House.

"You're a bit of an enigma yourself," Caspar began again, flinging himself into a chair opposite Polynice.

"In what way?" Polynice's tone was unconcerned, but he groped in his pocket for a cigarette and busied himself lighting it.

"I wonder sometimes why you went into the business; you never appear particularly enthusiastic over our schemes."

"I don't think you've had any reason to complain of my work, have you?" Polynice remarked stiffly. "I'm sorry I made that slip over the telegram I handed to Miss Westerham, but, as you admitted yourself, you didn't give me any instructions about it."

"No, it wasn't your work I was thinking about. It's just you . . . your queer aloofness." Caspar smiled, but there was a hint of chagrin in his tone.

"A legal training makes one inclined to be colourless. . ."

"You practised on the Gold Coast, didn't you?"

"Yes, and—other places." Polynice pricked up his ears. "Perhaps, if you don't want Mrs. Jansen to hear what you say on the 'phone,

I'd better go and delay her a bit; it sounds as though she might be coming back."

The telephone bell rang at that moment. Polynice slipped away while Caspar went to the instrument.

"Is that you, Maman . . .? Listen. What's that!" he almost shouted as he was interrupted by the mamaloi's shrill tone.

"Miss Bellenden?" His eyes flared—"and a man! Who? An artist . . . a friend of the girl; what do they want . . . how did you get hold of them?" He listen impatiently, the fingers of his free hand opening and closing spasmodically.

"Hell and damnation. . . I'll flay Joseph alive if he's made a blunder and the man is what he says he is. If he lives in the town, you could easily check up on it."

He listened again, fuming, for a moment, then: "Do with them?" he burst out violently, "what *is* there to do with them? Tell them it is all a mistake and the men were looking for some loony patients who've escaped, and let them go at once before they begin to suspect anything. What. . . they've put him in the stable. Oh, my God," he groaned, "now we are in the soup. . . Wait—the only chance is to give the man a hypodermic of the stuff I used for the blonde and turn him loose on the moor. It will look as if he's lost his memory. Better do the same with her, only keep her in the house. I'll be back as soon as I can. . . No—no thank you," he added, altering his tone as a voice broke in to ask if he wanted a further three minutes.

He strove to assume a normal air as Polynice pushed open the door for Mrs. Jansen, who was carrying a tray with coffee and toast.

"Thanks, that's good of you," he said affably, though he felt like wringing her neck. Then, as the necessity for calm thinking urged itself upon him, he forced a smile of gratitude.

"And now I wonder if you'd do something else for me?" he began on a new and less strained note.

The woman bridled. "Of course, Dr. Pettifranc."

"I want to get the girl you spoke of away as quickly as possible. There's a boat sailing from Lisbon in a couple of days and if Mr. Polynice takes her across to Paris by the plane she may be just able to make it. Could you have her at his office in Lincoln's Inn in a couple of hours—you'd better get her some new clothes first. . ." He brought out a well-filled wallet and began to count out a number of notes. The woman's eyes narrowed.

"Will two o'clock be all right; she'll want some lunch?"

"Perfectly—if Mr. Polynice should be out, let her sit in his office. I'll have a couple of dress boxes sent along and she can amuse herself looking over them . . . it will reassure her if by any chance she is suspicious."

"You needn't bother about that," Mrs. Jansen interposed with pride. "She's quite convinced by my story, and far too grateful for being alive to give any trouble."

"One hundred pounds." Caspar put the notes in the woman's palm, but contrived not to touch her fingers.

"Thank you, doctor." Her miser's fleshy hand closed and she got up to go.

"By the way—what is the girl's name; you didn't mention it?"

"Alice Sheldon. She's really quite a beauty—a bit anaemic just at present, but she'll soon plump up with regular meals," and with another meaning smile Mrs. Jansen departed.

The mulatto got up, opened a window and stood for a space, shoulders squared, breathing deeply. Polynice did not speak, only busied himself pouring out two cups of coffee. When Caspar turned, except for a more determined glint in his eye, he was his usual un-ruffled self.

He swallowed some coffee before reopening the conversation; took up a piece of toast, glanced at it distastefully, and went off into the kitchenette, returning with an apple.

"Walton and Westerham are our trump cards," said the mulatto. "With Walton's gas formula we can put a barrier round our capital that nobody in the world could cross . . . with what we hope to get out of Westerham and a few others, finance won't worry us any more. However, that can come later. The present position is that there's something very queer going on and we shall have to alter our plans." He drew his chair closer to Polynice and emphasized his points by tapping on the other's knee.

"Instead of having our initiation ceremony at full moon, I pro-pose to advance it to next Wednesday. Westerham ought to be in England before then and I shall have had time to make some more S.17 to use on Walton. I want you to go round to all the delegates and fix up with them for Wednesday night. The arrangements for transportation will be the same. If there's a Government function on for that evening, you must persuade the three leaders to speak to the Colonial Office and represent that the delegates have some personal business on for that evening."

"But, I thought—you said—the Great One would not appear unless there was a full moon and the ritual was in order," Polynice interrupted. He appeared upset.

"I did say so," Caspar returned quietly, though his eyes took on an odd gleam. "But the Ancestors have told Maman that it is not at all certain the Great One *will* appear on this occasion. They say he would prefer to postpone the First Court until the Inner Circle have proved their faith. That is why I have gone to so much trouble to prepare a . . . picturesque ceremonial. We know there are a number amongst those who will be attending who are sceptical. If by a certain amount of effect we can win their allegiance . . . tear away the scepticism bred of Westernisation and raise up the old primitive fears, then there will be no doubt about the Great One appearing to accept homage from his subjects. Until that time we must do the best we can for ourselves."

Polynice looked perplexed.

"You mean, you propose to have a—an understudy," he said.

Caspar shot a malicious glance at him.

"Would you consider that terribly immoral?" he asked ironically. "Don't you think the Great One would rather we carried out a little deception in his name with the object of insuring the conversion of the waverers sooner than risk making a personal appearance to a flock, some of whom might consider we were putting on an effective conjuring trick? Faith is the main thing, Polynice. Even the Christian teaching holds that it can move mountains. Produce that blind faith in the hearts of our future subjects and, whether the Great One manifests himself or prefers to remain hidden, we shall have no trouble with them. Why—what is the matter? You're trembling . . ."

"Nothing," Polynice answered. "I—I was only wondering if it might not be dangerous . . . if the Great One did not happen to take your view. Caspar? " he leaned forward and tried a couple of times to voice a question.

"Well—speak out, man," the mulatto said, impatient.

"Do you . . . are you honest in your faith and teaching or—are you only pretending, to serve your own ends?

Caspar stared at him for a few seconds in silence, a speculative look in his eye. Then he stretched out a huge hand and patted Polynice on the knee reassuringly.

"Of course I am honest," he answered.

Polynice's brow cleared.

"These séances? " he said and glanced at the pews. "I've often wondered why you bothered with a lot of foolish old women."

Caspar grinned. "Not so foolish, my friend, if one takes into consideration the fact that every one of them has a substantial bank balance, and that when I had prepared them sufficiently they would have handed out good round sums." He frowned. "Now it looks as if I should have to discontinue."

He broke off suddenly as the telephone rang once more.

"Well?" Caspar snapped. "What—you again, Maman . . . No more of Joseph's blunders, I hope." He hesitated just sufficiently long before the name to indicate that he did not consider her entirely blameless.

"The one-armed man! You've got him . . . splendid; that amply makes up for the other business. A private detective, eh? Hm, that explains quite a lot. Did you find out who is behind him?" The mamaloi's shrill tone clattered an explanation.

"Good," he said as her tale came to an end. "Post the one letter to the Chelsea address and burn the other. I'm glad about the bottle—let's hope the meddling idiot has left enough to do what we want. I'm glad that Dunkerley has come to see reason; it will help us a lot. I know . . ." his voice assumed a malicious note: "just to test him, tell him he has to operate on the detective—make him into a satyr. You might get him to give the hypodermic injection to the artist fellow. If he carries that out without jibbing, we can be fairly certain he won't let us down. Any news of the Zombies?" he listened, then chuckled. "Joseph headed them off and drove them over the cliff, eh; that's good. It might have been awkward if they'd been seen getting back into their graves. You remember what the Ancestors told you about another, younger girl coming along for the sacrifice . . . well, we've got her. Mrs. Jansen picked her up last night. I'll probably send her with Polynice to the house to-morrow if he can get away . . . I can't come myself; we've decided to have the Initiation earlier and there's a good deal to be arranged, but I'll call you up again to-night. Good-bye."

He rang off with an air of relief.

"A little better news," he said, turning to Polynice, who was sitting in his chair again. He recapitulated the events in Cornwall.

"You'd better trot along now and round up the delegates," he went on. "If you can, get the principal men to come to your office this evening between five and seven. I can prepare the way for Wednesday."

"Very good, chief." Polynice rose. The order seemed to make him happier. "And the girl—do you want me to drive her down to-night?"

"Probably, but I'll let you know definitely this evening. In the meantime take her to some quiet hotel. Tell her not to go out in case she is wanted."

"Shall I call you up here when I've seen the delegates?"

"No. I'll be at your office at five. We can have a bite at the Cafe de Paris after. I don't feel like using this place more than I can help at present. I'll probably take a room at a hotel myself to-night."

For several minutes after Polynice had gone the mulatto stared unseeingly at the door. Coming out of his reverie he opened the ebony press, took one of the books from the lower drawer, flung himself into a chair and began to read.

The dossier appeared to be perfectly in order and Polynice's bona fides genuine. And yet, a thin thread of suspicion that his associate was playing some strange game of his own obtruded in Caspar's mind.

"It would be a pity if Polynice should turn out to be a traitor," he reflected, closing the book and returning it to the press. He would set a trap for him. If he was genuine, he need never even suspect, but if he was playing a double game . . .

That matter decided, Caspar finished his coffee and then went to deal with Adolf. A pity the latter was not a real Zombie; as it was he who would have to be given a sleeping draft and conveyed to the Manor on Caspar's next journey down.

CHAPTER XVII

THE DRUG CALLED KINGO

WELL, SO you've come to your senses, I hear?"
Dunkerley, lying face downwards on his bed, stared
morosely into the grinning face of Maman Constance.

"The professor told me," she explained. "You're wise, 1 think;
probably spared yourself and that sweetheart of yours considerable
discomfort." She cackled shrilly and Dunkerley winced.

"Dr. Caspar's instructions are to test you. If you are honest and
don't try to play any tricks, you'll be treated as one of ourselves and
your pretty lady friend won't be interfered with. If not? " she
cackled again. "Is it safe to let you out, or do you want to change
your mind?" she continued.

"Don't think because I am alone you can get away," she added
tartly as she saw him glance round the laboratory. "There are three
of my men just outside. Well?" her tone was impatient.

"I meant what I said. I have no objection to your trying me."

"Good!"

He rose, stretched himself and moved forward a trifle shakily as
the front of the cage lifted on its counterweight and he was able to
leave his cell—for the first time in two weeks.

The mamaloi watched him, an odd appreciative glint in her eye,
as he came gradually to his full height and appeared to expand
physically. He was not as big as Caspar, but there was something
vital and extraordinarily attractive about him.

Maman had a decided penchant for good-looking men particularly blonde men with no colour taint. Of pure Arab-Negro descent
herself, she was not imbued with the constitutional hatred that animated the mulatto for both races. In her youth the mamaloi had had
several white lovers, some glamour still attached to them in her
memory.

Dunkerley reminded her a little of her first Ericcson, a Danish
author she had met when she was fifteen in Mozambique. An odd
thought came to her. . . if Caspar was so enamoured of Miss Bel-

lenden, why not let him have her and take this man, Dunkerley, for herself?

Her eyes, as her mind brooded on the idea, glowed with such dark intensity that Dunkerley shrunk back.

"What is it you want me to do?" he said, anxious to terminate the disturbing scrutiny.

She smiled; pleased that she had power to discompose him.

"Nothing very alarming. There is a young man—two young men—who are inconveniencing us slightly; spies are unpleasant people to have about—if anything should happen and we were interfered with, it is scarcely likely that you would be considered any more innocent than we . . . we should naturally take care of that."

"Go on," he said.

"In the case of the man we think maybe just a harmless fool, you will give him a hypodermic injection that will affect his mind. The doctor suggests two centigrammes, which should put him out of action for a couple of months. By that time we shall have finished what we have to do here and gone away. The other"—she glanced at him in evil amusement—"is more dangerous. The doctor proposes to add him to our collection of primitive creatures. I think you might perhaps try your hand at making him into a satyr: they are more spectacular than fauns and so Kucynski tells me, require more art . . ."

Dunkerley subdued a shudder.

"Do you want me to begin at once?" he asked, endeavouring to render his tone purely professional.

"Yes."

"Will—the professor be here?"

"Not unless you require him. Caspar feels that you should be allowed to work uncontrolled if you wish. You will want a nurse to assist you, though," she added.

"Later, yes. But at first . . ." he hesitated. "Would it be all right if I worked by myself on the preliminary stages—until I become more accustomed to the idea?" he ventured.

She surveyed him shrewdly, then made a gesture of assent. "If you get through successfully, I might ask you to carry out an operation on myself," she remarked. Her tone was casual, but there was a hint of anxiety underlying it.

"Is there something wrong with you?" he said. "You look strong enough to me—of course I can't say definitely without an examination." Even as the words were uttered he marvelled subconsciously that professional training was so much stronger than personal feeling.

"Nothing that a clever man such as yourself, doctor, cannot cure; but we can discuss that later."

It was apparent even to Dunkerley that for some reason she was inclined to be friendly. Actually it was his quick assumption of the professional air—even when she knew his nerves were all awry—that impressed her.

Observing this he decided to capitalise it to the utmost. She was a villainous old hag and he did not trust her an inch, but if by any means he could better his chances of helping the man who had talked with him, and escape, he would be a fool to allow personal feelings to come in the way.

"I shall be very pleased to do whatever I can," he said quietly. "You are sure it is nothing urgent?" He gave her another swift glance.

"No, nothing urgent. I will tell you when the comes," she returned; then, almost as if she were annoyed with her own weakness, "I will have the first man brought to you."

A couple of minutes later she returned with two Asiatics bringing between them their prisoner, his hands bound behind his back. Maman Constance followed, holding a small, yellow bottle. Dunkerley noted that this man? the one the old woman had designated "a harmless fool"—was a stranger.

He liked the face of this fellow, there was something ruggedly serene about him, and though he bore signs of having put up a losing fight, his eyes met Dunkerley's squarely. For a second the doctor thought one of them held the glimmer of a wink, but told himself he must be mistaken. If only the old hag could be got out of way for a space!

She handed him the bottle and again the odd sensation that she had some private intentions of her own concerning him forced itself upon Dunkerley.

"This is the drug. Two centigrammes," she repeated "Do you want him put on the table?"

"Oh, yes; I think it will be better . . . you see, I don't know what sort of reaction to expect." He took the glass stopper from the vial and smelled it cautiously, as the mamaloi made a sign to the two men to secure their captive on the nearest operating table.

"I've only seen it applied once," she confessed. "It seemed quite painless, but the girl had had an anaesthetic."

Dunkerley pricked up his ears at mention of the "girl." "There is no need for those men to remain," he said sharply as the two guards took up a stand like sentinels.

"They're none too clean, and even just for an injection I prefer to run no risks of sepsis."

"As you wish," she answered and was ordering them away when the doors were flung open violently and the professor came in, shaking with agitation. "Maman Constance—the girl—she's gone," he yelped. Then suddenly: "What's this . . . what's going on here? Work to be done—you never told me." He glared at Dunkerley and scuttled to the table, a crazy, gloating glint coming into his eyes. "Of course you can get an assistant if you want, but *I* take charge of all operations here."

He was cut short by Maman who, clawing one of his skinny arms, spun him round to her face. Dunkerley was amazed by the vitality she displayed. When the professor had entered her hand had flown to her throat, her face had turned grey, and he thought she was going to faint. But in less than five seconds she had recovered herself and was shaking the little man with such viciousness that his teeth literally chattered.

"You little fool," she hissed. "Answer—you don't mean that you've let her get away!" She stopped shaking him and held him at arm's length.

"No—no—the other—the blonde," he explained in a reedy gasp. "I took the new, dark one to her room, as you ordered, and when I got there she had gone. The nurse was under the bed, unconscious," he added in a puzzled tone.

"And, I suppose, whilst you came here to tell me that you let the other one go too," the mamaloi said bitingly.

"No—no, I didn't," he whimpered. "I locked her in the room; here is the key."

"You'd better come with me," Maman Constance said with grim-set mouth.

"But—he mustn't operate without me," Kucynski interposed. "This is my laboratory. I won't permit it. Besides he may kill the patient as he did the girl we were making into a . . ."

"Be quiet," snapped the old woman. "Dr. Dunkerley has Caspar's authority. Come," she repeated, seized his arm and pulled him to the door.

"A cheery collection of people you seem to have here," grinned Penberthy to Dunkerley. "I gather I'm for it. Is it possible to know exactly what you're going to do with me? I only ask because you don't look quite so sour as the rest."

"Are you a friend of the man with red hair?" Dunkerley inquired, after a swift glance towards the door, where the mamaloi was arguing with the professor.

"I'd like to know the object of that question."

Maman was out of sight now so Dunkerley dropped his professional stance. "Don't be silly, man. I'm in just as bad case as you are. The man—I don't know name . . ."

"Worthing," Penberthy prompted.

". . . said he had friends outside. He told me he was after a girl Caspar has kidnapped. I just wanted to make sure."

Penberthy stared at him as though not certain what reply. "Suppose the answer is in the affirmative?" he said at length.

"Listen carefully." Dunkerley drew nearer and pretended to be taking the other's pulse.

"I'm supposed to give you an injection; it has the effect of temporarily paralysing the memory. Sending one back to the mental condition of childhood."

"Probably 'Kingo,' " ejaculated Penberthy. "I've heard of it. It's an African drug used on the Congo."

"I don't know," said Dunkerley impatiently. "Anyway Maman Constance told me to inject two centigrammes, which she said would keep you harmless for a couple of months. I've been thinking—if I reduce the dose to a minimum there should be a chance of your coming round in a couple of days. I can't say for certain because I've had no experience with it. Now, if I do that, can you—when you come round—carry on as though you were still under the influence and work to help Worthing and me escape? They're fairly sure to have you watched, so unless you can play up we're all going to be worse off than before. Well?"

Penberthy nodded.

"I've always had a sneaking desire to play the village idiot. I can only do my best. Are you operating on Worthing, too?" he added as the surgeon proceeded to bare his arm.

"Unfortunately. I'm supposed to be doing a vivisection job on him."

Penberthy drew an uneasy breath.

"Those things in the stable. . . half goats, half men. . ."

"Aye, but don't worry. I'll find some way out. Ready?"

He stood for a second poised. "I hope to God this will react as I think it may. I can't see any other way out. My name's Dunkerley—when you come-to again."

"Shoot," said Penberthy, closing his eyes.

~ ~ ~ ~ ~

Ines was crouched on a chair in the room previously occupied by Bridget, trying to make herself believe that the whole thing was nothing but a horrible dream.

She regretted bitterly not having taken Penberthy's advice and remained indoors instead of foolishly slipping out to post a letter to Mrs. Townshend. And she had been captured so absurdly easily before she was able to reach the letter box not half a mile from the cottage. And if she had only the presence of mind to pretend not to recognise Penberthy when she saw him being interrogated by that evil old woman!

She knew by his expression when she uttered that stupid, revealing gasp, and by the gleam in the mamaloi's eye that she had given the show away. They had caught Pat Worthing, too; the woman had told her that in malicious glee. So now there was nobody to help them.

She dared not let herself think what might happen to them all.

One must keep one's thoughts occupied with other things. If they ever got clear of all this she must do something for Pat. It was funny how a person could barge suddenly into your life and make you feel that you had known him for ages and ages—and want to look after him. Perhaps that was the maternal instinct. And yet—it couldn't be entirely maternal, otherwise why should one have a kind of glow of satisfaction in knowing that it was she herself whom he had come to warn at the flat. Then—that amazingly consoling sensation of resting one's head against his shoulder. She had never felt like that with any man before . . . hoping he might kiss her and yet hoping he wouldn't! Notwithstanding her good resolutions she barely stopped a scream as the key turned and Maman Constance came into the room.

Except for casting a fleeting glance in her direction, the crone disregarded her, crossing to the bed and dropping on her knees to examine the unconscious nurse. Ines could not see what happened, but she heard her sniff. She then came over and stared resentfully at her. Ines tried not to flinch under the scrutiny, though it seemed to strip her of her clothes and leave her shuddering.

"How old are you?" she demanded suddenly.

"Nearly twenty-two," Ines returned, with a gasp.

The mamaloi nodded. "Older than I thought, but I don't suppose a year or so makes much difference," she pronounced cryptically. Her lips parted in a malicious grin. "Caspar wants you for himself, but I have other plans," she pursued. "It was thoughtful of you to walk in and save us. I suppose you came with your friend, eh?"

"The man I saw in the hall?" She endeavoured to appear ingenuous. "Yes, he is an artist. I've known him for years."

"I'm not talking about him," Maman snapped. "He's a fool but harmless, so far as I know. Anyhow he will be when we finish with him. I mean the other—the redheaded one, the detective." She leaned forward and sent her gaze boring into the other's face.

"I'm afraid I don't understand," Ines replied with a puzzled air. "Mr. Penberthy is the only man I know in Cornwall."

The mamaloi sniffed unbelievingly.

"You mean you didn't come with him?"

"I don't know what you're talking about," Ines returned. "I had no idea Bridget was here until you told me so. I thought she had gone to visit friends. I—I wish you would explain what it all means," she went on, racking her brain for some means of getting the other off her guard. She thought if Maman would remove her eyes for a moment she might be able to overpower her. But the black staring pupils paralysed action.

The mamaloi cackled. "In that case it won't upset you if we use a few primitive methods to make him tell us why he is here. Our little surgeon—you have met him—is very ingenious in using his knife upon parts that produce the most excruciating pain without doing the subject any permanent damage . . . I knew you were lying," she added in triumph as Ines shivered.

"I'm not—I'm not," she declared passionately. "It's just the thought of your beastly cruelty—"

"I only thought," Maman interposed, "if you were interested in him and *if* you wanted to spare him pain, you might have explained just why and how you came here together."

The door opened whilst Ines was trying to decide what to answer. Kucynski appeared, leading Bridget.

"She's quite all right," he tittered. "I examined her as you said and there is no sign of the drug losing its hold, so it must be the red-headed man who hid her away in the attic."

"Bridget . . ." Ines ran across to her friend, recoiling as she saw no sign of recognition.

"What have you done to her?" she demanded, turning on the woman fiercely. Then: "Bridget, dear—don't you know me?" she continued, drawing the passive girl into her arms.

Her whole mind was so concentrated that the sheet which Maman Constance whipped from the bed, descended over her head and shoulders before she could even turn. She kicked and struggled whilst Bridget, alarmed, began to wail loudly, but the professor and Maman wound the wrappings about her more tightly and bore her down.

Her last conscious sensation was a sharp pricking pain in her left thigh, and after that . . . oblivion.

CHAPTER XVIII

I FIND AN ALLY AND CHANGE PLACES
WITH A ZOMBIE

DUNKERLEY had conceived a plan; wholly crazy, but the only possibility. It came to him whilst he was still watching the effect of the injection on Penberthy.

He went across to the cages containing the Zombies, hurriedly taking stock of each.

He decided that one in the second cage might suit. Waiting only for a second to make sure that nobody was coming, he seized a pair of surgical scissors, opened the cage door, and proceeded to cut off the greater part of its grey beard and shaggy, long hair. The Zombie continued to sit on its pallet, staring with lack-lustre eyes at its own skinny hands.

When he had finished he made a sign to the object to lie down, and then covered him from head to toe in his rough blanket. Dunkerley secreted the hair in his pockets, keeping the two textures apart, and returned to Penberthy.

The latter had opened his eyes again. The doctor's heart quickened as he saw in them no recognition, but simply an inordinate, friendly curiosity.

"What am I doing here?" He glanced with interest at the strap confining him to the table.

Dunkerley hesitated. "You—you've been ill, but you'll soon be well again. You can get up if you like." He unfastened the thongs as he spoke.

Penberthy sat up, ruffled his hair, then grinned.

"Thanks. . . This is a queer spot. May I look round?"

Dunkerley nodded: admiration for the drug, mingling with fear that he might have given just too much or too little.

Penberthy trotted from cage to cubicle, commenting briefly on the queerness of the inmates, turned as the door of the laboratory swung open, and hurried back to Dunkerley's side, reaching for his hand as Maman Constance appeared. The surgeon felt his fingers tighten nervously as she came nearer.

"Good. I see you have made a success of the job. Wonderful stuff, isn't it; the professor just gave the girl a dose . . . she and her friend, the blonde, are cuddled up together now quite happily." She grinned. "I'll get you to try the antidote later. Are you ready to tackle the other operation?"

"You're sure you would rather I did that than look into your case? I don't want to appear an alarmist," he continued, gaining courage as she regarded him oddly, "but I was a little worried about your heart a wee while ago—when the professor came in."

"Thank you; I shall be all right," she returned, almost graciously. "I'll relieve you of your charge now and have your other patient sent in. The sooner you get started on him, the sooner Caspar will be satisfied you can be trusted."

"I should have thought *you* knew that already," he said boldly.

She shrugged. "Perhaps—but it's Caspar you have to please."

"Come," she said to Penberthy peremptorily, and held out her hand. The action had a totally unlooked for effect; instead of taking it, the other dodged on one side and sprinted for the door, just as the professor was on his way in.

In answer to the mamaloi's urgent cry to "stop him," Kucynski made a grab. Penberthy wheeled, feinted, and then charging, collared the little man by the legs, bringing him down with a crash to the stone floor.

Maman glared balefully at Dunkerley.

"If you've played a trick on me," she snarled, "you'll be sorry, young man. He can't get out—if that was what you hoped."

"Don't be silly," he retorted. "It's only what any kid would do if he thinks he's cornered." Even as he spoke a yelp floated down the stairs; evidently Penberthy had run into the hands of authority.

The mamaloi's face cleared. "You'd better look after the professor while I go and arrange for the other to be sent home."

Kucynski was unconscious, but Dunkerley's sensitive fingers could find no trace of a fracture. It had not seemed a very heavy fall: perhaps the abnormal thinness of the skull rendered him unduly delicate. As he bent over the figure and moved the little man into a more comfortable position he frowned. He stole another look at the prostrate man; reminding himself of all the horrible things he had seen on the operating table. Then, hastily, with set mouth, he reached for Kucynski's right arm, manoeuvred it and himself so that the portion between elbow and shoulder joint lay across his knee, and, clenching, his teeth made a movement like a man breaking a stick. The next second he lifted the arm gently and the lower portion hung limply awry.

Dunkerley got up rather uncertainly and wiped his forehead.

"Broken right arm," he said to Maman Constance, when she came back a few minutes later and found him busy putting it in splints. "He's all right except for that. He'll have to be put to bed though." He tried to keep his tone colourless.

The woman bit her lip angrily. The day had been one succession of annoyances. On the other hand, good had outbalanced bad on the whole. They knew now who the mysterious visitant of the studio was and had him safely by the heels; also they were safe from further interruption.

She hoped now that Caspar would be kept in London for a few days. If she found that Dunkerley could be trusted there might be time to get her own experiment over before the chief returned.

"That means all the more work for you," she commented briefly. "Can he be moved now?"

"As soon as I've finished with the bandaging." His deft hands manipulated the roll. "We can't do any more until he comes round."

"Very well. The men who are bringing the one you have to operate on can take him. I will have the goat sent in later."

"The goat?" For a second he was puzzled, then remembered. "Of course. You want him turned into a satyr, don't you."

"Yes, a satyr." A cruel evil glow came over her face "Can you manage alone?"

"I think so. If I want you—how can I let you know?"

"There is a house telephone by the professor's writing desk."

"Very good," he said and bent over Kucynski. "Don't put more strain on your heart than you can help," he added.

The remark was successful; she stalked out. The old dame's touchiness might be useful if he could play on it to keep her away from the laboratory.

He worked feverishly so that all might be in readiness for his plans when Worthing arrived. Fortunately he had watched Kucynski at work so long, he knew where to find everything. He then slipped into the Zombie's cage and gave the latter an unusually large shot of morphia preparatory to bandaging the upper part of his body so that it was almost as unrecognizable as a fully wrapped mummy.

He was interrupted as the two Asiastics arrived with me between them; a third man following with a black he goat, which struggled violently. Eventually it was trussed up, complaining loudly, on a second operating table contoured in places so that when the animal was pinioned on its back its head, chest and belly appeared almost human.

Dunkerley meanwhile grunted a few curt directions to my guards, who stripped me, threw a blanket over me and then bound me to the first table, which was drawn alongside of the one containing the goat.

I was more sick with horror and fear than I had ever been in my life until the white, masked figure gave me a reassuring nod. As the men started to remove my clothes he turned away again quickly; busying himself at a cabinet. After that I was able to allow myself to be strapped down, with a greater degree of equanimity.

He gave them directions to carry out Kucynski; adding instructions to tell Maman Constance that he was not to be disturbed for an hour.

"I only hope to God she'll do as I say, though I misdoubt it," he murmured, coming back to me as the door closed behind them. In one hand he had a sponge full of some soapy mixture and whilst he told me what had occurred he was hastily lathering my head.

"I'm sorry," he explained. "I've got to turn you into yon old grey-beard. If I can only get this part of the business through without interruption, I'll feel more confident. Funny, you know"—he was by this time shaving my skull, and I did not need any warning to keep still—"I felt worse over breaking the professor's arm than anything else I've ever done. It seemed such a low-down trick."

"What about Maman?" I asked nervously.

"If she gives me an hour, I'm not afraid of her."

"Do you know what they've done with Ines—Miss Bellenden?"

"No; except Maman said they'd given her a dose of stuff. You saw its effect on the other girl."

I subdued a groan; though it was better that way. At the same time I shivered. I dreaded her being in Caspar's hands.

Dunkerley mopped my head dry, spread it and my face with some kind of mucilage and then proceeded to apply the grey hair he had cut off the Zombie, trimming it carefully as soon as the gum was sufficiently set. He stood when he had finished and surveyed me gloomily. "Not so bonny as I'd have liked, but so long as you keep covered up and don't show more of your face than you can help it may pass."

"Now—quickly," he ordered, unstrapping me, "you've got to help me get the Zombie on the table and take his place."

Probably it was only a couple of minutes, though it seemed hours before the doped figure was safely in position and I had donned his horrible rags and was cowering under his unsavoury blanket.

Dunkerley was trembling as he dropped the door of my prison.

"Thank God that's done," he breathed. "Now, as you value our safety, keep still. You'd better not even look, it's a grisly business if you aren't inured to the operating room."

"All right: will you be able to talk to me later?"

"I expect so, but it will all depend on the old lady. I'll have to see about food for you, too. They don't give much to the Zombies. Might make them too heady." He gave a grim chuckle and I was at least thankful that he was able to treat the business lightly.

I was almost in a self-produced coma when, at last, Dunkerley came over and whispered: "I'm through for the moment." There was a glint of satisfaction in his eyes, though his face was white.

I glanced at the two tables rather nervously. The occupants were swathed in white bandages, stains of red showing on the one where the goat lay. I could see no sign of movement in it, but the Zombie was twitching spasmodically.

"Is it finished?" I asked.

"Good Lord, no; merely *preliminaries.* I'll have to get a nurse to help when I really start, but I've done enough to make your substitute unrecognizable to anyone but an expert."

There was a gleam of professional enthusiasm in his eyes and for a second I blenched.

"It is the only safe way of insuring they won't know it isn't you," he explained. "The patient won't be any worse off than he was before, and I'll see that he has an easy"—he hesitated a second—"return to the grave."

"I'm darned glad I had the luck to meet you," I murmured.

"I am, too, but we're not out of the wood yet—" He broke off abruptly and moved away as there was a buzzing sound outside the glass panelled door at the rear. The mamaloi entered and I recognized the preceding noise the descent of the lift.

"Well," she said sharply, as she reached the operating table, where Dunkerley was doing something to the bandages. "You said you wanted an hour, so I allowed hour and a half."

Dunkerley had left a space of a couple of inches between the cage door and the floor, so I could hear fairly plainly. She grinned at him after she had spoken, and I was struck by the change in her expression. He had definitely got on her softer side.

"Thanks," he replied. "It was only that I wanted to be sure of my own nerves before anyone watched me."

She made a movement to peer more closely at the patient's head bandages, but her attention was taken by a bowl where Dunkerley had dropped the hair as he shaved it from my scalp.

"Humph," she grunted, and pulled out some of the soapy strands and ran them through her fingers in malicious satisfaction. "So you've shorn our red-headed Samson of his locks, eh. Good. Caspar will be pleased when he returns."

"Is he coming back soon?" Dunkerley asked.

"He may be here in a couple of days, or he may not. That confounded red-head has upset some of his plans. Why do you ask?"

He led her over to the bandaged goat and entered into an explanation that I could not hear. It was, however, to her liking because I could see her nod several times.

"Do you want your lunch upstairs or will you have it here?" she inquired at length.

"Here, please. I want to keep an eye on the patient."

"Very well. I'll have it sent down." She moved a few steps to the door, then returned, almost awkwardly.

"Did you ever have any Danish relatives called Ericcson?"

"Not that I know of. Why?"

"You remind me of a man I—I once knew of that name in East Africa." It seemed to me she was disappointed. "If you want any help you have only to telephone," she went on in her ordinary tone, and disappeared through the door.

Dunkerley stared after her for a few seconds puzzled.

"I can't make head or tail of the old besom," he said. "One minute she's as mild as milk and the next . . . I'd say that if I'd never believed in witches she'd convert me."

"Don't make any mistake," I returned, "if she's mild, it is only for some devilish purpose of her own. With her here in charge I'm dead scared for those two girls. Listen, do they lock the 'lab' at night or is there a chance of getting into the house?"

"The cages are fastened from the outside. I can manage that part all right, but . . ." A look of alarm bred of the two weeks hell through which he had passed came into his face.

"Don't worry, I won't try to get away without you, but I'd like to find out a little more about the house. There's to be a big killing at the next full moon and, in case Penberthy can't help in time, I want to see what we can do to scotch it." A wild notion that it might be possible to get hold of Caspar on his way to the stone of sacrifice and take his place had burgeoned in my mind.

"I'm with you to the finish, you know that," he assured me hastily, as if to apologise for his momentary weakness.

"I know, old chap. Get hold of that Kingo stuff in its antidotal dose if you can. One of my biggest fears has been that we might get the girls away and then not be able to restore them to their senses. . ."

I broke off quickly as he turned towards the door. Fortunately it was only one of the servants with a tray containing Dunkerley's lunch. He set it down on a side table and civilly saying that if there was anything else the doctor required he had only to phone for it, left us.

We shared the meal with some difficulty as we dared not raise my barrier more than a couple of inches, so that every mouthful had to be pushed through on a fork at floor level. By the time our lunch was finished I had more than regained my optimism.

CHAPTER XIX

CASPAR HAS A TALK WITH THE INNER CIRCLE

CASPAR GAVE Adolf a sleeping draught which he calculated would keep him quiet for a good twenty-four hours. As he waited for it to take effect, Caspar went over the several points that had to be dealt with. There were two of considerable urgency—allay Mrs. Townsend's anxiety, and to check Polynice's loyalty.

He decided not to risk putting in the call to Mrs. Townsend from the studio, but to phone from a call office near the Chelsea Town Hall.

"I am speaking for Mr. Westerham," he began when, at last, Mrs. Townsend's voice, a shade flustered, came over the line.

"Oh, yes—how is he?" she demanded. "Miss Bellenden and a friend called last night on their way to Plymouth and said Bridget had had a telegram asking her to meet him because he was ill."

Caspar cursed Ines and the red-head under his breath. "I'm glad to say he is quite all right again now," he said, quickly, "only—as his business here is very private and important—he told me to ring you up and ask you not to let anyone know of his arrival."

"I've been too worried for poor Bridget to think of it. Is she with him?"

"Yes, and Miss Bellenden. But Miss Westerham will be along to see you as soon as her father can spare her. She was afraid you might be anxious," he lied glibly.

"I have been—very anxious." Mrs. Townsend's tone was plaintively aggrieved. "Who are you, Mr. Westerham's secretary?"

"Yes. He asked me to apologise for any uneasiness he has caused you, and Miss Westerham sent her love. I expect she will be writing to you herself shortly. Goodbye." Ringing off he emerged from the booth perspiring but relieved. In a week, or maybe less, he would ring up again and say the three had been called away to the Continent, and that would be the end so far as Mrs. Townsend was concerned.

He then put through another call to a small hotel where an envoy from Liberia was stopping. Caspar ordered him to call on Polynice and hint that he was not satisfied that the chief was carrying out the big scheme as its devotees considered proper, and to note the other's reactions

These matters dealt with, he hastened back to the studio and got Adolf into the chest.

As there was nothing of great importance until the meeting of the delegates at 5 P.M. he packed a small suitcase and taxied with it to the Hotel Russell, where he booked a room.

Eight dark-skinned gentlemen of mixed races were gathered round a large mahogany boardroom table in Polynice's office at five-fifteen that evening. At the head was Caspar and Polynice faced him.

On a wall a faded oleograph of Queen Victoria had been swung out of its frame, disclosing an oil painting of the "Great One," similar to the plaque in Caspar's studio.

Caspar, who had been sitting looking over some papers, merely nodding a welcome and exchanging with each newcomer as he entered a sign with the fingers of a cross reversed, now rose. The others stood up also.

"In the name of Zamiel, Prince of Darkness, to whose service we are pledged"—he bowed to the picture on the wall—"I give you welcome," he said gravely.

"His eye be ever upon us," the others intoned sombrely, also bowing to the picture and then to Caspar.

At a sign from him they resumed their seats and leaned back expectantly; he himself remaining standing.

"Polynice has explained why you have been asked to come here this evening," he began on an almost casual note, though his glance was shrewd and penetrating. "I regret that our plans have to be changed, but circumstances have arisen which render it imperative.

"If, for any reason, any of you—or the others, your companions who are not of the Arch Priesthood—are unable to attend the initiation on account of the change in date, I am going to suggest that they give to one of you power and authority to pledge their whole loyalty to the Great One when he calls upon you to testify. Are you agreeable?"

They answered "aye" to his question, and it was a murmur that assured him of their immediate compliance with whatever he might ordain. Only Polynice was silent, but as Caspar's principal lieutenant, it might be assumed that his agreement could be taken for granted. Nevertheless, for the fraction of a second, the mulatto's glance met that of a short, very fat and black negro, with a heavy jowled face and cruel, insolent eyes, sitting half way down the table. As their eyes met he gave the slightest perceptible nod.

"Good," said Caspar, though the signal disturbed him, conveying that Polynice was not entirely to be trusted.

"As all of you know," he went on, "there is a certain ritual to be observed in the ceremony we shall meet together to perform—if our sacrament is to be successful. It is essential that none of you shall touch food after noon of the appointed day. Purification will be performed by a Papaloi from Haiti, who has great experience of such rites and is being brought over specially. After the purification and when the mystic circles have been drawn, it is imperative that nobody shall either speak or move until the sacrifice of the black goat and the white virgin has been consummated. The consequences of breaking this instruction would be extremely danger-ous? possibly fatal."

The short, fat negro cleared his throat. "I should like to ask one thing," he said.

"Yes," Caspar remarked, the half turn of the speaker's head in the direction of Polynice not escaping him.

"In the event that the Great One does not see fit to manifest himself at the initiation . . . will it be necessary to defer action until another meeting can be convened?"

Caspar appeared to ponder the question whilst, unobtrusively, searching the faces of the remainder of the group. Only Polynice, however, seemed more than interested.

"I have every faith that that contingency will not occur," he pronounced suavely, "but if it did happen that the time and place were inauspicious, we would get Maman Constance to consult the Whistling Ancestors in the matter of holding another court. In re-gard to the institution of the kingdom—that will be proceeded with according to schedule. It is to make the final arrangements that I asked you to come here this evening.

"I have here," he went on, "the written details of the plans that the arch-priests will be requested to carry out. They will be put into action the day following the disbandment of the conference you are attending—in two more weeks. It is absolutely essential for the success of our scheme that the schedule is rigidly adhered to."

He picked up eight sealed envelopes each inscribed with a number.

"Number four," he handed to the man on his immediate right, a tall Ethiopian, "will proceed to Zanzibar and arrange for the migration and transport of those who have accepted the message, to the place upon which we have agreed."

Number four took the packet, rose, and turning to face the picture on the wall, kissed the envelope, saying: "As Zamiel commands that I will do." Then, with a slight bow to Caspar he made his way to the door and went out.

The same procedure followed in the case of the seven remaining men—rulers, hereditary chiefs, or representatives of the native kings or princes of the Belgian Congo, Portuguese East Africa, Italian Somaliland, the Cameroons and portions of the French East and West Africa. The instructions, in the case of a paler coloured, slim man, and another with Mongolian features, were the only ones that varied.

The first through the outer circles formed amongst the coloured "intelligentsia" in the principal cities was to inspire a demand from the United States for a free Africa. The Mongol would leave the night following the initiation for Northern China to report to certain Lamaistic monasteries in the north. Their duty was to raise a similar agitation amongst the depraved Buddhist peoples of the East.

As he who had asked the question about the "Great One" took his envelope, he contrived to slip a tiny note into Caspar's hand.

"Well, that settles everything, I think," Caspar said with a faint sigh of relief as he and Polynice were left alone. "Unless there is anything you want to discuss before we go to dine."

Polynice shook his head. "Only your plans for me. Have you decided whether it shall be India or Egypt?"

"Not yet. It is possible that I may ask you to remain with me. A good second-in-command is not so easy to find, you know. But come—let us go; you look as though a meal would do you good."

"It has been a heavy day, one way and another," Polynice admitted. "By the way, I took the Sheldon girl to the hotel."

"Good. I'll probably get you to run her down to the Manor this evening."

As they turned into Holborn and hailed a taxi, Caspar bought an evening paper. In the cab, one of the headlines arrested his attention.

"Suicide of a Woman in West End Flat," it ran, and beneath, in more discreet type: "Alleged White Slave Trafficker."

He read half a dozen lines feverishly, then came upon the name of the dead woman—"Lottie Schmalz, alias Marie Jansen." Her suicide was attributed to the fact that, torn up in the wastepaper basket were the fragments of a letter warning her that her activities had been discovered and that she would be arrested within the day. Caspar scowled and muttered a curse.

"Anything wrong?" Polynice, who had been gazing out of the window inquired, turning.

"No, of course not; what should there be?" He forced a smile and thrust the paper into his pocket.

The occurrence was peculiar, coming on top of the note given him a few minutes previously. It had said: "Agree suspicious. Believe acting for Prince Ali Singh; telephone Mayfair Mansions 7463."

Between cutlet and cheese he excused himself on the plea of ringing up the mamaloi. Instead of calling the number he had been given he first dialed the hall porter's office. A woman's voice answered and informed him that her husband was out and asked if she could take a message.

"No," Caspar replied. "I only wanted to know if a prince Ali Singh has a flat in the building. The telephone number is 7463, I believe."

"I don't think so, but I'll see if he's on the register," she returned.

"No, there's no name like that," the answer came after a short pause. "There's a foreign gentleman who has that number, but the name is Mirzaban."

Caspar started. Mirzaban was the name of the Parsi secretary who had on occasions signed letters for the prince. "Thank you, that is all I wanted to know, unless you can put the call through to his flat."

"I'm afraid I can't do that," the woman replied. "The telephone exchange is up in the renting office. But if you ring up 7463 you'll get him all right."

He hesitated a space, wondering if he could imitate Polynice's voice well enough not to arouse Mirzaban's suspicions. If Ali Singh had sent the secretary over without telling Caspar, there was definitely something in the wind. And that something could only bear one of two interpretations—that the prince was not genuinely with the movement or that he distrusted its leader. If Polynice had been detailed to spy on him and report to Mirzaban, then Polynice must be a pretty important person.

He cursed the circumstance that had planted doubt in the potentate's mind. Caspar, and his principal associates, had counted so much on his help in Asia amongst the better-class peoples. True, they had not seen fit to outline the whole of their plan, but had dwelt upon the idealistic side. And until Polynice had raised the issue of the Great One manifesting himself, Caspar had never dreamed that the prince knew of this angle.

Still . . . even if the prince withdrew his support, it need not affect the African and Mongolian plans. With sudden decision he called for the number.

"Yes, please, who is calling?" It was the Parsi himself at the other end; one could not mistake his voice.

"This is Polynice speaking," Caspar began, copying his lieutenant's tones as accurately as he could.

"Polynice?" Mirzaban repeated on a surprised note.

"Yes—I thought you would like to hear about the meeting."

"Oh, yes, the meeting."

Caspar could not decide whether the other was suspicious and fencing or being Oriental was merely interested in seeing what information he could gain. "Yes; it went practically as we expected except that I have an idea that possibly one or two besides His Highness are not quite satisfied. However, I have had another talk with Caspar and he tells me privately that he intends to do nothing further on the Indian angle until he has His Highness' approval."

"I see. Verree interesting." The comment was maddeningly non-committal.

"I may have to go to the country to-night," he proceeded, "so if you don't hear for a day or two don't worry."

A silence ensued and Caspar did not know if the other had put up the receiver or was thinking. All at once the voice cut in softly. "Gopal Singh," it said, "Gopal Singh, Kither hai?" (where are you).

Caspar's scalp prickled. Was it that Polynice might not be known to Mirzaban as Polynice but as—Gopal Singh.

"Speaking," he said softly. "I was afraid you had gone."

"I am still here. I wondered why you announced yourself as Polynice." There was yet a shade of doubt.

"I'm speaking from a restaurant," Caspar explained, chuckling silently.

"I see; my apologies. But, as you know, one must be careful. In view of what you tell me now, perhaps I had better wait for further news before cabling His Highness. If Dr. Pettifranc does not intend to move in India without His Highness's approval there is no urgency."

Caspar suddenly remembered—Gopal Singh was the name of Ali Singh's brother. "After all," he went on quickly, "so long as Caspar doesn't interfere with India—"

"Yes, please," prompted Mirzaban.

"? my brother isn't really interested."

"Perhaps—though I had thought His Highness might be concerned with the question of pandering to the forces of evil—but you know your brother best, naturally." There was a hint of flattery.

"No, I don't think so, at present, anyway. I will get in touch with you later," he added.

"Bohut accha, Huzzoor. I will await Your Honour's message."

The mulatto stared at the instrument for a full minute after he had replaced the receiver. Since Polynice was Gopal Singh he must not be harmed; the whole of the prince's influence and resources would be used to avenge him. Either he must contrive to win Gopal Singh over to his side, or—hold him until it was too late for him to do my mischief. India would have to be abandoned for the moment.

Polynice must not know he had been found out. That he had sent the warning letter to Mrs. Jansen Caspar was now almost certain. He shook his head, puzzled. There must be some reason behind the other's apparently contradictory actions if one could only get at it. However, the main thing was that he knew the worst and could proceed accordingly. He would send Polynice to the Manor at once and ask him to work in co-operation with Maman until his own return. By that time he would have decided on the next move.

When he rejoined him smiling amiably, Polynice was leisurely smoking a cigar, a copy of the evening paper open before him.

"Bad news, I'm afraid," he remarked, passing it to his chief. Caspar admired his poise even whilst he mentally cursed his impudence. He read the details of Mrs. Jansen's suicide nonchalantly.

"Hm," he grunted when he had finished. "I expected something like that one of these days. After all, we were only one of her clients. . . Personally, I'm not sorry," he continued, also lighting a cigar. "As I said this morning, she always gave me the creeps. And as Dunkerley has come to his senses we don't need her any more."

For a second silence reigned between them.

"I'm glad you take it that way," Polynice said at length, "though I should have told you in any event. It was I who sent the letter."

"I had an idea it might be so," Caspar returned coolly, "that was why I didn't say anything when I read the notice in the taxi. I presume you did it because you didn't like her either."

Polynice nodded. "When I saw the girl, Alice Sheldon, I knew Mrs. Jansen shouldn't be allowed to live," he continued. "What you intend to do with her is at least no more than she wished. But what that unspeakable fiend of a woman planned would have let her body live but would have killed her soul . . ." he broke off. "You think I'm a fool, I suppose."

"On the contrary, my friend, I admire you immensely. As a matter of fact you only forestalled me by a very few hours. For one thing I disliked her oiliness and for a second I knew perfectly well that the moment she believed I no longer needed her help, she would have begun to blackmail me. So you see—you really did me a very good turn."

CHAPTER XX

WESTERHAM ARRIVES AND
CASPAR SHOWS HIS TEETH

U P AT THE Manor the next two days seemed interminable though Dunkerley had the lengthy and delicate operation on the Zombie to perform. Maman Constance had provided him with a black nurse for an assistant, so with her cleaning up when he was not actually working, and the mamaloi popping in and out our chances of conversation were cut to a minimum. And Dunkerley was given a room in the wing where Ines and Bridget were confined.

One blessing was that, as he had to visit the girls in his professional capacity, he was able to tell me that, apart from the effects of the drug, they were both well. He was carrying out some experiments with the Kingo on another of the Zombies and hoped very shortly to be able to discover the amount necessary to bring persons back to their proper senses.

The only excitement during the first seventy-two hours was early in the morning of the second day. Someone called Polynice was bringing another girl from London in his car, but he had had an accident within a mile or so from the Manor. Polynice had been found unconscious and brought to the house on the Zennor Road, and then at night time to the Manor. The girl had disappeared, and the neighbourhood was being cautiously scoured for her whereabouts.

Dunkerley also told me that Penberthy had been seen generally behaving like a lunatic schoolboy.

Dunkerley was rather inclined to believe that Penberthy must have recovered by reason of his haunting the precincts. He had been several times to the lodge and left extraordinarily poorly spelled love letters addressed to somebody called Mabel.

Maman Constance, cackling over them, had shown Dunkerley one, but he could not make head nor tail of it.

It was just the sort of thing a man with Penberthy's quick brain would do, if he wanted to open up communication with me or

Dunkerley. I suggested Dunkerley should try to get hold of one of the effusions and propose sending a reply from the fictitious Mabel.

I spent the whole afternoon concocting an apparently harmless epistle. In it I said that Mabel's brother had measles and that the doctor had quarantined Mabel for the time being, but that if Sammy (Penberthy's notes were signed Sammy) was very good and did not worry, she might be able to see him in a couple of weeks' time. There was some more balderdash, but every fourth word, if read together, gave a clue to the position in the house.

On the fourth evening the nurse was told she need not remain on duty and Dunkerley managed to inform me that if I could get up by the lift to the left wing, he would leave his door ajar and we might talk.

"Only for the Lord's sake be crafty," he warned me. "I have an idea matters are coming to a head. Maman let out by accident that the big meeting is to be on Wednesday of next week, and she's all of a dither trying to decide whether she'll get me to do something or other to-morrow night. It all depends on whether Caspar comes back by then—she wants him out of the way until it is over."

His glance did not meet mine, so I surmised he had more than an idea what it was she desired but did not like to say.

"You may as well spit it out," I said.

He sighed. "She's got some weird notion that if I make a blood transfusion from a younger girl, that that together with what she terms her own magic arts, will turn her into a young woman again."

"Ines?"

"Yes, but don't worry. I'll find some way out."

My nerves were more on edge than ever after hearing this.

"Can't you give the old fiend a dose of something?"

"And then what? The whole bunch of them are twittering with nerves as it is. We've only till next Wednesday night—four days—to make our plans. If they get too rattled, they're liable to give us even less time."

"I expect you're right," I answered gloomily. "Only for heaven's sake try to get the note I've suggested to Penberthy. If Maman shows you his answer we'll be able to tell if he's playing the fool with a purpose or what."

"I'll do my best," he promised. "One blessing is that I'm fairly certain I've discovered the antidotal dose for Kingo."

He had to go then to visit the professor in a foul state of mind.

There was no way of telling the time in that cursed laboratory. What eventually put the wind up me completely was waking up with a jerk and discovering that I had been to sleep. Whether I had been unconscious five minutes or fifty I had no idea. However, I could wait no longer without going potty, so arranging the pallet to look as if I were still under the blanket, I raised the cage door.

I had to grope my way along the first corridor by touch. I was all right though, as soon as I turned the last corner, as the moon was shining through one of the windows. Dunkerley had arranged to draw the blind to indicate the whereabouts of his room, and I could see a slither of light coming from a slightly open door.

I was about to make a dash for it when I heard the sound of movement in the main hall. I recognised Caspar's voice giving an order and then, more clearly: "Now, Mr. Westerham. If you'll kindly sit in this chair, I will have the bandage taken off your eyes and we can have a little friendly chat. Maman," he went on, "will you mix a highball for our guest? I'm sure he must be thirsty after the long journey." There was an ironical note in his remark, and the mamaloi gave a shrill cackle.

I wished I dared go to the edge of the balustrade and look down, but it was too risky.

"Where is my daughter? You promised I should see her if I agreed to come with you," Westerham said as soon as he had, I surmised, glanced round the room and discovered she was not present. His tone was acid but restrained.

"All in good time, Mr. Westerham. There are several small details to be settled first," Caspar replied coolly.

"If you have brought me here on a fool's errand, or try to double cross me, I warn you you'll be sorry for it," Westerham snapped.

"I hope for your own sake as well as your daughter's you have not broken your promise and told anybody about our business arrangement," the mulatto said threateningly.

"Certainly not," the other returned. "When I say a thing I keep to it and I anticipated that for your own profit you would be equally honest."

Caspar chuckled. "You amuse me, Mr. Westerham; I dare wager that my financial undertakings are just as straight as yours—in perhaps a different way. I suggested a figure round about five hundred thousand dollars to guarantee her safety, didn't I?"

"As soon as I know she is safe and delivered to a party I shall name, I am prepared to give you my cheque for that amount."

"Splendid; that means we agree on the first condition."

I nearly gave the show away at that juncture, for I felt something move beside me. The next second my arm was squeezed reassuringly and I realised it was Dunkerley.

"What's going on; I was looking for you . . . been expecting you for the last half-hour," he whispered; putting his lips close to my ear.

"It's Westerham—the girl's father," I explained, trying not to lose anything of what was happening below. "Caspar is there and Maman, so we're safe for the moment."

"As an intelligent man you could hardly expect me to deliver Miss Westerham and let you go without insuring your future passivity. As a matter of fact I have such a high opinion of your qualities that one of my conditions is going to be your co-operation in my own plans. A brain like yours, with a sound financial house behind it, will be a very valuable asset in the international negotiations I shall want to carry out when we all go to Africa."

"Africa?" Westerham gasped.

"Haven't you been there before?" Caspar inquired, blandly. "You should have, considering how many interests your firm has in the country. Well, it will be an interesting experience for you, won't it, Maman?" The old woman chuckled in amusement.

"You're trying to scare me," Westerham bluffed at length.

"Not at all, my dear sir. Either willingly or unwillingly, you and your charming daughter will accompany me to a territory we have taken over, preparatory to asserting control of the whole continent. You will be my financial and legal adviser in dealing with such European powers as have to be convinced that we do not mean to be interfered with. You will have as a colleague another prominent countryman of yours. Maman, please remove that wrap you placed over Mr. Walton's head so that our friend here can identify him."

There was a horrified sound from Westerham as the Mamaloi exposed the second man to view.

"Mr. Walton, as you know, has acquired a new lethal gas, with which he is going to present us in due course. With that and a few other little things we have every hope that by the time the European *civilised* nations have finished slaughtering one another, we shall be in a position to enforce a more peaceful era."

"And if I refuse?" Westerham retorted stubbornly. "I suppose you killed Walton and mean to get someone to impersonate him."

"Oh, no, he's quite alive. At the moment he is drugged, a very special drug of my own invention. Your daughter is drugged, too. She is quite happy and active, but her mentality has been put back a few years."

"You swine," Westerham broke in. "If you've harmed her I will get you if it takes me all my life."

"Calm yourself, Mr. Westerham. She is perfectly safe, and when we reach Africa—so long as you are amenable—will be restored to her right mind. But first I require your promise to join us."

"I won't give it; I'll see you in hell first, you damned half-breed. Think to rule the world, do you? Let me tell you, neither you nor ten million like you could ever do it."

"I am sorry you are so childish as to resort to insults. Bad mannered children have to be punished. Perhaps a little lesson in what a 'half-breed' can do may put you in a more civil state of mind," Caspar said, and there was bitter hatred in his voice.

"Maman, will you wheel that little trolley closer to Mr. Westerham's chair—we will see what effect our high frequency sound wave has upon him—turn the reflector round so that it faces our friend's head."

"There"—we heard him move—"I think that should do. As soon as you feel that you can't bear it any longer providing you agree to my terms, you have only to raise your hand and I will stop. It is always interesting to see how different people react; in some, only the very high notes seem to register, whereas others are more susceptible to the lower frequencies, which they tell me affect the heart most."

We heard a click of a switch and a low humming as of a motor. With one accord we fell on our hands and knees and crawled to the balustrade.

Caspar and the mamaloi were out of range of vision, but we could make out Westerham—a distinguished-looking white-haired man of about fifty—bound in a big armchair, and beside him the curious contraption I had seen the professor wheel from the lift room the first day I was in the house.

As the whirring increased in intensity, surprise, then discomfort and, finally, acute distress came over the face of the unfortunate man.

"Peculiar sensation at first, isn't it?" Caspar gloated. "It seems to set all one's nerves vibrating in the wrong places. Of course it is possible to kill you, either by shattering the brain or speeding up the heart so that it bursts—but I have no intention of proceeding to such drastic lengths."

I felt myself being nudged viciously by Dunkerley. "Man, this is damnable," he breathed in my ear, "but yon machine is what I've dreamed of. If you could kill with it you could certainly cure, too? "

He broke off as a racking sound that started as a stifled groan and finished in a heartrending "hoo-hoo" was jerked from the sufferer.

"By God, I can't stand this," I muttered.

"Steady," he cautioned, "they're stopping now."

True enough the switch clicked and the whirring ceased.

"Another highball for Mr. Westerham, Maman, now that he has agreed to become one of us. These experiments exhaust one, don't they, Mr. Westerham?"

We saw the mamaloi hand the trembling man a glass, but his hand shook so she had to carry it to his lips. Caspar wheeled the machine aside, then released the strap round Westerham's waist that bound him to the chair.

"In the morning we will have another little chat and you shall give me the cheque; I won't trouble you now since you have accepted my terms," he remarked affably. "Can you stand? No"—as the other essayed to rise but sank back with a groan—"never mind, two of my attendants will carry you to your room. Later, when I have revived your friend Mr. Walton, I will have him put with you so that you can compare experiences."

He struck a small gong on a table. The sound was quite soft, but the vibration was sufficient to send Westerham's hands to his ears.

"If Caspar is going to work on Walton, you had better get back to the laboratory," Dunkerley whispered, as the two Asiatic servants came in, picked up the millionaire and started to carry him upstairs.

I started to crawl back as quickly as possible.

"I'll let you know to-morrow if anything further happens," Dunkerley murmured hurriedly.

I breathed relief when I was safely under the cover of my blanket again—foul as it was. It was none too soon either for, before I had been there five minutes, the door opened and Caspar came in with the mamaloi, and the two Asiatics carrying Walton.

He had the unconscious man deposited on a vacant operating table and dismissed the bearers. I gathered he was well pleased.

"Well, we shan't be very long now," he remarked, giving a quick, keen glance round the chamber. I was scared for a second that he would observe the slight opening between the door of my cage and the floor. "By the way what is the latest news of Polynice?"

"He is still unconscious," Maman replied shortly, "That was a bad business about the girl, Caspar."

"Yes, I'm sorry about that," he agreed, "though she isn't dangerous. She may have had another suicidal fit and thrown herself over the cliff. What is Dunkerley's opinion about Polynice?"

"He says he can't tell one way or the other. With concussion it may be a day or a week. Apart from that and a broken collar-bone, there is nothing seriously wrong."

"Hm," Caspar grunted. "Anyhow it will keep him quiet and out of mischief." He strolled across to the cubicle where lay the satyr creature Dunkerley was working on. It was swathed in bandages, but part of what had been a face was visible. At a distance it could not be distinguished from the mask of the black goat used in its creation.

"Quite a nice piece of work," he remarked. "I knew Dunkerley was a clever devil; he'll beat the professor at his own game yet—if he doesn't weaken. You feel very confident about him though, don't you?"

"Perfectly confident," she answered with decision. "I had no use at all for Kucynski when I saw how feeble he was in an emergency."

Caspar grinned. "You take strong likes and dislikes, don't you, Maman? Though, with you, I agree the other is the better man." He threw another glance at the cubicle. "At least your one-armed friend won't bother you any further."

Then he continued: "What would you advise about the sacrifice? If I use the blonde we'll lose Westerham, and his brains are going to be quite valuable. Of course, if the girl turns up, well and good; but if not, we've got to have a white goat from somewhere."

"Why not the dark one—her skin is fair enough," she suggested. Her tone was guileless, but there was a malicious leer on her face.

He checked a quiet retort. "Perhaps," he replied, "though a blonde would have been better. You might consult the Ancestors—they may be able to advise us. However, we'd better get on with Walton now, I have to get back to town to-morrow and put Westerham's cheque through. It's the devil how money flies."

"There's always the secret river," she returned, then glanced at him in sudden suspicion. "You haven't touched that yet, have you?"

"Of course not; how could I until the three are satisfied? The trouble is if Ali Singh backs out they may refuse to let us have the key. Still by Wednesday the worst of the difficulties should be over."

With swift decision he went over to one of the instrument cupboards and produced the bottle I had stolen at the studio.

"Thank goodness that interfering red-head left sufficient for what we want," he murmured as he selected a hypodermic and charged it. "Open his waistcoat and shirt will you, Maman?"

"That ought to do it," he said a few minutes later. "By ten o'clock he should be as well as he ever was. You might have some good beef-tea and tell Dunkerley to give it to him, after he's had his own breakfast, but not to wake him if he is still sleeping."

"Are you going to leave him here?" the mamaloi asked.

"It's better not to shake him up. You can put him with Westerham later."

He plunged the syringe into an antiseptic tank and yawned.

"Satan, but I'll be glad to get to bed," he remarked. "You're a marvel, Maman; you never seem to turn a hair."

"In a couple of days I may surprise you still more," she retorted.

Caspar swung round and faced her. "What do you mean?" he demanded.

"Nothing, *mon ami;* nothing at all," she answered, quickly. "Only that you know I am always at my best when there is work to be done."

I was rather amused by her evident regret over her incautious remark.

He grunted, though I did not think he sounded quite satisfied. A couple of minutes later I heard their footsteps disappearing.

I was tempted to have a closer look at Walton, but decided it was better to leave him alone. But for a long time my brain would not allow my body the rest it clamoured for. Only a few more days and so much to be done. If only we could rope in Walton and Westerham I felt that our chances of success were growing. I had a definite plan now taking more concrete form every hour, but the actual putting into action still lay on the knees of the gods.

The mamaloi's remark regarding the secret river and Caspar's reply about the "Three" also set me thinking. It was the first time there had been any mention of a superior hierarchy and I hoped it was not going to complicate matters for us still further. . .

When I opened my eyes again it was to see Walton being wheeled out of the laboratory in an invalid chair by Dunkerley.

CHAPTER XXI

THE CLANS BEGIN TO "GET TOGETHER"

POLYNICE had definitely made up his mind, by the evening of the restaurant dinner with Caspar, that somehow Alice Sheldon must be saved. But the moment he knew definitely that his chief suspected him, he needed to walk more warily than ever.

Within a few miles of the Manor he had been weighing up whether he could get the girl to some place of safety. Merely to drop her on the road side would help neither her nor himself.

He stopped the car a few hundred yards from Penberthy's cottage, and lighted a cigarette. Alice was asleep, and he was touched anew by her fragility and youth to such an extent that he got out of his seat, meaning to take a turn up and down the road while he thought out his plans.

Alighting, he was conscious of a pair of shrewd eyes peering brightly at him over a low, stone wall. The owner of the eyes suddenly rose up, grinned, leaped to the top of the wall, and squatted on it cross-legged, following the performance by levelling a toy pistol at Polynice.

"Hands up," he ordered, still grinning. "Nobody passes along this road without paying me toll." Polynice noticed that, notwithstanding the absurdity of his words, the glance he shot at the girl in the car was a particularly acute one.

"I'm sorry," Polynice answered affably. This odd person might well be the artist, Penberthy, concerning whose capture Caspar had been so annoyed. "Your name's Penberthy, isn't it?" he continued, watching the other's expression carefully.

He noted the quick reaction—covered instantly—in the other's eyes at the mention of the name and decided that the craziness was a clever pose.

"I am Dick Turpin," Penberthy returned.

"I beg your pardon. More than ever I am glad to meet you."

"Why?"

"I rather like highwaymen. I've always heard they loved to rescue maidens in distress." Polynice pursued and nodded his head towards the girl.

Penberthy appeared puzzled; hesitating whether to get down from his perch and come nearer or retreat.

"What is your name?" he asked suddenly.

"I'm known to one or two people—Dr. Pettifranc amongst them—as Polynice, but my real name is Gopal Singh," the latter answered, now reasonably sure of Penberthy. "I think if Dr. Pettifranc knew that though, he would probably kill me," he continued, "so I hope you won't think it necessary to tell him."

"No; I won't do that." Their eyes met then, with another quick survey of the road, Penberthy lowered his pistol with a grin.

"He'd probably kill me, too, if he knew I knew my name was Penberthy. What's the trouble?"

Polynice explained as briefly as he could.

"So you see how I stand. When I met you I was just considering faking a motor smash after sending Miss Sheldon on to an hotel somewhere, but she might be scared."

Penberthy pursed his lips.

"I'd take her to my place, but I'm fairly sure Caspar has it watched. . . I know—if you could drive back half a mile and leave her with Dr. King at the white house with the big copper beech in front, and say I'll explain later and that he's not to let her outside the place, she'll be safe for the present anyway."

"Right." Then he continued: "After that you are at liberty to see me wreck Caspar's car if you wish . . . only I don't want you to let any humane instincts intervene. It might be worse for both of us."

"Is there no other way?"

"I can't think of one—that will get me into the Manor without suspicion, and allow me to remain there dormant," Polynice smiled. "Where would be the best place to? er, stage it, by the way?"

"Well, there's a nasty blind corner just before you turn into the side lane leading to the house. You're liable to smash into a stone wall, if you're not careful."

"In that case, I'll be very careful," Polynice returned gravely. "Until we meet again . . ." he held out his hand.

"Good luck; and don't worry about the girl."

That conversation had been beating itself out over and over again in Polynice's fevered brain as he lay in bed at the Manor.

~ ~ ~ ~ ~

Dunkerley managed to snatch a few words with me later in the next afternoon.

"I've contrived to have a chat with Westerham and Walton, but they're so badly scared they are afraid to believe I'm on their side, I'll try to get you along to-night, and you may be able to convince them; though, unless I can shoot something into them to steady their nerves, they aren't likely to be much help. The trouble is that this place is about as private as a public library at the moment. . . That fellow they call Polynice bothers me, too; he hasn't any very serious injuries, yet his temperature stays up and he chatters nonsense from morning to night. From what I've gathered from Maman," he went on, "he is under suspicion for having made away with the girl."

He stopped, then burst out: "That crazy Jane is getting on my nerves most. Wants me to attend a séance of the Whistling Ancestors to-night, if Caspar doesn't come back, to find out if her operation will be successful. If they say 'yes,' she wants it done right away and Lord knows how I can put her off," he groaned.

"There must be some way," I said weakly.

"If she were an ordinary body, yes; but she has eyes at the back of her head, and half a dozen other means of registering what is going on. I've been trying to rig up a gadget under the bed so that I can stick one of their blasted goats there and do a switch from Miss Bellenden to it. Only I'm so scared the confounded beast will start bleating and blathering," he went on.

I sat up suddenly alert. "Is she going to have the operation only if the Ancestors say it will be auspicious?"

"That's what she hands at the minute," he replied glumly, "though she may change her mind half a dozen times before then."

"In that case, the only thing to do is to block the wires," I said. "If you can fix it so that she has the séance in the hall late enough to let me get up to the gallery, I think I can manage the rest. In the meantime have your goat all ready. Though I don't see how she would know anything if you give her dope first."

"But I can't," he argued. "It isn't necessary and she refuses."

"Oh well," I returned; "we'll have to see what we can do with the Ancestors. If that doesn't work, I'll tackle her myself if needs be. From the way Caspar looked at her lately, I don't think he'd be terribly sorry if she was *hors-de-combat.*"

"If it comes to the pinch," he said in a grim tone, "you'd far better let me do the job. You could carry on better than I, and I'm just

itching to have her quieted. Losh; she kens I'm engaged to be married, and yet—would ye believe it—she's already half hinting that
when she's a blithe lassie again we might make a match on't," he
said naïvely.

His face was so scandalised that it was all I could do not to
chuckle, but I knew it would have offended him beyond reparation.

"The wicked old besom," I said, "at her age, too."

He glared at me suspiciously and then left me. When he had gone
I had the first really hearty laugh I had enjoyed for a week.

CHAPTER XXII

I HOLD A SÉANCE WITH THE ANCESTORS
AND THE RESULT

WHEN DUNKERLEY made his final inspection for the night, accompanied by the mamaloi, he was able to give me a signal that all was clear for the séance, and that Caspar was not returning.

I lost no time in taking the lift to the upper storey, though I might have to hang around in hiding for an hour or more.

I had become fairly familiar with the ramifications of this particular bit of the house by now. Dunkerley had told me that, except for a young coloured girl detailed to attend on Ines and Bridget, the other servants were not allowed upstairs unless specially summoned.

I remembered that on my previous visit I had left my electric torch in the lumber room, and it occurred to me that if Penberthy were patrolling the roads—I might be able to signal to him from the turret window.

It was risky in a way, but with Caspar in London and the mamaloi busy with her own affairs, I thought I would do a little practising.

I sent out a succession of short and long flashes haphazard, not really expecting anything to happen; so when my second series was answered by a single beam flashing up at the window, I almost dropped my torch with excitement. But was it Penberthy?

If it was Penberthy and there was nobody else on the patch of road where he was stationed, he would be more than likely to repeat my sequence.

Within another half minute the light appeared again a series of long and short beams, like my own.

"Ines" struck me as the best bid for identification so I spelled the name out in Morse. There was a short pause and then the reply came—"Sam."

It was quick of Penberthy; I was nevertheless afraid to go on for the moment, so I merely signalled "O.K. News two a.m." and stopped. Almost at once he acknowledged it with a repetition: "O.K.2."

I put the torch handily on the window ledge and crept back down the stairs. It was by now going on for eleven-thirty and the séance should be fairly near at hand. Dunkerley's door was ajar, but the place was empty.

I knew that the next room was occupied by Ines and Bridget, but decided I had better get to the balcony.

I had noted, on the previous night, that alongside the balustrade was a refectory table spread with a white cloth, and a couple of trays containing the debris of somebody's meals. The table was clear now, but the cloth was still spread. I crept under it, and made myself as comfortable as I could.

I was fortunate in my timing. Just over a quarter of an hour later, by the chiming of the clock in the hall, Maman Constance's door opened, and she came out, followed by Dunkerley, and they went down the stairs. She was evidently impressed and annoyed by something he had been saying.

"Of course if you insist on it," she was arguing, "and give me your word as a doctor that it is necessary, I must do as you say. But if I am willing to take the risk without using an anaesthetic. . ."

"I admit that," he answered tolerantly, "but what would my position be with Dr. Pettifranc if anything went wrong? . . ." He went on, in subtle persuasion: "In the case of ordinary blood transfusion operations, the person receiving the blood is usually so weak that there is little or no resistance from the heart to the inward flow. But with you—mentally dynamic as well as physically powerful—it is quite feasible that the transfusion would be more in Miss Bellenden's favour than yours."

"Do I have to be under chloroform all the time?" she said.

"It would be better."

"And if I won't," she retorted tartly.

"In that case I must refuse to carry out the operation."

"Oh, well—we'll see what the Ancestors say," she replied grudgingly. "Will you please switch off all the lights except the small one on the table, and then sit down in that chair opposite, where I can see you. And on no account speak until I give you permission. . ."

Dunkerley turned off the lights, and I heard him take his place. A queer thick silence descended, yet a silence that seemed to vibrate in one's brain. I had not noticed this peculiarity when the séance was held in the church and it made me uncomfortable. I wondered if the spirits of the wretched, rest-deprived Zombies were clustering round and protesting. It was a fantastic notion, but anything seemed possible in the atmosphere of tense, spiritual ferment that made even the silence noisy.

I could see, by his face, that Dunkerley was unpleasantly affected by it, too.

A sudden fear came over me; suppose that what I proposed doing offended the Ancestors and they revenged themselves by throwing us all into chaos? It was with acute relief I heard the first faint chirrupings arise, and, with them, the air seemed to become suddenly clearer and the sensation of being gradually throttled by unseen forces vanished.

Turning slightly so that the sound should rise up towards the roof from which the other chirrupings appeared to emanate, I proceeded to copy the latter as nearly as I could; softly at first, and then with more volume, though keeping my notes in what might be termed a different key.

As if the Ancestors were angry with the interference, the whistlings rose to a crescendo—not unlike hundreds of angry snakes hissing. It took all the wind and will power I had to carry on and make my own "chirrups" audible over the rest. And still the volume of sound increased and with it arose an eddy of chill air.

I cowered as it passed; it descended through the opening over the hall like a cold, dank fog. At the same moment, from below, came the sound of a chair falling, followed by an agonised scream from the mamaloi of—"Stop! Stop!" and then a dull thud. With that the whistling stopped as abruptly as if it had been cut off by a switch.

I heard Dunkerley spring up, and crawling from under the table I stole as quickly as I could part of the way downstairs.

Dunkerley was bending over the mamaloi: she was lying on the floor and her lips were flecked with white foam.

I waited for a second, then as she did not move: "Is she dead?" I called softly.

"No—worse luck." He looked up. "I think it's a fit of some kind; I very nearly threw one myself. Why didn't you warn me what to expect?"

"It wasn't like that the last time," I explained. "I suppose I must have irritated the spirits. Do you want me to give you a hand?"

"No! Keep out of the way. I'll bide here for a wee, then if she doesn't come round, I'll get her to bed." He knelt down again and listened carefully. "It's all right. I thought she was coming to," he said, a moment later appearing round the corner of the stairs, so that we could talk more freely.

"I suppose that does the operation in all right?" I said.

"Yes; no doubt about that. I ought to be treating her for apoplexy by rights, I suppose, but I don't think it's that, and anyway, damn it, I'm not her family doctor," he grumbled.

"You'd better pop along and see Westerham & Co.," he continued. "Room next to mine. The key is in the door on the outside. I only hope your appearance won't scare them. If it wasn't for that I'd suggest your calling in at Miss Bellenden's room—but it might spoil your chances." He grinned dourly.

"What do you mean? Is she . . .?"

"Aye," he nodded. "I risked giving her a shot as my experiments had worked out all right. Thought if we had to tackle Maman, it would be better to have her co-operation. I didn't know what amount Kucynski had put into her," he pursued, "and she wasn't to be surprised if you didn't look the bonnie lad she remembered," he continued gravely, though there was a glint in his eye. "Lassies go a rare lot by appearances, so it's up to you."

"You didn't treat Miss Westerham, too?" I ignored his jibe.

"No, I daren't risk it. Not going, are you?"

"I hate to keep you longer from your lady friend," I replied and dashed up the stairs.

Ines was lying on a settee. I thought at first she was asleep, as was Bridget, who was in bed—but she opened her eyes when I went over to her. She sat up, then shrank back. I presumed Dunkerley had told her more or less what to expect, but until I saw the look on her face I did not realise what an appalling spectacle I presented.

"Don't be frightened: it's I—Worthing," I whispered hastily "I came to tell you that you needn't worry. Maman is out of the picture? for the time, at all events."

"Oh. . . I'm so thankful," she said, a nervous catch in her voice. "But—what have they been doing to you? You look so ill."

"It's nothing that can't be cured with soap and water and a razor. Though it will be a few weeks before my hair grows, I expect." I chuckled. "I had to change places with one of Caspar's Zombies, temporarily."

She stretched out her hand impulsively.

"I feel it is all my fault," she said. "I'll never be able to thank you. If it hadn't been for you—what you've done . . ."

"Nonsense; I've done precious little as yet. By the way you'll be glad to hear Penberthy is all right. I managed quite by luck, to establish communication with him to-night... So long as you're safe," I went on, then added, "—and Miss Westerham—that is all that matters."

"It will be wonderful to be away from this horrible place," she returned, a shade awkwardly. "When do you think . . ."

"Within three days at most—so cheer up. I have to go and talk to Mr. Westerham now, but I wanted to have a word with you first."

"You'll be careful, won't you?"

"Trust me for that."

I hesitated a second outside the door of Westerham's room, wishing that my appearance was a little less unpleasant.

The two men were sitting over a chess board when I opened the door. The turning of the key brought them round with a jerk and their strained faces took on an even greyer tinge as their eyes fell on me.

"It's all right: I'm Worthing," I reassured them. "Dr. Dunkerley said you would be expecting me."

Of the pair, Walton was the quicker to pull himself together.

"Worthing? Oh, yes; you're the gentleman who hopes to get us out of this infernal tangle, I understand."

His tone was polite but he spoke with some effort, and I guessed was disappointed in the type of man he saw. He was a shortish, pompous individual, with a full, heavy face and chilly eyes that stared unfriendly through a pair of steel rimmed spectacles. He looked entirely different from when I had seen him laid out in the bed in the studio. He nettled me.

"Yes, if you are game to co-operate," I returned, and I could see the curtness of my reply rather surprised him. I did not wait for an answer, but turned to Westerham.

"I've just seen your daughter, sir," I began, and the blankness in his face lifted a shade. "She was asleep, but Miss Bellenden was with her. Dunkerley has managed to get her right, but he is waiting until things are more settled to tackle Miss Westerham. She knows nothing of what is going on and therefore isn't under any strain," I explained.

"I am sure you are doing all you can, Mr. Worthing," he said courteously; but there was no hope in his tone.

Walton broke in. "Dunkerley says you have a plan, but that it entails our pretending to accept that damned mulatto's conditions . . . how are we to know that you're not in league with the scoundrel?"

"I have no way of convincing you other than my word. Of course, I know I must appear a pretty disreputable person at the moment," I answered, "but that's because I have had to do some fairly un-pleasant pretending myself—perhaps Dunkerley told you? However, I can assure you that I'm honest in hating Caspar, even more than you do."

He studied me grimly and Westerham struck in. "If you have the run of the house why can't you get out and bring the police?"

"It isn't so simple as all that," I returned quietly, though the attitude of the pair was irritating.

"For one thing," I explained, "I'm still in captivity, but supposed to be harmless. If my absence were discovered—Dunkerley would pay the penalty. Not only that, but they'd take the alarm and clear out. If they couldn't take you with them, they'd probably murder you. I don't know if you realise it, but they have a thundering big scheme afoot. I'm hoping to scotch their game, but to do that we have to wait for the big meeting next Wednesday."

Walton emitted an indignant sound, but I continued unruffled.

"I had hoped to get Miss Westerham away and then pursue the business unfettered. But when they snaffled Miss Bellenden, and my friend Penberthy—who was going to help us—and then I ran against Dr. Dunkerley, and found he had to be cared for, too, it was too late. . ."

"If you slipped out and fetched the police," Walton put in irritably, "they'd take care of all that."

"Caspar is in London at present, and there are others besides him," I retorted, beginning to lose my temper. "If you won't help—well, it makes two men less when the fighting starts, but I expect we can manage."

"I didn't say I refused; I only stated that, in my opinion, you're wasting valuable time," Walton said in the sort of tone I could imagine his using at a meeting of a Board of International Armament Directors.

"What exactly do you wish us to do?" Westerham asked, with a half reproachful glance at his companion.

"To appear to accept Caspar's terms. When the right time comes Dunkerley or I will get word to you and you'll help to overpower whomever is in the house. I don't know whether you"—I turned to Walton—"have handed over the gas formula they're after; if not, I suggest you either do so or offer them a faked one."

"What the hell do you know about the gas formula?" he rapped.

"No more than that if it hadn't come into your possession, you probably would not have been here to-day."

"You can rely on me, Mr. Worthing," Westerham interposed quietly. "I only wanted to make sure we—we were not being hoaxed. Besides I owe you something for trying to protect my daughter."

"Thanks," I said.

"I shall reserve my decision until I've talked the matter over with Mr. Westerham," Walton said non-committantly.

It was his way of accepting the situation graciously.

"Good," I returned. "By the way, I suggest you should exercise discretion when you confer." I put a tinge of irony in my tone. "Walls have eyes as well as ears in this place," and with a friendly nod to Westerham I left them.

The door of the mamaloi's room showed a light through an opening. I crept closer and heard Dunkerley moving around, but no sound from Maman.

I "chirruped" very softly, after the manner of the Ancestors. A second later he came to the door.

"Okay," I said; "they'll co-operate, but the Lord spare me from any more like Walton."

"Oh, he's all right; a wee bit pompous, maybe, but 'tis the nature of the animal," he grinned. "I'm glad you persuaded them, though. She's still out? " he nodded in the direction of the mamaloi's room. "I'm thinking maybe it's a cataleptic attack. . . Seen your girl? I hope she liked your hair."

"She's not my girl, but I saw her, thanks. You know Walton asked me why I didn't slip out and fetch the police or make a dash for it now, while Caspar is away," I continued. "What do you say?"

"Have you any idea how this place is guarded?" he asked scathingly. "No? Well I have. Apart from that I'm taking no chances until I'm certain Caspar hasn't got his hands on Sheila. Besides, even if we got Caspar and Maman, there are half a dozen others who'd carry on unless we put the wind up them so badly that they'll go chasing back to Africa with their tails between their legs. I'd feel a waster for the rest of my days. . ." He was quite excited.

"Thanks," I said, "I'm going to signal Penberthy now, and tell him to have all ready for Wednesday. Mind you, Caspar's my meat, when it comes to the show down," I insisted.

"As you wish, laddie. I'll take the professor and Carol . . . Losh, I'm sorry, though, Kucynski isn't a whole man. I'd have loved to break his arm in a fair scrap."

CHAPTER XXIII

CASPAR SHOWS ANOTHER SIDE OF HIS CHARACTER

DUNKERLEY WAS LATE in coming to the laboratory the next morning. I spent the irksome wait going over in my mind the details heliographed by me to Penberthy at two A.M. and my instructions to him.

Dunkerley had been told by the mamaloi that lest the Manor was seriously threatened the whole of the underground laboratory and stable containing any dangerous evidence had had explosives concealed and wired so that they could be set off from a point of safety outside.

It was therefore up to the three of us to deal with the inmates of the Manor, and I was more than content that this should be so. My main worry was that we had no arms, but whilst the initiation ceremony was going on the probabilities were that most of Caspar's men would be occupied in the barrows. Penberthy and several of his friends would have guns. His only appeal to authority had been to get in touch with a friend in the Colonial Office and ask the latter to come down and spend a few days with him, to act as a witness.

Dunkerley came in alone and looked strained. He made straight for my cage and produced a ham sandwich and handed it to me apologetically.

"Best I could manage," he said. "I've had the devil of a time answering Caspar's calls. We've had two since breakfast. He was slavering mad over the Ancestor's séance; scared, too. Told me to take charge and he'd get a plane to the nearest landing ground as soon as he could. By the way—you asked me about his Papaloi's outfit; the togs are in his room—in a cupboard by the window,"

"How's your lady friend?" I asked.

"She's come round; she's scared, too, but her vitality is amazing. I had the de'il's own difficulty in making her keep her bed until Caspar turns up. There's a queer look in her eye, but she won't say a thing. I'd dearly love to know what yon whistling Ancestors told her, but I can't force her to speak. I did ask, but she merely mumbled something about having to wait until after the initiation for the operation and changed the subject. She's a bit cheered since Carol came in with the girl; found her wandering round the barrows."

"What?"

He nodded. "*She* won't talk either, except to keep on saying—'Why didn't you let me do as I wanted . . .' "

I did not know at this point, of course, anything beyond the fact that Polynice had been bringing her, and that her non-appearance had caused dismay in the house. I groaned at the thought of still another person whose safety had to be insured, although, if she was destined for the sacrificial stone it would be Penberthy's affair.

"One more thing," he went on, after a quick glance round, or rather, two. "First, I've located two or three useful pokers, and I'll give them to you and Westerham and take one myself. Carol has the guns, but I can't see any way of getting one out of him. The second is, that either you or I must put these wretched creatures out of their misery before we tackle the folk upstairs."

I shuddered. "I'd rather you did it. I'd probably make a mess of it."

"If I can get down I will, if not, before you leave the 'lab' take a lancet from one of the trays and just plunge it as deep as you can here"—he pointed out a spot on his own chest. "I must run now. Maman is like a cat on hot bricks whenever I'm out of her sight for more than ten minutes, but I'll be back as soon as I can." He turned. "Ines sends her love and says not to worry about her."

"Thanks," I said weakly.

~ ~ ~ ~ ~

Caspar arrived shortly after lunch. He had calmed down a little, but I could see, when he accompanied Dunkerley, that he was still jittery.

I stole a glance at the monstrosity when Dunkerley removed the bandages from its head for Caspar to see. It gave me a shock more on account of the thought that but for Dunkerley the gruesome object might have been myself.

Caspar clapped the surgeon on the back. "Good work, Dunkerley; very good work. You've actually beaten the professor at his own speciality. If your loyalty is as sound as your skill, you shall have no regrets at throwing in your lot with mine, I promise you."

"And Miss Stuart?"

Caspar grinned, but for once it was a friendly grin.

"You don't trust my word; I am just as good a friend as I am an enemy. So long as I am convinced that you are not trying to deceive me, you need have no fear for Miss Stuart."

"Where is she?" Dunkerley demanded.

"In Edinburgh. Directly we have finished with our business the day after to-morrow, and your first public appearance assures me that I can trust you wholeheartedly, you will be at liberty to communicate with her. If you like, you can even be married before we go to Africa."

"Africa? You never said anything to me about that," Dunkerley returned, with an assumption of sharpness.

"Didn't I? I said you were to become one of us. As a matter of fact, owing to certain changes that have taken place, I am going to make you my chief of staff in place of Polynice—if you continue to be sensible."

Dunkerley made no comment, and for a second or so there was silence. The mulatto appeared at a loss how to continue. He took a turn nearly to the door, then came back to the surgeon.

"What exactly happened at the séance last night?" he said suddenly.

"I told you. The whistling began, worked up to a crescendo like a hundred angry kettles boiling, and then Maman Constance flopped," Dunkerley replied.

"It has never happened before," Caspar said accusingly.

"Are you blaming me?" Dunkerley retorted.

"No—only it is odd." He considered for a pause, then shrugged his shoulders. "Well, it may mean nothing, or anything. Unfortunately I can't interpret the messages myself; that's Maman's speciality. In any case it won't affect my plans. Will Maman be well enough to assist me on Wednesday night?"

"She might have another cataleptic attack."

Caspar plucked at his chin broodingly.

"Oh, well, we shall have to see how she is later," he said. "I have a good deal still to do in town; luckily Walton and Westerham have decided to be sensible—but I'll be here without fail on Wednesday morning to make the final arrangements. I will give you your instructions then. By the way, that girl who was brought in yesterday. What is wrong with her?"

"Nothing very serious. Suffering from nerves mostly. She isn't in a fit condition to be questioned."

"I see." Caspar nodded, then moved nearer impulsively and placed his hand on Dunkerley's shoulder.

"You're a close man, Dunkerley, but that's no great fault. I like you and one of these days I hope you may come to like me, notwithstanding the bad moments you've had." He broke off as if rather ashamed, and going over to the operating table again stared moodily at the patient.

"This was only a small test, Dunkerley. If you had failed me in that I should have known you were not what I sought. . . I need hardly tell you that if what you have done here were to get out, no country in the world would be safe for you."

I was surprised by this unexpected transition on the mulatto's part. It showed that he was still considerably rattled.

A few days before, haunted with the uncertainty regarding his fiancé, the surgeon would probably have quailed under the onslaught, but now he was a different man. His answer, which astonished Caspar quite as much as the latter's tirade had startled us, was certainly the most calculated to provoke a storm; though, as it happened, it had just the opposite effect.

"Eh, man, I sometimes wonder if you're not still just a small urchin flourishing a toy gun," Dunkerley said, wagging his head chidingly. "I'm here and I canna get away, let alone being the only person in this fantastic place that has their full wits about them. And yet you waste time in talk like that. It's rideeculous, man."

I had hard work to subdue a chuckle as I watched Caspar's face.

"Do you know what you're saying—who you're talking to?"

"Weel—I did hear you called 'doctor,' though I don't know what your qualifications are," Dunkerley returned.

"But if you're a doctor you should know enough not to waste good breath on the obvious."

Caspar scowled, then his face cleared and he actually laughed.

"You're a great fellow, Dunkerley. I'll see you on Wednesday morning, then." He looked as if he was going to hold out his hand, but the other frustrated the gesture—busying himself in readjusting the bandages on his satyr.

"You've mentioned that already," he remarked.

"In that case I'll merely add 'good morning.' "

"And that's the man who thinks to start a new empire," Dunkerley said ironically, when sufficient time had elapsed to be certain Caspar had gone for good. "Did you hear him?"

I grinned. "Yes, but that doesn't make him any the less dangerous. You just happened to strike one of his weak spots."

"One—he fairly bristles with them."

"So do half the world's present dictators, but so long as it isn't generally known they can get away with it," I remarked.

He stared at me.

"Maybe you're right," he said, and looked puzzled when I laughed. It was nerves in part, but also I was so almighty thankful that Dunkerley had regained his own cantankerous manhood.

The ensuing forty-eight hours seemed as lacking in the elements of time and substantiality as a dream. There were successions of space that represented aeons, when I was alone in the laboratory, hours that passed as a flash when, after 11 P.M., I was flitting like a ghost in the upper part of the house. I had to see Walton and Westerham steal a few precious seconds with Ines and ascertain for myself the exact whereabouts of the Papaloi's robes which I intended to use. Then there was a further spell of signalling to Penberthy and, finally, a stealthy investigation of Polynice.

Unless I knew definitely if he were friend or foe it was impossible to forecast what he would do in an emergency. If he was on our side he would have to be looked after; if on Caspar's then he would still have to be taken care of, but in a different manner. And, whilst a temperature, such as he was supposed to be running, is generally considered an accurate indication of something being wrong, it is not infallible. An Indian Yogi can increase his temperature or decrease his heart beats practically at will.

With Dunkerley's sanction therefore I went to the sick man's room, after I had finished my flashlight talk with Penberthy, at 2 A.M. on the Wednesday.

I stole in as quietly as I could, hoping to find him asleep and, by waking him suddenly, judge by his reactions whether he was malingering.

There was a shaded light upon a chest and, as I entered, I could have sworn the man moved. When I reached the bedside, however, he was lying with his eyes closed, but began to talk ramblingly.

I sat down on a chair by the bed and waited for about five minutes. If the man was malingering they must have been at least a hundred per cent longer and more anxious for him than for me. As he made no sign, I thought before disturbing him abruptly I would try another ruse.

As if talking to myself, I commenced to speak on a low note.

"Either the girl was released by Polynice before the accident or she ran off after it occurred. In the former case, then Polynice evidently wanted to save her from Caspar, but if that were so then he would surely have found some place of safety for her to go to." I paused, trying to decide if his breathing had quickened.

"The fact that she was picked up close to the Manor in a state of apparent exhaustion seems to indicate she ran away after the accident," I pursued. "Of course, she can be made to speak—and there are means of doing that then Caspar will know whether Polynice is with or against him."

This time there was a definite catch in Polynice's breath.

"A temperature is not always an indication of fever," I went on ruthlessly. "In India I have seen Yogis who could send their temperatures up ten degrees within a few minutes. Caspar apparently doesn't know this, but there are others who do. Some, maybe, who would like to help Polynice if they were certain of his motives."

I stopped again to prolong the suspense.

"There are seven prisoners in this house," I began again, "the red-head, Dr. Dunkerley, three girls and Walton and Westerham. It would be awkward if, by any chance, they succeeded in breaking loose on the night of the initiation and did not know Polynice was no friend of Caspar."

I stood up noisily and looked down on him.

He opened his eyes and smiled up at me. "I thought it must be the red-head," he remarked. "Ever since Caspar told me of the trouble you've given him I had a desire to meet you."

"Thanks. My real name is Worthing—I'm getting a little tired of being referred to as the 'red-head'," I grinned back.

"I beg your pardon, Mr. Worthing," he corrected.

In spite of my assurance I was still not quite comfortable.

At length: "My cards are on the table," I said. "You have only to tell Caspar and my plans are ruined. How do you stand?"

He reflected. "You say the girl was brought back? That is curious, considering I gave her into the charge of your friend Penberthy," he said at length. "We met before the accident and he said he would see she was safe. Does that mean he has been taken too?"

"No; he is all right."

"Hm." He reflected. "Perhaps he has some reason." He looked at me squarely in the face. "I hope you will believe me when I say that in no circumstances would I have permitted her or the other two girls to come to harm."

"And yet you assisted Caspar to kidnap Miss Westerham."

"I had to: to enable me to carry out my work."

I suppose my face showed incredulity. "It is true," he insisted, "and if Caspar had not been rendered unduly suspicious by your visit to his studio, I should never have been suspected." His tone held a shade of bitterness.

That stung me a bit.

"How did you propose to do it?" I demanded bluntly. "It seems to me you were taking pretty long chances."

He sighed. "Yes, I realise that now, but until a couple of days ago I thought what I had to offer as a bargain would have persuaded him. I—I am not so sure now."

"And *I* am perfectly sure that you would have been let down— unless you had something to offer considerably more valuable than I can imagine," I remarked.

"I had the key to India—through my brother, Prince Ali Singh, if Caspar agreed to give up his devil worship and go out simply for the peaceful freeing of all coloured races."

"And you expected Caspar to agree to *that,* when he looks forward to becoming a second Jenghiz Khan and Cetewayo rolled into one," I scoffed.

His eyes clouded. "Yes, but . . . I did not know his full intentions at the time."

"Well, you ought to realise them pretty well by now," I returned, half sorry for, half annoyed with the man. As an idealist he was fine, but as a practical plotter he was ludicrous.

"Anyway, it's too late to consider what might have been," I pursued, rather peremptorily. "All I'm concerned with now is to be sure you won't take Caspar's part."

"I can promise you that, certainly. In fact," he went on slowly, "I should rather like a chance to help on the other side."

"That depends on circumstances," I replied. "If anything happens and I can get word to you, I will." I moved to go. The interview had taken longer than I anticipated.

"Is Miss Bellenden all right?" he asked in sudden anxiety.

"Quite safe so far," I answered.

"Thank you." He smiled again faintly. "And thanks for coming to see me," he added.

"Not at all. Good night," I returned.

Dunkerley was asleep and I saw no need to disturb him. Either, within the next twenty hours, we should all be safely out of the Manor and Caspar's schemes would have been finally squashed or . . . I refused to consider that alternative.

I also declined to think of what would happen to me when the business was over, and I had to return to my ordinary life again.

CHAPTER XXIV

THE ROUNDING UP OF THE ANCESTORS
—FIRST STAGE

THE VARIETY OF EVENTS which took place between ten P.M. and midnight of that fateful Wednesday is difficult to set down coolly.

The hours between my waking up in the morning and noon—when Dunkerley popped in for a few seconds and told me Caspar had returned—were some of the worst I have ever known. After the mid-day meal it would have been even worse, except that Dunkerley had given me a sleeping draught which enabled me to doze for a good four hours.

The poker was hidden under my blanket; Dunkerley had smuggled it in to me after breakfast. He also told me then that he had instructed Ines how to give Bridget the antidotal injection of Kingo.

Caspar paid a fleeting visit during the early afternoon to look at the satyr, but he was far too worked up over the coming ceremony to concentrate. There was little or no danger that he would notice anything wrong and I determined to make a move for the upper storey earlier than I had originally intended. As it turned out it was lucky I changed my plans.

Dunkerley made his final inspection earlier than usual, as Caspar had ordered him to come to his room at nine o'clock. He informed me that the delegates and certain other important people, thirty in all, were arriving by specially chartered planes at Exeter at six P.M. There they were being met and were being motored by devious routes to the barrows. Caspar had interviewed Polynice, and had deputed him to receive the delegates at the barrows, and show them to their places, since he now appeared well enough for the task. The mamaloi, however, had informed Dunkerley that an usher was being provided to help Polynice and had instructions to knock him on the head if he evinced any sign of treachery.

Dunkerley was ordered to take charge of Alice Sheldon, and lead her to the sacrificial stone, where the Haitian Papaloi would then assume authority. The Papaloi in question had arrived with Caspar and was in the stable feasting his depraved senses on the horrible exhibits.

Dunkerley said that he was a poisonous specimen.

Penberthy's plans I knew in the main, but they were to be governed entirely by the elements of opportunity and expediency.

At a little before nine I took the lift to the top floor, and stole along to the stairs leading to the attic window.

As I turned the corner of the landing I noticed a light in the room in which I had formerly hidden Bridget. It was as serious a thing as could have happened because I had arranged to try and switch that light on as a signal to Penberthy that Caspar had left for the stone, and its presence now was misleading.

I laid down my poker and crept up as quietly as I could, but not quietly enough to take the occupant by surprise. As I peered through the door my eyes met those of a gaunt skeletonian-like black fellow; naked except for a scarlet cloak, a head-dress of feathers, and a necklace of human finger-bones. I realised I was gazing at the Haitian Papaloi.

He was squatting on the floor and ranged round him were half a dozen dolls, and he had been decorating them with feathers taken from a dead cockerel that lay on the floor beside him.

He nodded and then turned to the circle of dolls. "I found these in one of the boxes . . . I thought I would dress them for the great occasion."

His eyes turned to mine again and his skinny fingers plucked at the bone necklace on his parchment-like chest.

"That's all right," I said; "only it is rather dangerous to have the light on . . . hadn't you better switch it off?"

"I never thought of that," he replied. "Yes, I will if you think it best."

Unsuspectingly he got up and as the light went off I sprang at his throat. He gurgled and struggled and tore at me with his talons desperately. He was considerably stronger than I had expected, but I held on, cursing myself for being so impetuous. It was a ghastly shock to me when, with another choke, he suddenly dropped forward limply and I found I had killed him.

However, it was no good worrying now, and I debated what was the best way of disposing of the body. It would be dangerous to leave in it the attic, in case Caspar came later to look for him. Then it struck me that I might put it in my cage in the laboratory.

It was only when I had got it safely ensconced that the thought occurred to me that possibly its robes might come in handy. I stripped it as speedily as I could, bundled the roll under my arm and returned to the attic, where I hid the clothing in the bottom of a drawer under some old curtains.

By not later than nine-fifteen I was standing by the swing doors leading to the balcony, wondering if it was safe to peep through.

I could hear Caspar's voice booming in his room; I could not make out what he was saying, but judged it would be quite safe to push the panel ajar, when I might be able to distinguish his words. I squinted through the opening cautiously and nearly gave myself away by a gasp when I saw Maman Constance in an attitude of furtive listening outside Caspar's door. Her room was next to his so that she could be back in her own quarters in a flash if the mulatto gave sign of coming out.

She was stooping down and I could see by the set of her back that she was in a violent rage, yet, apparently at the same time scared. She must have been dressing for the ceremony when she heard Caspar's voice raised and stole out to investigate. The lower portion of her attire was a kind of skirt on to which rows of different coloured feathers had been stitched, but the upper only consisted of a white chemise

We must have remained crouching in our respective positions a full ten minutes. Once she hissed and shook her fist vindictively.

"It's no use arguing, Dunkerley, you've got to do it," I heard Caspar shout menacingly. "This thing has got to through to-night in my way or your girl pays the penalty. Nobody can possibly recognize you aren't what you're supposed to be in that light. I intended to do it myself, but I'm afraid of Maman making a scene. If you do it and she doesn't know, she'll take you for the real thing."

If Caspar could have seen the venomous poise of the mamaloi at that instant he would have had the surprise of his life.

Dunkerley said something I could not hear.

"Never mind the girl," Caspar replied. "Carol can take her to the stone. This is much more important. Will you do it? . . . all the things are ready in that suitcase."

"All right, I'll do it." Dunkerley's voice was loud and confident.

"Good. I promise you you won't regret it. Now you'd better get along and see how Maman is. Don't let her out if there's the slightest chance of her cracking up . . ."

The door opened and Maman was back in her own room, hastily tearing off the skirt as she fled.

"After that, you'd better give a shot of the Kingo to the girl before she leaves the house. I don't want her screaming all over the place and ruining the show," Caspar proceeded, accompanying Dunkerley to the door and giving him a friendly thump on the shoulders. The action was jovial but the mulatto's face was a study in sheer, triumphant mischief. I hated and feared him more at that moment than I had ever done. Whatever there was of white in him had been wiped put as by a sponge and the residue was unadulterated animal brutality, which the assumption of a good nature merely emphasized.

Before, I was not sure that he had not at least a partial belief in the mummery he was planning to stage, but now I saw he had none and was simply using it to further his own ascendancy.

"What about the two other girls?" Dunkerley asked on a casual note which I applauded enviously.

"Leave them where they are. We shan't want them now we have the younger one. I must go to the barrows now. I'll talk to Miss Bellenden myself when it's all over."

I had the greatest difficulty in restraining myself from dashing out; the leering viciousness on his face when he mentioned Ines' name was so foul. Fortunately he gave me no opportunity to make a fool of myself, but with a snap of his fingers he started off hurriedly to the stairs.

"Pst," I sounded just in time to stop Dunkerley.

He came over, carrying the suitcase as if on the way to his room.

"I thought you'd better know," I whispered, when we were behind the swing panels. "Maman was listening outside Caspar's door."

He framed a whistle. "The devil: that's a complication. I wonder now—will she go for me or will she save her venom for Caspar?"

"What's the trouble?" I asked.

He shook the suitcase and grinned. "Nothing—only that I'm to impersonate Zamiel? the Great One. These are the duds."

"Good Lord."

"Exactly. First I'm to be assistant to the Lord High Executioner and then the Devil, and God knows what kind of a time I'm in for with Maman. Ten to one she tries to bribe me to double-cross Caspar."

"I've just strangled one of them myself . . . Your ugly friend the Papaloi," I said. My tone was cool, but I was a little scared what he might say.

"The deuce you did." He eyed me enviously.

"I was afraid you might think I was too hasty," I added.

"Weel," he reflected? "who's going to officiate for him?"

"I have his clothes."

"It *is* a masquerade," he murmured joyously. "Losh man, it's worth that two weeks of hell."

"We haven't started yet. The only thing I can't understand is how you've managed to get so thick with Caspar?"

"Needs must when the devil drives," he answered. "Polynice is in disgrace; Maman has the vapours and there's nobody else here on the inside of the house. Though, mind you, he intends making away with me directly once I've served his purpose; I could read it in his eyes." He paused.

"By the way," he continued, "I've a wee present here for Miss Bellenden. Tell her not to have any compunction in using it in self-defence if yon old beldame goes to her room, and tries to murder her." He produced a revolver from his pocket and handed it to me. "It's Maman's."

"You don't think . . ." I began.

"You never know with a jealous woman," he replied. "See you later." He left the suitcase beside the swing door and went off to visit the mamaloi.

I waited for a second, then, as all appeared quiet, I went to Ines' room and tapped gently on the door before unlocking it. She met me on the threshold.

"I guessed it was you," she breathed. "Is all well?"

"So far." I handed her the revolver and explained its object.

"You don't think she will come, though, do you?" she said, startled.

"No, but it's best to be prepared. You're quite sure you know what to do," I said hastily. "I mean later . . ."

"Three knocks on the door and I'm to take Bridget to the third room on the right and wait for further orders, with Mr. Westerham."

"Correct. And for the love of Heaven, if that old fiend comes to your room and looks likes mischief, shoot to kill. Remember, she's quite as dangerous as that tiger you went after with your father."

"I will? " she said resolutely. "Is there anything else?"

"That's all."

"Quite all?" she asked and there was a queer look in her eyes.

I did it then. It was a mad night and we were none of us quite responsible for our actions. I kissed her squarely on the mouth, then pushed her back and closed the door, hurriedly, before I made a still more utter fool of myself.

Suddenly I saw Dunkerley's suitcase and chuckled softly. He had
said it was a masquerade—well, one more absurdity in those circumstances could do no harm.

Within ten minutes I had removed the costume from the case,
substituted the Papaloi's robes, and taken the other to the attic where
I changed into them. As soon as Caspar returned, I would let him see
his Great One face to face.

~ ~ ~ ~ ~

Ensued another period of waiting, which I spent, every nerve alert,
in finding what cover was available in the corridor that communicated with the servants' quarters. There was precious little, but on
the first landing I found a housemaid's cupboard which gave me just
room enough to crouch.

Through the open landing window I heard several cars. A clock
in the distance struck ten, and then the quarter, but there was no sign
of Caspar.

I was beginning to wonder if he had changed his mind and meant
to remain all the time at the barrows, when I heard hurried footsteps
in the lower corridor and his voice calling for Alfonse and Antoine.

A moment later the two servants answered the summons.

"You, Antoine, stay in the hall and keep watch," Caspar ordered.
"Don't let anyone in or out unless I, Maman Constance or Dr.
Dunkerley tell you to. If anybody tries to get away shoot them—in
the leg if you can. Alfonse—go and fetch the Papaloi from the attic
room and take him with you to the entrance to the underground
passage. Tell him to wait for me there. Then stand by, yourself, by
the outside of the stables and keep your eye on the sky through the
grating. When you see a light go on, open the door and drive the
people from the stables down the first corridor to the stone. Whatever you do, use the first passage—the one that was completed on
Sunday; do you understand?"

"Yes, chief," Alfonse answered eagerly.

"Send the two Mongols up to me right away. I want them to take
the girl to the stone; make them understand they must use the second
passage. Carol will meet them at the far end and take charge of her
until she is needed. Is that quite clear?"

"Yes, chief."

"Tell Charles and Svend to stand by in case they are wanted.
Mackson and Slim, with the Mongols, when they've taken the girl,

had better go to the circle and remain in the higher ground to drive back any of the stable folk, if they try to break away."

"Very good, chief."

"One more thing. If the—the Great One should appear in the corridor, don't be scared, but on no account go near him. That's all; now get along and see you don't make any mistakes."

They were evidently glad to be gone and Caspar rushed up the remaining stairs and through to the balcony.

I wondered whether it would be better to deal with Caspar or the servants first, and decided after a second's thought on the servants. The two Mongols came by and went through the swing doors. I concluded I would let them get out of the way with the girl and allow the others to reach their posts before I made a move. Penberthy would be on the spot at the stone and, if we held up the girl, some of our best evidence regarding the mulatto's fiendish designs would be missing.

They returned within five minutes, and as they set off I risked a peep and saw they were carrying the girl. She appeared quiescent though awake, and wore a white, flowing garment. A second later the door communicating with the servants' quarters clanged again and several more pairs of feet could be heard going along the lower corridor.

I reckoned it was time now to deal with the remaining two.

Charles and Svend, were sitting smoking over a table, playing cards, when I pushed through the door. They looked up incuriously and then their faces set in an expression of absolute terror. Their teeth chattered but they never stirred when I went over and touched them on the shoulder. As a matter of fact I was quite as much disconcerted as they. I had looked for a scrap and here I was with two scared men on my hands. The only way was to carry off the business as one imagined the Great One might have done.

"Come," I said, touching the nearest on the shoulder. "Zamiel commands. You too," and I faced the other.

He rose at that and, driving them in front of me, I walked over to a further door which I thought might lead to a scullery. If I could lock them up for the time being it would be fine. I motioned to the foremost to open the door, which he did, disclosing a moderate sized pantry. The window, fitted with wire gauze, showed me at once it was no place for a prison.

Apparently the second man misunderstood my motives, for he pushed past the other and seizing a leg of lamb that stood on a dish, he bowed and held it forward to me humbly. My jaw dropped and I suppose the very human look on my face showed through the black gauze mask I wore and betrayed me.

"My God, it's a man," he gasped, dropping the dish.

Even then I might have saved the situation if I had kept my presence of mind, as neither of them knew who I was or my business. But unfortunately I raised the poker. The next second we were at it tooth and nail.

I got the first, and biggest man, on the side of the head before he could collect himself. The second was more agile and quicker to action.

There was very little left unbroken in the pantry within a minute or so, and I was terrified the noise of smashing china would bring some others in. I stuck to my poker, laming in with it whenever I could. If I had not clinched I should have suffered more badly, but though he planted some hefty blows on my face and nearly bit through to the bone on my shoulder, I escaped any serious damage. He yelled for mercy when I got a welt in with the poker that nearly broke his arm, but I dare not risk letting him off. As he staggered back, throwing up his hands, I dropped the poker and caught him full on the chin with my right. He collapsed without a sound and after robbing the two of their guns, I tied them up back to back with a length of clothes-line I found on a shelf.

I gagged them with pieces torn from their own shirts—and locked the pantry door on them. It took me about five minutes to make myself presentable—one eye was puffed and threatened to become black and my shoulder had to be staunched—and then I was ready for the next adventure.

I made a cursory inspection of the kitchen quarters, discovered a room where some maids were sleeping, turned the key on the outside, and then set off for the balcony once more.

Below I could see Antoine on duty, but I had no time for him for the moment. It was Caspar now I thirsted to settle with.

CHAPTER XXV

ROUNDING UP OF THE ANCESTORS—SECOND STAGE

I HAD HEARD Alfonse coming helter skelter along the corridor of the far wing just as I was on the point of entering it by the swing doors, and had barely time to conceal myself under the refectory table before he appeared, made a dash for Caspar's room and knocked, announcing breathlessly that the Haitian Papaloi was missing.

"I told him to wait in the attic until I sent for him. Here—get out of the way: I'll go and see for myself."

Caspar pushed Alfonse aside and sprinted past my hiding-place and through the panel. Alfonse irresolutely followed.

I wondered what had better be my next move. Time was getting on and within a quarter of an hour events ought to be in full swing at the barrows.

At that moment I heard a soft movement on the balcony. I looked out furtively, afraid that it might be one of our band. Then I saw it was the little professor in his pyjamas, and if ever clear, stark madness shone in a man's eyes, it did in his.

It was a nasty shock to see his maniacal face, his mouth working spasmodically, and in his usable hand a cruel-looking surgical knife, wet with blood.

For an awful moment I thought he might have been butchering the girls, but then Caspar must have heard some outcry. I was on the point of diving from under the table and tackling him when instinct halted me.

A second later he was in front of the mamaloi's door, where he paused, glanced cunningly up and down the balcony and then bent down with his ear to the keyhole. At almost the same instant the door opened and Dunkerley appeared. It was too late to cry a warning; Dunkerley's unexpected advent and the opening of the door threw the little man off his balance and he fell forward on his knees. As he did so the knife dropped on to the floor, and Dunkerley caught it with his foot and sent it spinning a half dozen feet along the balcony.

With a scream of rage Kucynski was up and after it like a flash, Dunkerley behind him, and at the same moment Caspar—mad with fury—burst through the panels.

"Hold him . . . hold the crazy devil," he shouted.

Dunkerley was the stronger man and Kucynski was handicapped by his arm, but his frenzy endowed him with superhuman power.

At sound of Caspar's voice he hurled Dunkerley from him and with a savage snarl picked up the knife and sped round the corner of the balcony to meet the mulatto.

"You . . . you . . ." he shrieked in his reedy falsetto. "It was you who turned me out of my laboratory. . ."

I heard a cry of alarm from Maman Constance, who had come to the door, drawn by the noise, an impact and a curse from Caspar, and then a horrible scream and a crash from below, followed by an exclamation from Antoine, who had come running up and was now within a couple of feet of me, peering over the railing at the crumpled body on the hall floor. Caspar must have hurled him over his shoulder.

"The mad fool," he went on angrily, as Dunkerley examined his shoulder which had suffered a glancing cut. "No wonder we couldn't find the Papaloi. Kucynski murdered him and stowed him in the lab; he's butchered everything in the place, and I suppose came along here to finish up with us."

"The girls . . ." Dunkerley's tone showed his anxiety.

"No; only those in the laboratory. Well, Maman," he continued, to the mamaloi who was watching the scene in inscrutable silence, "it looks as if you would have to perform the purification ceremony as well as the sacrifice."

She grunted sneeringly. "I told you in the first instance that it was a waste of good money bringing that man over," she retorted.

"Are you ready? If so you'd better get down," he snapped. "They'll be wondering what we're waiting for," and with a curt, "Then you, Doc," to Dunkerley, I heard him move along the balcony.

"You ought to have that cut dressed," the latter said.

"I can't spare the time now, it isn't serious. You go on down and wait, Maman, I'll be with you as soon as I get my things on. You have your instructions, Dunkerley," he continued. "I'll see you later."

The old woman cackled.

"Always so polite when you want a favour, aren't you, *mon ami?*" she said on a derisive note. "So you won't be able to do without poor old Maman after all."

"I never suggested doing without you," he returned a shade too emphatically.

"No? *Eh bien,* I hope for your own sake you never will," she cackled again, but it was a sinister sound. "But since you need me and the cause comes before everything, I'll help you. A warning though, Caspar," she called, halting on her way to the stairs.

"What is it this time?" he said irritably.

"A clever man may fool others, but only a fool tries to fool himself," she said meaningly, and resumed her stately descent of the stairway.

He paused for a second, looking after her, then shrugged.

"Antoine—clear away the mess in the hall," he ordered, "and afterwards remain on watch as I told you. Alfonse, you'd better come and help me change."

As Antoine lumbered down the stairs and Caspar's door slammed behind him and Alfonse, I crept from my cover and set off for Dunkerley's room. I reckoned it would take at least five minutes for the mulatto to get into his robes.

Dunkerley was sitting on the edge of the bed, his shoe and sock off, ruefully examining his ankle.

"Curse that professor, this would happen," he said viciously. "Did it when we were grappling for the knife."

"Anyway, here's something to comfort you," I said, and handed him one of the revolvers. "I've rounded up the kitchen crew, so there's only Antoine in the hall and Alfonse at the moment. What I want you to do now is to switch on the light in the attic to warn Penberthy . . . you can make that, can't you?"

"I could crawl that far."

"Good. After that stand by in the corridor here. If I don't come back within a quarter of an hour it will mean Caspar's got me and you'll have to take charge. In that case take the girls and Westerham and Co. to the attic. Switch off the light and signal with the flash-lamp you'll find on the floor under the window. Dot-dash, dot-dash and continue. That will tell him I've failed. Wait . . . take off your coat and trousers," I added, myself peeling off my own garb hurriedly. "This dress will give you the run of the place. I'll take Caspar's—if I am lucky."

There was no time to put on a collar and tie, so I buttoned up Dunkerley's coat and left it at that.

Caspar was in practically full panoply when I entered his room.

He had his back to me, but turned as Alfonse, who was adjusting the feather anklets on his legs, gasped when I closed the door.

I had removed the Zombie's grey hair from my chin and head, but my own skull was still practically bare, so that for a second or so he did not recognise me.

"Hands up," I said, and reached to my coat pocket for the revolver. Automatically they put up their arms.

I have never in all my life felt such a complete and utter idiot as I did at that moment, when I discovered that, in my haste, I had omitted to put the gun in my pocket. I had laid it on a side table when I was changing.

"So—it's the red-head again and Dunkerley has double-crossed me." The icy, bitter rage in the mulatto's tone, coming on top of my own stupidity, will remain with me to the end of my days.

There was only one thing to be done and that was to go all out for the mulatto before either of the pair realized my predicament.

"Well," Caspar sneered, "you seem to have a positive genius for making yourself a nuisance. What is the next item on the programme?"

"Keep your hands up and turn round and face the wall," I ordered.

Alfonse turned, but the other merely laughed.

"Thanks, but when there's danger around I prefer to face it."

"You'll turn round, or? " I went up to him, and poked him in the ribs with my thumb, praying he would take it for the gun.

He turned unwillingly. I tautened to fling myself upon him, but before I could do so he kicked backwards, catching me on the knee and, as I doubled under, he whirled round and threw himself on top of me. I could have managed him alone in my desperation, but with Alfonse clinging to my feet I hadn't a chance.

Caspar did not let up for a second until I was senseless, and I believe he intended to strangle me to a finish. I came round to find myself swathed in rope and Alfonse morosely keeping guard. Caspar had gone.

I felt as sick as a dog and my throat had the sensation of being torn apart, but my physical anguish was nothing to the deadly nausea that overcame me when I thought of my own stupendous folly. Now all turned on Penberthy.

"Where's Caspar?" I croaked, hoping Alfonse might talk.

"He's busy—but he'll be right back," Alfonse grinned spitefully. "He said to tell yo' the next time he's going to deal with yo' himself and it won't be no picnic either," he gloated.

"Has he gone to the stone?" I pressed.

"You mind yo' own business," Alfonse retorted, leering.

I stifled a groan. If by some means or other I could call Dunkerley. I began to sing at the top of my voice. "Loch Lomond" was an air I knew Dunkerley would gather came from me.

"Stop that," Alfonse shouted, then, as I continued to croak even more lustily, "stop it, d'ye hear," and launched a vicious kick at my ribs.

I rolled over to lessen the blow, but my last bars died out in a gasp, because as I turned my eyes fell upon another roped and prostrate body on the floor a couple of feet away, naked except for its underclothes.

A small pool of blood was forming round the thigh nearest to me.

It was Dunkerley.

CHAPTER XXVI

ROUNDING UP OF THE ANCESTORS—THIRD STAGE

AT A LITTLE BEFORE 9 P.M. Penberthy with his friend Motton, from the Colonial Office, set out by a circuitous route for the barrows.

"I wish you would tell me what all the mystery is about," Motton remarked, for at least the tenth time since his arrival.

"Now look here, Edward," Penberthy was beginning to get irritated. "You're a pal of mine and you know me well enough to realise that I'm not trying to make a fool of you."

The other grunted. "Yes, but? "

"You've always held that hearsay evidence is no evidence. If I told you what to expect you would either think, as my housekeeper does, that I'm potty, or you'd become all official and say you must ring up the Prime Minister for instructions and spoil all the fun."

"If it's as serious as that," Motton began, and halted.

"Don't be an ass, Edward," Penberthy compelled him on. "I tell you I don't know myself exactly what you're likely to see. All I know is that a kind of meeting is being held in some early British ruins near here which may be interesting. I want an unbiased witness to check up my own impressions."

"Oh, very well, but I still consider? "

"The camera I gave you—you're quite sure you know how to use it?" Penberthy cut in.

"Of course I do. But you can't take pictures by moonlight—not instantaneous ones."

"You'll have plenty of light for that, if I'm not mistaken. But for the Lord's sake don't get so excited that you forget to shoot at the crucial moment."

"I never get excited," Motton replied stiffly.

"No, I've never seen you yet, but you might. And, if you really want to snap something unique don't attempt to move from the nice little cubby-hole I've got ready for you. Will you promise me that much?"

"Certainly." There was doubt in his tone, but Penberthy felt he would keep his word.

He deposited Motton in the cubby-hole—an ancient burial urn whose roof had caved in a little to the left of the main excavation and the track, but near enough to see and hear the performance.

After that he made a detour to a broken-down barn on the outskirts of the Manor, where he found half a dozen men waiting his arrival. Each was dressed in black clothes and had a stockinette mask.

Here they waited in silence until Penberthy saw the lights of a car coming up the road that led to the barrows. There were a number of cars in all, and as each one arrived, Penberthy crawled out with one of the party and guided him either to the shelter of a mound or a clump of gorse within a hundred yards of the excavations.

By the time the last of the cars had deposited its passengers, Penberthy had his men in a ring round the top of the crater. He himself made his way, inch by inch, to a spot inside the bowl that he had previously marked down. A longish wait ensued with a good deal of subdued conversation between various members of the delegation. Penberthy counted twenty-five in horse-shoe formation round the stone, and two, apparently more important personages, who were placed on either side of it. Above it was an arc light suspended from a pole with wires running down to some point by the main subway.

Penberthy caught sight of Polynice and noted that wherever he went he was followed by another man who kept a suspicious eye on him. He came up to the artist in passing and said:

"Good evening. Is everything all right?"

"Okay," Penberthy replied. "I sent the girl along for special reasons. Don't worry, though, she'll be looked after."

A few seconds later Caspar, in evening clothes, appeared, and a quick hush fell upon the gathering.

Using the stone as a platform, he bade the delegates welcome, and recapitulated briefly the reason of the meeting. He then produced a paper from which he read certain questions. The responses were given by the whole gathering and there seemed to be no doubt as to their unanimity.

"I will now leave you for a little while," the mulatto announced, "and fetch the appointed one to carry out the ceremony of purification. When that is complete the mamaloi and myself will perform the sacrifice of the white virgin, and if all is propitious, the Great One, Zamiel himself, will appear and bless our enterprise.

"Whilst I am gone, two of the exalted three will address you and tell you the arrangements that have been made for precipitating trouble between Europe, America and the Far East."

There was subdued applause when he took his leave, and the man sitting at the front on the left of the stone—a tall, finely-built man of Arab type, not so big as the mulatto, but giving the impression of purer blood—rose.

He recapitulated the plans that had been made amongst certain powerful East African tribes to take over various tracts of country and, when he sat down, his place was occupied by the second of the three—a jovial, plump little individual, almost white, with shifty eyes and a Mongolian cast of face. He gave a similar resume of plans affecting northern China and Tibet.

It was so like a dull, political meeting up to that point that Penberthy was very nearly bored. Still, he reflected, if Motton had his ears open, he should be finding enough to keep his mind busy.

After that a strain of soft music was heard stealing through the barrows; it held sadness, yet there was a hint of savagery in it that stirred the pulses; a peculiar drum beat resembling the throb of a heart, and though it was so gentle as to be barely perceptible a few yards from the crater, it had a strangely powerful effect upon the senses. Even as he was peering round to try to locate from whence it emanated, Penberthy found himself swaying with the rest of the crowd.

It swelled a little as the two Mongols, with Carol in attendance behind, appeared at a break in the horse-shoe which afforded a straight passage from the main underground runway to the stone. All three were naked except for loin cloths, and the two foremost carried above their heads a kind of litter upon which the girl—Alice Sheldon—was secured with gilded chains. Under the thin, white silken sheet that covered her the young slimness of her unclad form could be seen clearly outlined.

Two negroes followed, leading by a silver chain a huge black goat whose horns were garlanded with white and red flowers. In their free hands they held aloft torches that burned with a slightly reddish flame.

The Mongols paced slowly to the stone, laid the bier down and then proceeded to bind the girl to the stone itself by the steel chains fitted to the sides.

The tempo of the music changed and appeared to grow faster and louder. The swaying bodies grew more frenzied; some of the darker-coloured men started to champ their jaws and utter spasmodic, guttural grunts. Foam came dribbling from the lips of others.

As soon as the girl was secured the two negroes hoisted the goat on to the stone, placing it about a couple of feet away from the girl, and tethered it to another chain. Following that, Carol deposited a wickedly gleaming, short sharp sword at the head of either intended victim.

And still the insidious tempo of the music continued, lashing the brutal, sensuous emotions of the gathering. Penberthy assured himself that it was a record, relayed probably, through a loudspeaker from the Manor—but beads of sweat started out on his brow as he strove to keep sane and calm.

There was a longish pause after this, though the music went on, and several of the more hypnotised members of the party began to cast impatient glances towards the dusk of the underground passage, licking their lips feverishly. Their passions were aroused and they were anxious to see blood flowing over the stone and to gather and drink it from the polished copper bowls that lay in a semi-circle round the base.

Just when it seemed that the tension was beaming unbearable and that a number of the worshippers would leap to the stone and themselves consummate the sacrifice, Caspar and the mamaloi appeared at the end of the aisle leading to the altar.

The music stopped, as pacing slowly, they reached the plinth. The two arch priests assisted them reverently to mount the altar itself and everybody rose. After a dead silence lasting several seconds, Caspar raised his arm and made the sign of the Cross reversed.

With a sigh like the escape of the last breath from a weary man the worshippers sat down. The two negroes handed up a triple decanter containing oil, water and wine, which Caspar poured out gravely into a trough that had been chipped out between the feet of the two sacrifices. Then he and the mamaloi fell on their knees and carried some of the mixture to their mouths, drank of it, murmured something and, finally, sprinkled it on the heads and feet of the goat and the girl.

The pair now got up, Caspar moving to the back of the stone, and Maman Constance remaining at the front. The music started again on a different theme, and plucking up the sword that lay at the head of the goat the mamaloi began to dance, slowly at first, then with ever-increasing tempo, at the same time chanting an incantation.

Faster and faster she spun, like some monstrous human teetotum. The crowd beat with their feet on the ground and slapped their knees in time with a line that the mamaloi repeated at the end of each stanza.

All at once, without the slightest warning, she came to a standstill in the middle of her chanting, and with an inhuman screech plunged the sword into the goat's breast, herself falling prostrate across its writhing body.

There was a movement as though the assembly would storm the altar to get at the spouting blood, but Caspar quelled it with a cry of warning, and signalled to the two negroes and the Mongols to catch the blood in the bowls and take it round to the worshippers to drink. Meanwhile the music had stopped.

Whilst this was proceeding he served Maman with a drink from a special silver bowl handed up by Carol and, as soon as she had recovered herself, escorted her to the back of the stone, where she stood at the head of the girl, blinking maliciously around upon what was taking place.

When the last man, including Penberthy, had drunk of the blood, Caspar came to the front of the altar and held up his hand again.

"The purification has been performed," he said. "We shall now make the sacrifice of the white virgin to Zamiel the Great One. If it is acceptable, as we pray, then Zamiel with some of his beloved court may come amongst us in token that our kingdom to be has his benign blessing."

Penberthy, with a quick glance at his nearest neighbours and a fleeting look in the direction of the high ground surrounding the crater, drew two revolvers from his pockets and slipped back the safety catches.

"I exhort you all," Caspar continued solemnly, "on no account to move, whatever happens, until I give you permission to partake of the sacrificial drink."

The music recommenced; this time on an even more primitive beat with drums whose "boom, boom, boom," drowned the other instruments. As if it had been prearranged a cloud scudded over the moon, and in the distance could be heard a dull rumble of thunder. At the same time a sudden gust of wind pricked up, and catching the torches, extinguished them.

It could only have been prelude to a sudden, summer thunderstorm, but it acted on the wrought-up nerves of the assembly as though it was the trump of doom. Somebody gave voice to a ghastly wail, and from a group of others came a frightened groan of "Zamiel . . . he comes. . ."

Right on top of this there was a woman's terrified scream, followed by the cry of "Caspar—Polynice . . . help!", then a commotion at the back and a pattering of hooves and again the exclamation "Zamiel . . ." in a horrorstricken gasp from the worshippers.

Penberthy, springing to his feet, heard the mulatto shout furiously: "Light—curse you, turn on the light."

A second peal of thunder, which seemed to come from right overhead, rolled and as it died so the electric arc went on, lighting up a writhing group of figures on the stone.

Caspar was struggling with Polynice for possession of the sword at the girl's head. As they struggled a figure dressed as Zamiel was battling to make way through a milling score of the stable people. Maddened with terror by the thunder and the commotion, the wretched creatures grunted and bleated and whined, running this way and that amongst the unnerved worshippers, to escape the whips of Mackson and Slim who were trying to drive them back into the passage.

Penberthy recognised me at the same moment as did the mulatto.

In his fury Caspar swung Polynice round, and with superhuman force hurled him by the neck clean over his shoulders at me. As I dodged I thought I heard the sound of his neck breaking.

The mamaloi gave an eldritch screech and seized the sword with the intention of plunging it in the girl's breast. Before she could raise it Penberthy fired and the weapon crashed on to the stone.

For a second neither Caspar's servants nor the delegates suspected that I was not truly the Great One, so I was able to reach the base of the altar unhindered.

Caspar cried to his men to seize me and Penberthy but as they still shrank back, quivering beneath another and still louder crash of thunder, leaped down himself and grappled with me. As he did so a number of dark figures appeared on the edge of the crater, and pointing shotguns and rifles at the thoroughly disorganised members of Caspar's circle, bade them throw their hands up.

There was another banshee-like wail and the mamaloi slid off the stone and, head between her hands, ran round the outer edge of the ring and disappeared into the underground passage. One of Penberthy's men fired, but she escaped.

"I'm going to shoot you like the foul swine you are," I cried, my revolver at the mulatto's heart.

What held my hand I don't quite know myself except that before I executed justice I wanted to be sure that Ines and the others were safely out of the Manor. Caspar, alive, could be used as a hostage for their safety if anything unforeseen had occurred since Ines rescued me and Dunkerley from Alfonse at the point of her revolver, shooting him, and then promptly fainting. I had had to leave her in Dunkerley's charge.

I saw them at that moment, Dunkerley leading limpingly, emerging from the tunnel, and was about to give Caspar his deserts—though even then I hated firing in cold blood—when two things happened simultaneously.

"I must protest," said a strange voice, breathlessly, and looking up my eyes fell upon a shortish, spectacled man in a Norfolk suit who had pushed his way to the front. "While I agree that this—er—person's death is probably well merited, I must, as a representative of His Majesty's Government, insist that? er—justice . . ."

He broke off as the electric arc was extinguished and a violent explosion was heard from the direction of the Manor, followed by a shower of sparks and then a flare that seemed to light the whole sky. Instinctively we all turned towards the house, and in that instant Caspar saw his advantage and, before I could move, was gone.

"You damned fool, you've ruined everything," I stormed, sweeping the pompous, meddling idiot aside roughly and dashed off in the direction I thought Caspar had taken.

With the extinguishing of the light and the ominous sound of the fire, pandemonium broke loose in the barrows. Fortunately Ines and her party, under Dunkerley's leadership, were outside the zone of the panic, and their activity in shooting to kill the stable creatures prevented any of the maddened crowd encroaching upon their position. Amongst the latter, friend and foe were tearing at each other in crazy impartiality.

Dunkerley and the others held fire as I reached them.

"He didn't come this way," he shouted. "Maman went down the second passage, but she was by before we could stop her, and I daren't leave the girls to go after her." He raised his revolver and shot Antoine, who was trying to make a circuit to reach the runway.

I looked round. Penberthy's crew held all the ways out of the crater so far as I could judge.

"Did you see where he was heading?" I demanded.

"No; the light going out suddenly blinded us for the moment."

"He must be somewhere," I returned irascibly. "I wonder if he is hiding in one of those damned holes in the ground." I stared at the series of caves that bordered parts of the circle and ran under the banks of the surrounding higher ground.

"We can look," Dunkerley said. "Westerham can take charge here." He called instructions to the latter, who nodded impatient assent.

"You go round one side and I'll take the other," I said, and started off on the left. The rain was now beginning to come down in torrents, and there was a lull round the stone. Motton had climbed on top and was haranguing the crowd.

"I am a representative of the Colonial Office," I heard him shouting, "and I must insist that you gentlemen stop this tomfoolery. To-morrow you will report in person to Sir Henry and give him an explanation of your extraordinary behaviour. . ."

I left it at that and went on with my search. Again I blamed that fussy Government servant. At the same time if it had not been for his speechifying I should probably have noticed that Ines was following me. Only when I heard her cry out in alarm did I realise she was near.

"Pat—he's here," she shouted.

I whipped round like a flash, just in time to catch her, propelled like a bolt by the figure that had been crouching behind a pile of fallen debris. He was up upon the bank with a great bound before I could recover myself. I fired a couple of shots, but the air was becoming thick with smoke from the Manor, and I could not tell if I hit him.

I scrambled to the top of the crater, but by the time I was up he was nowhere in sight. A second later the noise of a car being started up in the distance came to my ears and I knew that for the moment, anyway, my score with Caspar would have to stand.

"I'm terribly sorry, Pat," Ines said as I returned despondently, "only I didn't see him until we were past. I thought something moved behind that pile of earth and then, when I turned to go back, he sprung out on me."

"Nonsense, it wasn't your fault. If it hadn't been for that confounded ass braying on his soap box I'd have seen him myself," I said. "And if you hadn't had the marvellous pluck to come and look for me when you heard me singing 'Loch Lomond' and rescued me and Dunkerley, we'd all have been burning in the Manor now. So really you saved the situation."

On this she began to cry softly. I patted her shoulder—she was leaning against me—and comforted her as well as I could, but I was so afraid of making and saying more than I should that I probably seemed more matter of fact than fervent.

"If you're all right we'd better join Penberthy," I went on as I saw the group by the stone beginning to break up, and still under the guns of the men on the bank, climb up to make their way, crestfallen, to where the cars were parked. The rain was now coming down in sheets.

Caspar's gang, such as were not lying injured on the ground, were huddled together under the stone.

My tone was curt because if I had not rigidly controlled myself I should have taken her in my arms.

She drew away and stared at me for a long second oddly, then her eyes dropped and she shrugged her shoulders.

"Certainly," she replied, and moved off in advance of me.

~ ~ ~ ~ ~

"Well, well—I think I managed that really very nicely. Of course they wouldn't have hurt the girl—really—just a piece of showmanship; nevertheless it was just as well you sent for me," Motton remarked in a self-satisfied voice as he joined us all.

The veterans of the campaign were gathered together, waiting until the fire engines should arrive.

Penberthy had his arm round Miss Sheldon; it was evident they had reached a satisfactory mutual understanding, and I envied them bitterly. Bridget and her father were together. Walton and Ines had linked up, and I was feeling rather lonely and sore.

Penberthy chuckled at Motton's remark and winked at me.

"Of course they wouldn't, Edward; as you say it was merely a very impressive bit of showmanship. And if it hadn't been for you we might have committed one really satisfactory murder. As it is you hold all the honours."

CHAPTER XXVII

IN WHICH THE BUSINESS IS CONCLUDED
FAIRLY SATISFACTORILY

DUNKERLEY AND I had accepted Penberthy's invitation to spend a couple of days with him at the cottage. After, the excitement of the past week I felt unutterably flat.

We had met Walton and Westerham the morning following the fire and inspected what remained of the Manor. The female servants had been saved, and were now under surveillance pending proceedings which had been instituted by Walton against Antoine, Joseph and others of the male staff for complicity in his abduction. Both men had then thanked me for what I had done, but it seemed to me that they appeared ill at ease in my company.

The remains of Maman Constance were found by the entrance to the stable. Her skull gave evidence of a heavy blow, and there was a slight wound in her arm, but no other sign of injury. She must have died within a few minutes of operating the switch that set off the explosives. In death she looked a singularly small, frail and peaceful old lady.

A corps of men, sworn to secrecy, were interring the remains of the stable creatures killed in the barrows.

The afternoon of the second day found me smoking a pipe alone in the garden. Mrs. Thompson had brought out a table with afternoon tea laid, but I thought I would wait for Penberthy.

To keep myself from brooding I tried to think what Caspar's future movements were likely to be and how I could get on his trail.

Maman's phrase about the secret river came to my mind. Was it some African river or was it merely a catch phrase? It had something to do with money, because Caspar had said he couldn't get the key until the "three" were satisfied.

Supposing there did actually exist in Africa a river—a source of gold that would make Caspar and his associates financially independent? And, if such a river did exist—maybe the source from which the Queen of Sheba's wealth came—that would be where I should be most likely to find Caspar.

I paced up and down the garden path, trying to concoct plans for getting to Africa, and was so wrapped up in my imaginings that I did not notice Penberthy had come up to the garden.

"Planning another campaign?" he remarked when, all at once, I became aware he was there, and pulled up self-consciously. "I see Mrs. Thompson has brought tea." He appeared uneasy and was fidgeting with a small parcel he carried.

"What's on your mind?" I asked bluntly.

"Well ... one or two things. This principally." He held the package out. "Mr. Walton asked me to give it to you with his compliments and deep gratitude." He subdued something very like a snort of disgust.

"What is it?"

"A gold watch in token of his appreciation of your services."

I laid down the packet on the table unopened.

"Quite unnecessary, though I expect he felt just as awkward about sending it as he knew I would be about accepting it," I said.

"Yes. Maybe that was it," he returned flatly. He opened two telegrams, then handed me one. "This is to your account," he grinned. "It's from Caspar."

"What?" I snatched it from him. It had been sent from Paris.

"Tell the red-head offer of job still holds good. In any case, to our next meeting. Pettifranc."

"At least it gives me something to live for," I commented.

"Yes, you might look at it that way, I suppose," he remarked drily. "Mine's from the estimable Motton; like to hear it?"

"Please."

"Siena Studios fired by unknown person yesterday. Stop. Chief has congratulated me on handling of delicate situation. Stop. Conference delegates assure Government no disloyalty intended but were misled. Stop. We are nevertheless taking steps to guarantee future good behaviour. Stop. Police warned to apprehend Caspar. Stop. Chief wishes to add his thanks to mine for your assistance also to your friend Worthing. Motton."

I laughed.

He began to pour the tea.

"Walton has gone to Plymouth on business. Westerham and his daughter and Miss Bellenden are leaving for London by the night train," he vouchsafed.

I said "Oh," and helped myself with grave deliberation to a scone and Cornish cream.

"I suppose you'll be going yourself soon?" he continued, dourly, keeping his eyes on his cup.

"To-morrow morning—unless I'm in the way," I answered.

"Oh, well." he still kept his eyes averted. "We'll be seeing you down here again for the inquest on Maman and the others. I hope you contrive to spend the weekend with me."

"I'll look forward to it more than anything I know? except meeting Caspar again," I grinned.

We shook hands on it.

~ ~ ~ ~ ~

Two mornings later I took up my abandoned pitch at the corner of the square. I could hardly realise, as I set my chalks on the pavement, that I had been away over a week.

I was busy sketching the outline of my ship picture when I heard a cough. Looking up I saw Westerham.

I grinned, I couldn't help it.

"Mr. Worthing," he said "In my position, as you may possibly realise, it is difficult to get hold of men? the right kind of men? who have a flair for tracking unusual things down to their source."

"Yes," I answered, half in a daze.

He came a little nearer. "I can't tell you all about it now, but for quite a long time I and most of the bigger financial concerns in Great Britain and America have been puzzled as to what is really happening to the world's gold as it comes on the market. Some? a considerable portion? is bought on Government account by the various powers, but the residue, no mean amount, just . . . vanishes."

"I have sometimes puzzled over that myself." I remarked.

"Good. If a young man like yourself, Mr. Worthing, considered five thousand a year and his expenses sufficient inducement to undertake the investigation of this peculiar? er? problem, my firm would consider themselves extremely lucky in finding him."

I stared at him. His eyes met mine frankly and fairly.

"I mean what I say," he added as I still kept silent. "We have had it in mind for some time, but we could not find the right man."

"Thanks," I said. "I'd like it better than any job I know of, but I did want to find Caspar and settle accounts with him."

"You might combine the two," he said thoughtfully.

"Yes," I admitted, the phrase about the secret river still ringing in my brain.

"Fine. By the way," he went on casually, "that cheque I gave Caspar; it hadn't been put through, so that little expense was saved. I should like to have given you a—er—small bonus on it, but Miss Bellenden said you would be upset if I suggested it."

"I would rather leave things as they are," I replied.

"I thought so." He nodded and held out his hand. "Come to my office to-morrow."

~ ~ ~ ~ ~

Within two minutes of his departure Ines came along.

"Well?" she said without preface.

"Well," I returned.

"Of course I'd hate to take you from your work if the big boss is around," she smiled, "but I'm dying for a cup of coffee and there is a place quite handy."

"I'll take you, but only on one condition," I returned firmly.

"Oh, conditions—is that fair?"

"That you'll marry me." My heart was thumping more quickly than it had ever done at the Manor.

"As bad as that?"

"From the first minute I saw you," I said.

"I simply must have that coffee," she said.

I gathered my chalks together, dumped them into my disreputable cap—all but a stick of white—and placed them between the railings of the church.

With the white chalk I wrote on the pavement:

"This space to let. No reasonable offer refused," and pitched the crayon into the gutter.

"Idiot," she murmured affectionately as I took her arm.

I paused for a second at the church door, then pulled her in and kissed her. "Would you mind if we get married here?" I asked.

"If you want to. Why, though?"

"I think the Ancestors would like it," I said, and kissed her again.

THE END

RAMBLE HOUSE's

HARRY STEPHEN KEELER WEBWORK MYSTERIES

(RH) indicates the title is available ONLY in the RAMBLE HOUSE edition

The Ace of Spades Murder
The Affair of the Bottled Deuce (RH)
The Amazing Web
The Barking Clock
Behind That Mask
The Book with the Orange Leaves
The Bottle with the Green Wax Seal
The Box from Japan
The Case of the Canny Killer
The Case of the Crazy Corpse (RH)
The Case of the Flying Hands (RH)
The Case of the Ivory Arrow
The Case of the Jeweled Ragpicker
The Case of the Lavender Gripsack
The Case of the Mysterious Moll
The Case of the 16 Beans
The Case of the Transparent Nude (RH)
The Case of the Transposed Legs
The Case of the Two-Headed Idiot (RH)
The Case of the Two Strange Ladies
The Circus Stealers (RH)
Cleopatra's Tears
A Copy of Beowulf (RH)
The Crimson Cube (RH)
The Face of the Man From Saturn
Find the Clock
The Five Silver Buddhas
The 4th King
The Gallows Waits, My Lord! (RH)
The Green Jade Hand
Finger! Finger!
Hangman's Nights (RH)
I, Chameleon (RH)
I Killed Lincoln at 10:13! (RH)
The Iron Ring
The Man Who Changed His Skin (RH)
The Man with the Crimson Box
The Man with the Magic Eardrums
The Man with the Wooden Spectacles
The Marceau Case
The Matilda Hunter Murder
The Monocled Monster

The Murder of London Lew
The Murdered Mathematician
The Mysterious Card (RH)
The Mysterious Ivory Ball of Wong Shing Li (RH)
The Mystery of the Fiddling Cracksman
The Peacock Fan
The Photo of Lady X (RH)
The Portrait of Jirjohn Cobb
Report on Vanessa Hewstone (RH)
Riddle of the Travelling Skull
Riddle of the Wooden Parrakeet (RH)
The Scarlet Mummy (RH)
The Search for X-Y-Z
The Sharkskin Book
Sing Sing Nights
The Six From Nowhere (RH)
The Skull of the Waltzing Clown
The Spectacles of Mr. Cagliostro
Stand By—London Calling!
The Steeltown Strangler
The Stolen Gravestone (RH)
Strange Journey (RH)
The Strange Will
The Straw Hat Murders (RH)
The Street of 1000 Eyes (RH)
Thieves' Nights
Three Novellos (RH)
The Tiger Snake
The Trap (RH)
Vagabond Nights (Defrauded Yeggman)
Vagabond Nights 2 (10 Hours)
The Vanishing Gold Truck
The Voice of the Seven Sparrows
The Washington Square Enigma
When Thief Meets Thief
The White Circle (RH)
The Wonderful Scheme of Mr. Christopher Thorne
X. Jones—of Scotland Yard
Y. Cheung, Business Detective

Keeler Related Works

A To Izzard: A Harry Stephen Keeler Companion by Fender Tucker — Articles and stories about Harry, by Harry, and in his style. Included is a compleat bibliography.

Wild About Harry: Reviews of Keeler Novels — Edited by Richard Polt & Fender Tucker — 22 reviews of works by Harry Stephen Keeler from *Keeler News*. A perfect introduction to the author.

The Keeler Keyhole Collection: Annotated newsletter rants from Harry Stephen Keeler, edited by Francis M. Nevins. Over 400 pages of incredibly personal Keeleriana.

Fakealoo — Pastiches of the style of Harry Stephen Keeler by selected demented members of the HSK Society. Updated every year with the new winner.

RAMBLE HOUSE's OTHER LOONS

The End of It All and Other Stories — Ed Gorman's latest short story collection

Four Dancing Tuatara Press Books — *Beast or Man?* By Sean M'Guire; *The Whistling Ancestors* by Richard E. Goddard; *The Shadow on the House* and *Sorcerer's Chessmen* by Mark Hansom. With introductions by John Pelan

The Dumpling — Political murder from 1907 by Coulson Kernahan

Victims & Villains — Intriguing Sherlockiana from Derham Groves

Evidence in Blue — 1938 mystery by E. Charles Vivian

The Case of the Little Green Men — Mack Reynolds wrote this love song to sci-fi fans back in 1951 and it's now back in print.

Hell Fire — A new hard-boiled novel by Jack Moskovitz about an arsonist, an arson cop and a Nazi hooker. It isn't pretty.

Researching American-Made Toy Soldiers — A 276-page collection of a lifetime of articles by toy soldier expert Richard O'Brien

Strands of the Web: Short Stories of Harry Stephen Keeler — Edited and Introduced by Fred Cleaver

The Sam McCain Novels — Ed Gorman's terrific series includes *The Day the Music Died, Wake Up Little Susie* and *Will You Still Love Me Tomorrow?*

A Shot Rang Out — Three decades of reviews from Jon Breen

Mysterious Martin, the Master of Murder — Two versions of a strange 1912 novel by Tod Robbins about a man who writes books that can kill.

Dago Red — 22 tales of dark suspense by Bill Pronzini

The Night Remembers — A 1991 Jack Walsh mystery from Ed Gorman

Rough Cut & New, Improved Murder — Ed Gorman's first two novels

Hollywood Dreams — A novel of the Depression by Richard O'Brien

Seven Gelett Burgess Novels — *The Master of Mysteries, The White Cat, Two O'Clock Courage, Ladies in Boxes, Find the Woman, The Heart Line, The Picaroons*

The Organ Reader — A huge compilation of just about everything published in the 1971-1972 radical bay-area newspaper, *THE ORGAN*.

A Clear Path to Cross — Sharon Knowles short mystery stories by Ed Lynskey

Old Times' Sake — Short stories by James Reasoner from Mike Shayne Magazine

Freaks and Fantasies — Eerie tales by Tod Robbins, collaborator of Tod Browning on the film FREAKS.

Six Jim Harmon Double Novels — *Vixen Hollow/Celluloid Scandal, The Man Who Made Maniacs/Silent Siren, Ape Rape/Wanton Witch, Sex Burns Like Fire/Twist Session, Sudden Lust/Passion Strip, Sin Unlimited/Harlot Master, Twilight Girls/Sex Institution.* Written in the early 60s.

Marblehead: A Novel of H.P. Lovecraft — A long-lost masterpiece from Richard A. Lupoff. Published for the first time!

The Compleat Ova Hamlet — Parodies of SF authors by Richard A. Lupoff – A brand new edition with more stories and more illustrations by Trina Robbins.

The Secret Adventures of Sherlock Holmes — Three Sherlockian pastiches by the Brooklyn author/publisher, Gary Lovisi.

The Universal Holmes — Richard A. Lupoff's 2007 collection of five Holmesian pastiches and a recipe for giant rat stew.

Four Joel Townsley Rogers Novels — By the author of *The Red Right Hand: Once In a Red Moon, Lady With the Dice, The Stopped Clock, Never Leave My Bed*

Two Joel Townsley Rogers Story Collections — Night of Horror and Killing Time

Twenty Norman Berrow Novels — *The Bishop's Sword, Ghost House, Don't Go Out After Dark, Claws of the Cougar, The Smokers of Hashish, The Secret Dancer, Don't Jump Mr. Boland!, The Footprints of Satan, Fingers for Ransom, The Three Tiers of Fantasy, The Spaniard's Thumb, The Eleventh Plague, Words Have Wings, One Thrilling Night, The Lady's in Danger, It Howls at Night, The Terror in the Fog, Oil Under the Window, Murder in the Melody, The Singing Room*

The N. R. De Mexico Novels — Robert Bragg presents *Marijuana Girl, Madman on a Drum, Private Chauffeur* in one volume.

Four Chelsea Quinn Yarbro Novels featuring Charlie Moon — *Ogilvie, Tallant and Moon, Music When the Sweet Voice Dies, Poisonous Fruit* and *Dead Mice*

Five Walter S. Masterman Mysteries — *The Green Toad, The Flying Beast, The Yellow Mistletoe, The Wrong Verdict* and *The Perjured Alibi.* Fantastic impossible plots.

Two Hake Talbot Novels — *Rim of the Pit, The Hangman's Handyman.* Classic locked room mysteries.

Two Alexander Laing Novels — *The Motives of Nicholas Holtz* and *Dr. Scarlett*, stories of medical mayhem and intrigue from the 30s.

Four David Hume Novels — *Corpses Never Argue, Cemetery First Stop, Make Way for the Mourners, Eternity Here I Come*, and more to come.

Three Wade Wright Novels — *Echo of Fear, Death At Nostalgia Street* and *It Leads to Murder*, with more to come!

Eight Rupert Penny Novels — *Policeman's Holiday, Policeman's Evidence, Lucky Policeman, Policeman in Armour, Sealed Room Murder, Sweet Poison, The Talkative Policeman, She had to Have Gas* and *Cut and Run* (by Martin Tanner.)

Five Jack Mann Novels — Strange murder in the English countryside. *Gees' First Case, Nightmare Farm, Grey Shapes, The Ninth Life, The Glass Too Many.*

Seven Max Afford Novels — *Owl of Darkness, Death's Mannikins, Blood on His Hands, The Dead Are Blind, The Sheep and the Wolves, Sinners in Paradise* and *Two Locked Room Mysteries and a Ripping Yarn* by one of Australia's finest novelists.

Five Joseph Shallit Novels — *The Case of the Billion Dollar Body, Lady Don't Die on My Doorstep, Kiss the Killer, Yell Bloody Murder, Take Your Last Look.* One of America's best 50's authors.

Two Crimson Clown Novels — By Johnston McCulley, author of the Zorro novels, *The Crimson Clown* and *The Crimson Clown Again.*

The Best of 10-Story Book — edited by Chris Mikul, over 35 stories from the literary magazine Harry Stephen Keeler edited.

A Young Man's Heart — A forgotten early classic by Cornell Woolrich

The Anthony Boucher Chronicles — edited by Francis M. Nevins
Book reviews by Anthony Boucher written for the *San Francisco Chronicle,* 1942 – 1947. Essential and fascinating reading.

Muddled Mind: Complete Works of Ed Wood, Jr. — David Hayes and Hayden Davis deconstruct the life and works of a mad genius.

Gadsby — A lipogram (a novel without the letter E). Ernest Vincent Wright's last work, published in 1939 right before his death.

My First Time: The One Experience You Never Forget — Michael Birchwood — 64 true first-person narratives of how they lost it.

A Roland Daniel Double: The Signal and The Return of Wu Fang — Classic thrillers from the 30s

Murder in Shawnee — Two novels of the Alleghenies by John Douglas: *Shawnee Alley Fire* and *Haunts.*

Deep Space and other Stories — A collection of SF gems by Richard A. Lupoff

Blood Moon — The first of the Robert Payne series by Ed Gorman

The Time Armada — Fox B. Holden's 1953 SF gem.

Black River Falls — Suspense from the master, Ed Gorman

Sideslip — 1968 SF masterpiece by Ted White and Dave Van Arnam

The Triune Man — Mindscrambling science fiction from Richard A. Lupoff

Detective Duff Unravels It — Episodic mysteries by Harvey O'Higgins

Automaton — Brilliant treatise on robotics: 1928-style! By H. Stafford Hatfield

The Incredible Adventures of Rowland Hern — Rousing 1928 impossible crimes by Nicholas Olde.

Slammer Days — Two full-length prison memoirs: *Men into Beasts* (1952) by George Sylvester Viereck and *Home Away From Home* (1962) by Jack Woodford

Murder in Black and White — 1931 classic tennis whodunit by Evelyn Elder

Killer's Caress — Cary Moran's 1936 hardboiled thriller

The Golden Dagger — 1951 Scotland Yard yarn by E. R. Punshon

A Smell of Smoke — 1951 English countryside thriller by Miles Burton

Ruled By Radio — 1925 futuristic novel by Robert L. Hadfield & Frank E. Farncombe

Murder in Silk — A 1937 Yellow Peril novel of the silk trade by Ralph Trevor

The Case of the Withered Hand — 1936 potboiler by John G. Brandon

Finger-prints Never Lie — A 1939 classic detective novel by John G. Brandon

Inclination to Murder — 1966 thriller by New Zealand's Harriet Hunter

Invaders from the Dark — Classic werewolf tale from Greye La Spina

Fatal Accident — Murder by automobile, a 1936 mystery by Cecil M. Wills

The Devil Drives — A prison and lost treasure novel by Virgil Markham

Dr. Odin — Douglas Newton's 1933 potboiler comes back to life.

The Chinese Jar Mystery — Murder in the manor by John Stephen Strange, 1934

The Julius Caesar Murder Case — A classic 1935 re-telling of the assassination by Wallace Irwin that's much more fun than the Shakespeare version

West Texas War and Other Western Stories — by Gary Lovisi

The Contested Earth and Other SF Stories — A never-before published space opera and seven short stories by Jim Harmon.

Tales of the Macabre and Ordinary — Modern twisted horror by Chris Mikul, author of the *Bizarrism* series.

The Gold Star Line — Seaboard adventure from L.T. Reade and Robert Eustace.

The Werewolf vs the Vampire Woman — Hard to believe ultraviolence by either Arthur M. Scarm or Arthur M. Scram.

Black Hogan Strikes Again — Australia's Peter Renwick pens a tale of the outback.

Don Diablo: Book of a Lost Film — Two-volume treatment of a western by Paul Landres, with diagrams. Intro by Francis M. Nevins.

The Charlie Chaplin Murder Mystery — Movie hijinks by Wes D. Gehring

The Koky Comics — A collection of all of the 1978-1981 Sunday and daily comic strips by Richard O'Brien and Mort Gerberg, in two volumes.

Suzy — Another collection of comic strips from Richard O'Brien and Bob Vojtko

Dime Novels: Ramble House's 10-Cent Books — *Knife in the Dark* by Robert Leslie Bellem, *Hot Lead* and *Song of Death* by Ed Earl Repp, *A Hashish House in New York* by H.H. Kane, and five more.

Blood in a Snap — The *Finnegan's Wake* of the 21ˢᵗ century, by Jim Weiler

Stakeout on Millennium Drive — Award-winning Indianapolis Noir — Ian Woollen.

Dope Tales #1 — Two dope-riddled classics; *Dope Runners* by Gerald Grantham and *Death Takes the Joystick* by Phillip Condé.

Dope Tales #2 — Two more narco-classics; *The Invisible Hand* by Rex Dark and *The Smokers of Hashish* by Norman Berrow.

Dope Tales #3 — Two enchanting novels of opium by the master, Sax Rohmer. *Dope* and *The Yellow Claw.*

Tenebrae — Ernest G. Henham's 1898 horror tale brought back.

The Singular Problem of the Stygian House-Boat — Two classic tales by John Kendrick Bangs about the denizens of Hades.

Tiresias — Psychotic modern horror novel by Jonathan M. Sweet.

The One After Snelling — Kickass modern noir from Richard O'Brien.

The Sign of the Scorpion — 1935 Edmund Snell tale of oriental evil.

The House of the Vampire — 1907 poetic thriller by George S. Viereck.

An Angel in the Street — Modern hardboiled noir by Peter Genovese.

The Devil's Mistress — Scottish gothic tale by J. W. Brodie-Innes.

The Lord of Terror — 1925 mystery with master-criminal, Fantômas.

The Lady of the Terraces — 1925 adventure by E. Charles Vivian.

My Deadly Angel — 1955 Cold War drama by John Chelton

Prose Bowl — Futuristic satire — Bill Pronzini & Barry N. Malzberg .

Satan's Den Exposed — True crime in Truth or Consequences New Mexico — Award-winning journalism by the *Desert Journal.*

The Amorous Intrigues & Adventures of Aaron Burr — by Anonymous — Hot historical action.

I Stole $16,000,000 — A true story by cracksman Herbert E. Wilson.

The Black Dark Murders — Vintage 50s college murder yarn by Milt Ozaki, writing as Robert O. Saber.

Sex Slave — Potboiler of lust in the days of Cleopatra — Dion Leclerq.

You'll Die Laughing — Bruce Elliott's 1945 novel of murder at a practical joker's English countryside manor.

The Private Journal & Diary of John H. Surratt — The memoirs of the man who conspired to assassinate President Lincoln.

Dead Man Talks Too Much — Hollywood boozer by Weed Dickenson

Red Light — History of legal prostitution in Shreveport Louisiana by Eric Brock. Includes wonderful photos of the houses and the ladies.

A Snark Selection — Lewis Carroll's *The Hunting of the Snark* with two Snarkian chapters by Harry Stephen Keeler — Illustrated by Gavin L. O'Keefe.

Ripped from the Headlines! — The Jack the Ripper story as told in the newspaper articles in the *New York* and *London Times.*

Geronimo — S. M. Barrett's 1905 autobiography of a noble American.

The White Peril in the Far East — Sidney Lewis Gulick's 1905 indictment of the West and assurance that Japan would never attack the U.S.

The Compleat Calhoon — All of Fender Tucker's works: Includes *Totah Six-Pack, Weed, Women and Song* and *Tales from the Tower,* plus a CD of all of his songs.

Totah Six-Pack — Just Fender Tucker's six tales about Farmington in one sleek volume.

RAMBLE HOUSE

Fender Tucker, Prop.

www.ramblehouse.com   fender@ramblehouse.com

228-826-1783   10329 Sheephead Drive, Vancleave MS 39565

www.ingramcontent.com/pod-product-compliance
Lightning Source LLC
Chambersburg PA
CBHW030328020726
47493CB00004B/1192